ELIMINATION

KELLY KELSEY

Edited by Foxtale Editing

Proofreading by Black Lotus Editing

❋ Created with Vellum

ACKNOWLEDGMENTS

To anybody who fell in love with somebody they shouldn't have.
Don't punish yourself. Sometimes we don't get to choose what the
heart wants.

PLAYLIST

Jessie Ware – Wildest Moments
    Jose Gonzalez – Heartbeats
    Ed Sheeran – Bad Habits
    Switchfoot – I Dare You To Move
    The Goo Goo Dolls – Iris
    Lady Gaga – Always Remember Us This Way
    Birdy – Wild Horses
    Alex Roe – Enough
    Snow Patrol – Crack The Shutters
    Johnny Cash – Hurt
    Sheryl Crow – The First Cut Is The Deepest
    Sam Smith – Stay With Me
    John Major – Free Fallin'
    Robyn – With Every Heartbeat
    Ed Sheeran – Kiss Me
    Shakira – Underneath Your Clothes
    One Night Only – Just For Tonight
    James Blunt – Goodbye My Lover
    The Sundays – Wild Horses
    Beyonce – Broken Hearted Girl

Dave Matthews – Some Devil

Beyonce – Irreplaceable

Marshmello, Jonas Brothers – Leave Before You Love Me

Taylor Swift – Lover

Taylor Swift – Wildest Dreams

Kings of Leon – Sex On Fire

Mimi Webb – Dumb Love

Adele – One And Only

Ed Sheeran – Kiss Me

Nelly Furtado – Try

Pink – Who Knew

Jubel – Klingande

***

"Love that we cannot have is the one that lasts the longest, hurts the deepest, and feels the strongest." – Unknown

Chapter One

THALIA

Excitement courses through me as I spot the imposing sign on the brick wall.

Rhodes Farms.

The place I have wanted to train ever since I watched Mr. Theodore Rhodes, himself, compete at the Global tour in New York a few years back. I was mesmerized by him. The way he rode. The way he was at one with his horse. His riding was an art form. He won the whole competition, and I knew then I wanted to be just like him.

Theodore Rhodes is the number one show jumper in the world and the one person who can help me achieve my show jumping dreams. He won individual and team gold at the last Olympics - his third time competing for Team USA.

After much discussion—and begging on my behalf—my parents agreed to let me train with him, with the stipulation that I finish high school first. Of course, I agreed, and I graduated from St. Constantine's private all-girls school a couple weeks ago. Now my journey can really start. I will be a showjumper. I will prove to my parents that this is what I want.

We pull through the wrought iron gates. I scan the area through the blacked-out SUV windows, taking in the lush green grass and palm tree lined drive before the barn comes into view. I smile knowing I am going to see my horses in just a couple more minutes.

Zeus and Lolly.

I have had them for a couple years now, competing on the East Coast whenever I had the chance between modelling, filming, and school. I want to take the next step now and that can only happen if I get the right trainer.

Coming to a stop, I open the door before the driver gets the chance to do it for me and hop out. I hear my father's stern voice but that doesn't stop me as I race toward the stalls. I have never gone this long without seeing my horses, so the excitement is real. Spotting a woman, I come to a halt.

"Hey, do you know where my horses are? Zeus and Lolly?" Her eyes widen before she composes herself.

"You're Thalia Maxwell?" I nod in confirmation. It's only when her mouth gapes that I remember what my name means.

Thalia Maxwell, daughter to the owner of the world's biggest diamond and jewelry corporation, Christian Maxwell III, and America's sweetheart, movie star, Elena Maxwell. She straightens, clears her throat. I frown. I don't want to be treated any differently from anyone else here.

"Uhh, yeah. Follow me." She spins on her heel, and I follow her lead. "I'm Tessa by the way. Barn manager at Rhodes Farms."

"Hey," I reply. She glances over her shoulder with a small smile then carries on to my horses' stalls. She comes to a stop at a door. I peek over, smiling when I see Zeus. He is gray in color and around 16.2 hands, big compared to my five-foot six height. Spotting me, he neighs. I open the door, strolling in and wrapping my arms around his neck.

"Hey boy. Did you miss me?" I ask even though he can't reply.

"Zeus and Lolly have been very well looked after," Tessa says. I glance over at her and smile.

"Thank you. This is the longest I have gone without seeing them," I tell her. Both my horses were transported from New York to Florida over a month ago. I know it sounds cliché, but I have been lost without them.

"Lolly is next door," Tessa adds. I release Zeus and make my way to Lolly. I grin at my girl. She is around 16 hands and brown in color with a black mane and tail. She is beautiful. Opening the stall door, I walk in and wrap my arms around her just the same as I did with Zeus. I breathe her in, breathe in the smell of horses.

It feels like home.

I hear footsteps approach and I know it is my father. My mom couldn't make it today, as she is on location for a new movie she is filming.

"Thalia?" I release Lolly, stepping out of the stall to find my father with his cell in hand and a frown marring his face.

"Here, Daddy." He glances up at me with a smile.

"Come. Mr. Rhodes is in his office." I swallow down my nerves as I follow my father. I have never met Theodore Rhodes in person, but I have seen pictures. He is known as the hottest guy in show jumping and it is not hard to see why. With his dark hair, striking blue eyes, and chiseled features, he is a god. Beautiful. I have been around good-looking men, worked with them on several modelling campaigns, but Theodore Rhodes beats them all. Unfortunately for all women that covet him, he isn't single. He has been with his girlfriend for six years and as far as I know, there has never been any rumors of him being unfaithful. Not like you would be if you were dating British socialite, Melody Whitworth. With her blond hair and brown eyes, she is gorgeous and together, they look like the picture-perfect couple.

Coming to a stop at a big oak door, my father knocks. A few seconds later a deep male voice responds, sending a shiver down my spine.

"Come in." My father pushes the door open before stepping through. I follow behind him only to come to a stop when I spot the man behind the desk. My breath hitches. I swallow.

Hard.

Jesus. Pictures do not do this man justice. In person, he is even more god-like. Noticing my stare, he clears his throat and holds out his hand for me to take. "You must be Thalia?" My cheeks heat in embarrassment at being caught ogling him. I take his hand.

"Yes," I breathe. He smirks. A smirk I feel right down to my... pussy? I frown, stunned by my reaction. This never happens to me. I have never been interested in men, choosing to focus on my horses, yet for some reason, this stranger has my stomach in knots with lust.

This is bad. Really bad.

The guy is not only in a long-term relationship but is twelve years older than me. I glance at my father who would, for sure, have me back on our jet and back to the East Coast if he heard my thoughts right now. Being the baby of the family, I am my father's little princess. The good girl. Never had a boyfriend and I am sure he would like to keep it that way. My father takes a seat, dragging me out of my thoughts.

"Nice to meet you, Thalia. I'm Theo, but I am sure you already knew that," He says smugly, releasing my hand. The instant loss leaves me cold. I shake my head trying to compose myself.

"Nice to meet you, Theo," I say in a voice I don't quite recognize. I need to get it together before my dad realizes something is wrong. And anyway, Theo is way out of my league. A grown man with a girlfriend who I am sure has no interest in me other than training. I am a paying trainee. He is my trainer. I chant the words silently to myself, reminding myself to keep my head in the game and off this glorious specimen in front of me. He smiles once more before rounding his desk and taking a seat.

"So, Mr. Maxwell—" My father holds his hand up to stop him.

"Please, call me Christian." He nods before carrying on.

"Christian, I know we spoke in detail before about Thalia's ambitions and what she is looking to achieve from training with me. We discussed her accomplishments so far and that she is now looking to step up a level, move up the ranks." Theo's gaze moves to me. I blush at the intensity in his blue eyes. "Is that correct Thalia?"

Clearing my throat, I nod. "Yes. I have followed your career for a long time now, Mr. Rhode's..." I trail off at the look on Theo's face.

"Please call me Theo. If you are going to be training with me, I would rather we be informal with each other. Mr. Rhodes is far too formal when we will be working closely."

I nod. "Like I was saying, I have been following your career for a long time now, Theo. Your performance at the Beijing Olympics was extraordinary. It is what inspired me to want to do more. To be better. I have wanted to train with you for a long time, but I needed to finish school."

Theo's eyes light up at my hero worship and my tummy flutters with excitement that I have pleased him. "I want to compete at a higher level. Do the tours in Europe. Maybe make the nations cup teams. I understand I have a long way to go but I am willing to do what it takes." I feel my father's stare at my speech, but my eyes stay locked on Theo's. My gaze drops to his lips when I see them twitch.

"You are passionate, Thalia; I will give you that. But I need you to understand the work that will go into getting you to that level. It does not and will not happen overnight. Show jumping is one of the toughest sports." I frown at his words, but he continues. "But with your parents' backing, I think you have as good a chance as any. Show jumping is also a money sport, you have that. Your father has already informed me that you will have your parents full support in whatever we need to do to get you to where you want to be."

"Whatever it takes," my father cuts in. Theo nods.

"I have schooled both your horses and studied videos of you competing. While they are both nice horses, they are average at best. They need to be exceptional to compete at the level you want to." My jaw clenches, fists ball at the audacity of this man. How dare he speak about my horses this way. Before I can stop myself, the words tumble out of me.

"My horses are just fine. They may not be competing at top level yet, but they can," I hiss. I feel my dad's eyes on me, but I don't move my gaze from Theo. Something flashes in his eyes, his lips curving into a smirk.

"Thalia," my father warns. Being childish, I shoot Theo an indignant look before he carries on like the arrogant asshole he apparently is.

"As I was saying. While they are both nice animals, I feel that to compete at top level, you need a top-level horse. Fortunately for you, I do have one in mind and although the owners aren't desperate to sell, I have it on good authority from the current rider that they are willing to allow you the chance to view and purchase him. We will need to be discreet, but I think it will be the perfect horse for what you are looking to do." Theo glances at my father then back to me.

"You know my position, Theo; I am willing to spend the money to get my princess," I cringe at my dad calling me that in front of this man, "to where she wants to be. What sort of figures are we looking at?"

Theo clears his throat. "I have been told he is going to be in the high six figure numbers. That being said, it will be worth it if it gets Thalia the results and exposure she wants. He is competing at top level in Europe and is on all the Dutch Nation Cup teams with very good results. I think it would be the perfect fit." I frown at his words. Although it would be exciting to have a new horse, I don't want to sell my current ones.

"I don't want to sell Zeus or Lolly. I won't." I look at my dad, shaking my head as if to drive the point home. My father's eyes soften.

"Princess, we won't be selling them. I just think that if you want this as much as you say you do, you are going to have to take Theo's advice. He knows what he is talking about and if that means buying a better horse then that is what we will do." I smile before my gaze moves to Theo. Something passes in his eyes that I can't quite decipher before he speaks.

"I think this is the right move, Thalia. Of course, we will spend a couple of weeks getting to know one another, so I can see the level you are at with both horses. But ultimately, I think buying a horse or even a couple of horses that have good records competing at top level is the best way forward."

I nod, feeling my anger at his earlier words dissipate. "Of course. I want this and I trust your advice. I wouldn't be here otherwise." He eyes me for a long beat before he nods.

"Good. I am glad we cleared that up. Now onto the next thing. You will have two assigned grooms and one stable hand which are included in the price of your monthly fees. I will introduce you to them later today. You will also meet my whole team. I have three other students here training with me and they all live on site, as do the staff. Your father mentioned you will be living off-site in a condo purchased for you." My father cuts in.

"Yes, that is correct. It is around ten minutes from here and Thalia has a vehicle to travel back and forth."

"Good. I also understand you will be taking college courses online so I will take this into account when working out your schedule."

"This is important," my father says in a tone that leaves no room for argument. "Thalia knows that it is part of the condition of being here, so she knows to take her studying seriously." My father shoots me a stern look to remind me that I promised to continue my studies. The fact I can study online is a bonus. I don't want to go to a classroom.

"I am sure we can come up with something that suits us all. With two horses, Thalia will only need lessons four or five times a week. The rest will be trail rides, flatwork, or the horse exerciser." The way Theo says my name has my core clenching. I didn't know my name could sound so sexy on someone's tongue.

"That is what I want to hear. Studying is important and although I know Thalia is determined to make a career in show jumping, I still want her to continue her studies. She is a very bright girl." My father beams at me while my eyes slide to Theo to find him watching me intently. Something in his stare makes goosebumps break out all over my body and wetness seeps between my thighs. What the hell? That's new. I squirm and as if he knows what he is doing to me, Theo grins before his eyes move back to my father.

"Theo, I would also like to discuss the NDA. As you know, my wife is a very high-profile actress. But not only that, Maxwell is one of the biggest names in the US and while I trust you to be discreet during Thalia's training with you, it is something I insist on being signed by yourself and the people who will be working closely with my daughter." Annoyance flashes in Theo's eyes before he schools his features.

"That won't be a problem, Christian. Consider it done." I don't miss the bite in his tone. I grimace that he is having to do this, but it comes with the territory. When you are the daughter of a world-famous actress and one of the richest men in the world, it is something that must happen.

"Good. Now that the formalities are over, I would like to take Thalia to her condo and then tomorrow, she is all yours." My father pushes to a stand, holding his hand out for Theo to shake. "It was nice to meet you in person, Theo. I trust you will make sure my daughter gets settled once I leave." It's not a question. My father expects Theo to take care of his 'princess'.

"Of course, Christian. I will make sure she feels at home here at Rhodes Farms." Theo's eyes slide to me before going back to my father. I push out of my chair, my gaze on Theo as I flash him a small smile. He smiles back causing my stomach to twist. Ignoring it, I rush out of his office and back to the waiting car that will take me to my condo.

Chapter Two

THEO

Thalia Maxwell.

My new trainee student. And a distraction.

I knew she would be attractive. Expected it, what with her being the daughter of Elena Maxwell.

What I didn't expect was for her to be so god damn beautiful, she made my eyes hurt and my cock weep.

With her long dark hair, olive skin and gray eyes, she is otherworldly. Breathtaking.

I had to blink just to make sure she was real, and I wasn't imagining this beauty in front of me. It wasn't just her looks that caught my attention. No. Her smart mouth and defiant attitude made my dick want to jump out of my pants and run right to her.

I groan in frustration. This is bad. Not only is she young, but she is the daughter of one of the most powerful men in not only America but the world. He would ruin me if I so much as looked at her wrong let alone touch the girl. That's not my only problem. As soon as Thalia walked in here, I seemed to have forgotten all about Melody, my *girlfriend*. I might see our relationship as more of a business arrangement but that doesn't change the fact that I have been with her for six years.

Jesus, what is wrong with me? I haven't looked at another woman the whole time I have been in a *relationship*—let alone a barely legal one—and trust me, that is hard considering the sport I am in. Women constantly throw themselves at me when I am at competitions, but I've dismissed every single one of them. Not because I love Mel. But because her father owns my top horses and if I upset her, they will be taken away from me. I can't let that happen. It is because of him and his investments that I have made it as far as I have in my show jumping career.

So why do I suddenly feel like a horny teenager over this girl? Like I would give it all up just to have one taste of her.

Sighing, I scrub a palm down my face. I am a professional. I can keep my relationship with Thalia strictly business. I have done it with the rest of my clients.

A knock at my office door drags me from my thoughts. "Come in." The door opens revealing Tessa, my barn manager. She smiles nervously.

"Theo, hey. I just wanted to ask about Miss Maxwell's horses. Will she be coming back to ride them?" I shake my head.

"No, can you make sure they are exercised? Miss Maxwell will be back later to meet her personal grooms. Can you make sure Maria, Jess, and Milo are ready at 4.00 P.M? They will be assigned to her."

"Of course. I think they are just getting settled into their accommodations, but I will let them know."

"Thank you, Tessa. I will also need you to let every member of staff, and my other trainees, know that I will need them to come by my office to sign some paperwork regarding Miss Maxwell." Tessa's eyes widen before she nods. I have had some very rich students train with me over the years but have never been asked to sign an NDA. This could, of course, have to do with who Thalia's mother is. I guess when your mom is movie star Elena Maxwell and your father is one of the richest men in the world, discretion is necessary.

"I will let them all know." With that, she turns on her heel and leaves me alone with my thoughts.

Thoughts I have no business having.

———

After sorting out all the NDA paperwork, I make my way out to the stall's only to stop when I find Thalia outside in conversation with Tessa. I study her. Every part, from the tips of her toes to the top of her head, groaning when I find her long legs covered in the thin, tight material of her white jodhpurs. I didn't think it was possible for any human to look good in equestrian attire, yet Thalia is proving me wrong. I clear my throat to get their attention. Two pairs of eyes dart to me but my attention falls on the gray pair.

"Thalia? I didn't think you would be back so soon."

"My father had to get back to New York. I wanted to ride my horses, but Tessa informed me they have been exercised today."

"Yes, that is correct. Tomorrow we will start with training. Since you are here, I will introduce you to my team of staff and the other trainees." Thalia nods before stepping towards me. My skin prickles in awareness and my cock twitches the closer she gets to me.

Jesus. I need to get a grip of myself. I am not going to let an eighteen-year-old girl have this kind of hold over me. Even if she isn't aware of the fact. I turn away from her, stalking back to my office. Coming to a stop at the door, I shout.

"Tessa, have all the staff and students come to my office." I don't look at her when I bark this order. I know she will be confused by my tone. I am an arrogant bastard, but I have always treated my staff with respect. Which is why I manage to keep them.

"Of course, Thh-Theo," she stutters. Shame courses through me. It's not Tessa's fault that I have a hard on for my new trainee.

I round my desk and drop down in my chair, glancing up at Thalia who is as quiet as a mouse as she takes a seat. Her inquisitive mesmerizing eyes dart around my office, no doubt taking in my medals of achievement. I clear my throat, her gaze snaps to me.

"So, Thalia, did you get settled into your condo?" She nods, pushing a strand of her dark hair behind her ear.

"Yes, thank you. What time will I be training tomorrow?"

She's eager, I like it. "You can get here around 9' and we will start. I want to see what I am working with and go from there." She scowls but hides it quickly. I bite back a smile. Before she can answer, there is a knock at my door.

"Come in." The door opens and my staff pile in. I don't miss the way their eyes dart to the girl sitting in front of me as they spread themselves around. A possessiveness I have never felt before slithers through me. I want to throw Thalia over my shoulder, run away, and hide her from the world.

"Thank you all for coming. I would like to introduce you to Thalia," I wave towards her. "My newest trainee." They all murmur a hello as she smiles brightly, throwing them a small wave. "Zeus and Lolly both belong to her, and I have assigned Milo as her stable hand and our newest members, Jessica and Maria, you will be Thalia's grooms. Home and competition." They both nod their agreement. I turn to the girl who has gained my attention. "This is the rest of my staff who you will see on a daily basis, so I would like to introduce you to them." I point to my left and start with one of my oldest members of staff who has been with me since I bought this place. "We have Roland, Juan, and Dally, the stable hands. You've met Tessa, my barn manager. Then we have Josephine, Curtis, Rosa, Jorge, Bonnie, Lara, Tiffany, and Stella, the grooms. They all live on site, so you will be seeing a lot of them."

"Nice to meet you all," Thalia says softly, the sound going straight to my cock. They all smile at her, and I don't miss the way the younger guys—Curtis and Dally, to be precise—eye her up.

My heart beats wildly in my chest. I want to claw their eyes out for even daring to look at her.

"You can go," I snap without meaning to. They all flinch and scramble out. Thalia looks at me, a frown on her face. I don't get to say anything because the door knocks again. "Come in," I regret saying it the minute the door opens and Carter Vanderberg, one of my other trainees saunters in. His eyes light up as his gaze rakes all over Thalia's body. I clench my fists, so I don't do something stupid like throat punch the smug fucker.

"Ah, so you must be the lovely Thalia Maxwell?" he drawls arrogantly, and I have never wanted to hit someone as much as I want to hit him right now. Christ, what the fuck is wrong with me? This girl is not mine nor will she ever be.

"Hey," she smiles, so sweetly it makes my teeth ache.

"Carter," I snap. His gaze meets mine, a smug grin in place.

"Yes, Theo? I am just being polite and introducing myself to the beautiful lady." He smirks. My chest rumbles with a possessive growl. I've never liked the kid. Yeah, he pays good money to train with me, but I always thought he was an arrogant asshole that thought he was better than he is. "We will have none of that. You are here to train." He flashes me a smile that tells me everything I need to know; he doesn't care what I say. Just then, my other two trainees stroll in saving me from saying anything else to the asshole.

I glance at Thalia who is staring at me with a perplexed look on her face no doubt picking up on the atmosphere in this room. I clear my throat. "This is Carter Vanderberg, Marissa Massey, and Kiara Stanton. They will be training alongside you."

"Hey, I'm Thalia," she says with a smile and wave. It's so adorable the way she does it. So innocent. So...mine. My eyes widen at that thought. No, she is not mine. Fuck, I need to control myself. I am thirty years old. A man. I've been around plenty of attractive women and managed to keep my hands off, so I can do it with her...but then why does it feel like I have no control over myself? I want to touch her. Feel her soft skin. It's almost as if it's a necessity.

"Hey," Marissa and Kiara greet whilst Carter just eyes her with a look in his eyes that I do not like one bit.

"I just need you to sign some paperwork and you can go." I grab the papers and a pen so they can sign the non-disclosure, not missing the embarrassment that covers Thalia's cheeks. Once that is done, they leave but not before Carter shoots her a flirty wink. Possession claws at my chest and when the door shuts, I turn to her.

"You stay away from him, you hear me?" She rears back like I slapped her.

"Excuse me?" she demands, fire in those gray eyes.

"Stay. Away. From. Him." I enunciate every word for her, just in case she is hard of hearing and doesn't understand. She leans forward.

"I don't think you have any say on who I do and don't stay away from Mr. Rhodes." She hisses my name, but the sound of it from her lips makes my cock jerk.

"You either want to reach your goals or you don't. If you want to run around chasing boys then I suggest college is the way forward, not training with me." I shrug nonchalantly.

Her tiny fists ball, anger radiates from her. "I don't want to chase boys but if I do choose to date, that is up to me. Show jumping is my priority."

Choose to date? What the fuck? No way will I let that happen. I know I am being irrational but for some reason, in the couple of hours I have spent with her, she has brought out this visceral side of me that I didn't even know I had.

"Dating?" I chuckle. "By the time I have finished with you, you will not have time for dating." Her beautiful eyes widen. I don't know what I am saying or why I am saying this—I never have to anyone else who has trained with me - but I cannot seem to stop myself. I don't want her attention anywhere but on me. It's ridiculous. But it's how I feel.

"Are we done? I need to get back to do some schoolwork," she says, ignoring my outburst but I know I got through to her.

"You can go. Just make sure you are here and on a horse by 9.00 A.M."

She glares at me; I have to bite down a laugh at the feisty little kitten. She pushes out of the chair and pulls my door open without another word. I let out a breath I didn't realize I was holding and fall back in my chair.

Jesus, this is bad.

The absolute nerve of that man. Who the hell does he think he is, talking to me like that? I pace my apartment, still in shock at his outburst. I wonder if he is the same with his other students.

I hope not.

Although I am pissed, a part of me likes that he came across as jealous when Carter showed an interest in me. Or maybe that is wishful thinking, and he doesn't really give a damn. He has a girl-friend after all. She is beautiful. Older. British. Not just some eighteen-year-old girl paying to train with him. I flop down on my couch and sigh. I don't want to read into his reaction, but I can't help it. He was normal, professional, until Carter came into the office. I want to know why he acted the way he did.

My cell rings dragging me out of my thoughts. I grab it off the coffee table, smiling when I see my sister's name on the screen.

"Hey Aria," I chirp in greeting.

"Hey little sis, how's Florida treating you?" I chuckle at the excitement in her voice.

"I have only been here about six hours and in that time, I have seen the farm and my condo." Aria sighs dramatically and I know without seeing her she is rolling her eyes.

"What's the hottie show jumper like?" I still at the mention of Theo. Before I came here, Aria and I did some research on him. To say my sister was impressed is an understatement. Let's just say, she nearly packed her bags and came to Florida with me. She doesn't even like horses. "Thalia?" Aria presses. I clear my throat.

"He's okay. I haven't really had much to do with him so far. I have my first training session at 9 A.M." I don't mention the threats Theo issued; Aria would look into it deeper than I already have.

"Jesus Thalia, I mean is he as good looking as he looks in his pictures?" she chuckles.

I sigh in exasperation. Aria is all about the men. She is two years older than me and is currently studying jewelry design at NYU and will eventually work for my father, hoping to one day have her own line at Maxwell's.

"I can confirm that yes, he is hot, Aria." She shrieks so loud I pull the phone from my ear. "Jesus Ari," I snap. She knows I mean business when I call her Ari.

"Sorry, sorry. In his pictures he just looked so damn gorgeous. I'm coming to Wellington the first chance I get." Something a lot like jealousy slithers through me. It's irrational. I know that. I only just met the guy; he was a dick to me, and he has a girlfriend. I need to keep reminding myself of that.

"Have you spoken to Evan?" I ask, quickly changing the subject. Evan is our older brother. At twenty-four, he graduated in International Business and Politics and is already working for our father. He is currently on vacation with his model girlfriend. When I left New York, I never got to say bye.

"No, I have not. I think he gets back from the Maldives tomorrow. He will miss you; you know. You are his and dad's favorite," she grumbles but I know she isn't really bothered. It's because I am the youngest, they are protective of me. Aria and my mother are the same. It can be quite suffocating at times which is why I was so excited to come here on my own. Where Aria is a wild child and a free spirit, I am quite reserved, almost shy. I don't know why I am like that. I was a child model and have appeared in several of my mother's movies.

"I will send a message to the sibling group chat. I think he said he would be in Miami for business at the end of the month, so I'll see him then."

"Of course, he will. He has to make sure no Floridian boys are sniffing around you." I can almost hear her eyes roll. "Anyway, baby sis, I better get going. I am going to a club opening tonight." Of course, she is. Aria loves all that shit.

"Okay. Have fun and be careful. I flove you," I say the revised word we have said to each other for the past several years. It's a mix of fucking and love. We are not allowed to curse around our parents, so we made up our own words that wouldn't get us grounded.

"Flove you too." And with that we end our call.

———

The next morning, I am up early so I can work out before I go to training. Riding horses keeps me fit, but keeping a strict fitness routine helps, especially strength training. I can't be weak when I have 1200 lbs of horse between my legs.

Showered, I get dressed in my jodhpurs and boots. Making my way down to the parking lot, I hop in my SUV and drive to Rhodes Farms.

I feel nervous. Today is the day Theo will assess me. Not only do I have the stress of that, but I still cannot believe what he said to me yesterday. I am here to become a better rider, hopefully work up to a higher level, and that will need all my focus. But if I choose to date, that is up to me. My choice. Not Theo's.

Twenty minutes later, I pull up to the barn. The place is alive with activity and my nerves fray again. I jump out of my vehicle and make my way inside where I find Tessa barking orders at the staff. Hearing my footsteps, she turns to me. She looks flustered. I can't say I am surprised. It takes a whole lot of effort to run an operation like this.

"Good morning, Thalia. You're early." She states glancing at her watch. I nod.

"Yeah, I was actually going to help muck out the stalls." Her eyes widen, no doubt surprised that I said that. I am sure she is used to rich bratty kids that don't want to get their hands dirty and only turn up to ride their horses but that is not me. I may be privileged but I am not above cleaning out my horses' stalls. She clears her throat.

"Don't worry about that, Milo has that covered. Jessica and Maria are just grooming Zeus and Lolly and they will be ready to go for 9.00 A.M. Theo will meet you in the arena."

I smile. "Thank you, I will go and see how they are getting on." I find my horses tied up in the grooming stalls. One of my grooms is with Zeus and one working on Lolly.

"Good morning," I greet, making both their heads shoot toward me. They both smile, stopping what they are doing. The shorter of the two steps towards me, brush in hand.

"Morning, we met yesterday but in case you have forgotten, I am Jessica," she says, holding out her free hand. I take it, giving it a shake.

"Hey. Thalia, in case you forgot." I repeat her words. She chuckles, making me frown.

"I wouldn't forget. We know who you are. Everyone does." I smile shyly as the other woman—Maria—steps up.

"Maria," she speaks with a Spanish lilt. I take her hand like Jessica took mine and give her a firm handshake.

"I was just finishing brushing off Lolly and then I will saddle her up." Jess glances at the watch on her wrist. "Theo will expect you in the arena in fifteen minutes and not a minute later." She grins before turning and heading back to Lolly.

Ten minutes later, I am leading Lolly out to the arena. Nerves dance in my stomach but I will not show them. No way. I spot Theo in the middle, phone to his ear, deep in conversation. I take a second to study him. I have never thought men look hot in jodhpurs, but Theo? Wow. The man is gorgeous. His thick thighs fill every inch of the material, looking like he should be modelling them. My eyes stop on the prominent bulge on display, and I swallow. Jesus. It should be illegal for a man of his...size to wear something so tight. Looking at him is an accident waiting to happen with the way it distracts me. I shake the thought away and continue my perusal. My gaze rakes up his body - safe territory - to the tight black shirt he wears. It showcases every inch of his muscular chest and abs. I stifle a groan. No wonder he is lusted over by so many women in the equestrian world. Me, currently being one of them.

The man is sex personified.

"He is hot, huh?" I startle at the voice, my eyes snapping to the right to find a girl I met yesterday—I think her name is Marissa—standing there, a grin on her face. I smile.

"Umm, yeah I guess," I shrug nonchalantly. She laughs.

"You don't need to lie; we all think it. It won't get you anywhere though. He has been with Melody for six years. They look so in love. Wait until you see them together." For some reason, her words make me feel sick with jealousy. I have no right to feel like this. He isn't mine, never will be. I smile tightly and continue to the arena where Theo has now finished his call. He glances up, pocketing his cell.

"Ah Thalia, nice to see you this morning." He glances at his watch, and I *know*. I just know he is checking I am not late. Asshole.

"Morning Theo." I shoot him a saccharine smile. I swear I see his lips twitch.

"Okay, go over to the mounting block and hop on. Then we will get started." I stride to the block with an air of confidence I don't feel. I bring Lolly to a stop, climb the three steps and get on. I adjust my position and put my feet in the stirrups. God, it feels good to be back on a horse. I give her a squeeze and do a lap around the arena in a walk, just letting myself get a feel of her.

"Trot on Thalia, we do not have all day," Theo barks, I resist an eye roll. Surely, he should allow me to get settled in the saddle. Instead of arguing my point, I kick into a trot, working Lolly's head into a nice outline. I have never been one for dressage, but I do like my horses to be schooled nice.

After warming up in a trot, I push into a canter. I am in my own little world, enjoying being back on my horse when Theo's voice breaks through.

"Sit up, Thalia, you look like a sack of potatoes," he shouts. My head snaps to him and I scowl. The man may be hot, but he is a douche. I drop down into a trot, groaning when Theo calls me to go to him. I stop in front of him, not even bothering to hide my glare. He clenches his jaw.

"I don't know if it is just because you are nervous, but I expected your standard of riding to be higher than this." I open my mouth to argue but he cuts me off by grabbing my leg. Electricity shoots through me as every nerve ending in my body comes alive at his touch. I know he feels it too when his eyes shoot to mine, and he swallows. "Heel down, Thalia." He shoves my heel into position and moves his hand further up my leg. Goosebumps trail my skin; my lips part and my breathing picks up.

"Squeeze with your legs and grip with your knees," he murmurs before letting me go. His gaze meets mine, the heat in them has my eyes widening. Theo shakes his head and clears his throat. "Now, go into a canter. I will put some jumps up and see what you are capable of. From watching you so far, I don't have high expectations." My mouth drops open at the audacity of this asshole. Ignoring me, he turns on his heels and heads to the jumps, leaving me determined to prove the arrogant bastard wrong.

Chapter Four

THEO

I am in hell.

I knew it would be hard training Thalia after my...visceral reaction to her yesterday. I just didn't think it would be this hard. Watching her smile in her element as she rides her horse. Her pussy grinding against the saddle as she sits in it.

I groan.

Never did I think I would be jealous of a saddle but here I am. I want to pull her from it and get her to grind on me like that. My brain has malfunctioned and all I can think about is her riding me. Taking my cock as I sink inside of her. My dick twitches in my jodhpurs and I now wish I had worn sweatpants or jeans. Not something that clings to me and shows every outline. I quickly move to stand behind one of the arena decorations, hiding my erection as I call out to her.

"Thalia, come down to the upright, then turn left and jump the oxer," I shout. She does as I say, jumping the fences I have set out for her. She isn't that bad of a rider, to be honest, and her horse is okay. It won't be good enough for what she is aiming to achieve. If she wants to be the best, to step up a level, then she needs to listen to what I tell her, even if she doesn't like what I have to say. She jumps them a couple more times and I have seen enough.

"Okay, that's enough. Hop off and hand Lolly to Jessica to cool down. Maria is bringing Zeus out." She nods, jumping off and passing the horse to Jessica. She spins and starts towards me. I stand frozen behind the artificial plant, my dick hardening at the sight of her in those tight white jodhpurs that cling to her every curve.

Jesus. She needs to walk the other way before she sees the bulge in mine. I am not exactly small and if she gets any nearer, she will easily see the outline of my cock. My heart rate picks up as she gets closer, and I know I need to do something. I clear my throat, ready to tell her to go and see where Zeus is, when I spot Maria bringing him out of the barn. I sigh in relief. Crisis averted.

"Thalia, hop on Zeus," I almost snap. She frowns before spinning and spotting her horse. She marches toward him, her heart shaped ass bouncing as she walks away. I have never seen such a perfect ass in my life.

I groan.

Again.

What the fuck is this girl doing to me? I have never had such a reaction toward a woman before.

Thalia comes to an abrupt stop by the side of him and bends.

She. Fucking. Bends.

Her ass is now in full view of me. My dick jerks, as my jaw clenches. A wolf whistle sounds and my head jerks to the viewing area where Carter *fucking* Vanderberg watches Thalia like she is his next meal. My blood boils and I see red.

"Go and get suited up, Carter, you're up next," I bark, making his head whip to me, a knowing grin on his face. I want to kill the bastard. In fact, I just might. That or end his contract with me. He stares at me for a long beat before mock saluting—because he is an asshole—and walks away. I glance at Thalia, who is studying me intently. Like I am a puzzle she must solve.

"Get on the horse, Thalia, I don't have all day," I drawl. She scowls and I bite back a smile. The girl is feisty. I like it.

I like it a lot.

———

After finishing my second session with Thalia and Zeus, she hands him off to Maria and I take her to my office. She needs to understand that as much as she loves her horses, they are not quite good enough. I have a deal ready on the table for a world class level horse that I think would be a perfect fit for her. Yes, I will be set to earn a nice cut—like most trainers do—but it's more than that. She has dreams and I want to help her succeed in them.

I take a seat behind my desk, tracking Thalia's every move as she walks from the door to the chair in front of me. She drops down in the wingback, takes a breath as if she is readying herself for my wrath, and then her gray eyes meet mine as she nibbles that plump bottom lip. My cock jumps and I silently beg the fucker to behave.

He needs to realize this girl is off limits.

I need to remember this girl is off limits.

One wrong move. *One* wrong touch. Everything I have built in the last six years will be destroyed.

Her family is powerful. One of the richest families in the world. I have no doubt her father would come for me if I ever made a move on her, ever touched her in a way I am not supposed to.

She clears her throat, snapping me out of my thoughts. I steeple my fingers and eye her.

"So, Thalia. From what I have seen today, Zeus and Lolly are not good enough for what you want to achieve," I start, and I know my words are going to annoy her. Her facial expression tells me I am right. "I have a horse lined up for you to view in Europe.

I think we should discuss plans to fly there in the next couple of weeks," I finish, waiting for her response. It's a bad idea really. Me flying to Europe with her. On our own. But if we don't move quickly then someone else might snap him up before us. Thalia clears her throat and I brace myself for what she is going to say.

"Theo, while I respect your comments on both my horses, how can you tell from one session how talented they are? I already agreed to view the horse you have lined up, but I will be running Zeus and Lolly alongside any other horse my father purchases." Her voice is calm, but I can tell she is pissed. I don't care. Because now I am pissed. How dare she question my words.

"Thalia, you told me you want to be the best. You want to step up a level, compete in the Global tour. No disrespect but Lolly and Zeus are not capable of that. They are one meter thirty horses at best. If you are going to question me at every turn then I would rather you train with somebody else. I have been in this game a long time. You either listen to me or you find someone else to put up with your attitude. Because I will not. I am not here to play My Little Ponies with you. I am here to make you the best."

Her mouth gapes—no doubt because the princess has never been spoken to like that before—and her eyes widen before she schools herself, purses her lips, and plasters on a fake smile.

"Whatever you say, Theo. I will speak with my father and see when it is suitable for me to use the jet. What days are you thinking you would like us to go?" Of course, the Maxwells have a private jet. God forbid if they had to fly commercial.

"We can fly out next week if that works for you and your father. I know he is a busy man."

———

"Darling, how are you?" Melody's posh British accent comes over the speaker of my cell. I glance at the time. It's just past midnight here which means it's very early in London. There was a time I thought I could love her. She is beautiful. Fun. But over the years, I realized I can't. I have used her to further my career. Which makes me a complete asshole. Don't get me wrong, I like the woman but sometimes I wonder why the hell I stay with her. I know it's the horses, but I could find other investors now that I am number one in the world. It's just easier to be with her. I don't feel too guilty though. She uses me as much as I use her. Melody loves the attention that comes with being with me. And me? I love the money her father invests to keep me at the top. She trained with me when I was based in Britain. She was never great, just a rich girl playing with daddy's money. I knew she liked me, and I used it to my advantage. Eventually she gave up show jumping and convinced her father to buy horses for me.

"I'm good, Mel, it's just been a long day. What are you doing?"

"I am just going for an early yoga class. What is Thalia Maxwell like?" she asks excitedly. Melody is a big fan of Thalia's mother. When I told her she would be training with me, it was like she had won the lottery. Not that she needs to. Melody's parents are rich. Not Thalia Maxwell rich but rich enough that Melody doesn't have to work. I scrub a palm down my face at her question and make a mental note to make sure she signs the NDA involving Thalia when she comes back to the states.

"Melody, she is like any other of my trainees. Do not go all fan girl when you get here. It's business" I scold. Melody chuckles.

"Calm down, Theo, I was only asking. I have seen pictures of her, she is very attractive." I swallow harshly at her words. Thalia is beyond attractive. Not only that, but she has this innocence about her that I want to taint. I want to dirty her up. Watch her lips part, eyes widen, hear her moans as I shove my cock in her. The thought has my dick hardening to stone.

I quickly shake the thoughts away, not wanting to go down that road. I have already agreed with myself that I will stay away from her in any way other than in a professional capacity.

"I haven't noticed," I lie. "She is a job to me Melody, just like Carter, Marissa, and Kiara."

"Theo, darling, I am not stupid. Even a blind man could see that the girl is attractive." She laughs out and I wonder why she is pushing for me to admit this.

"When are you coming here?" I ask, changing the subject.

"In the next couple of weeks. I have some events to attend for my father and mother first. I would like you to join me, but I know that will not be possible with your schedule." I don't miss the accusation in her tone. She has been begging me to join her in England for the last month. For some reason, I don't mention to her that I will be flying to Europe in the next week or so to view a horse with Thalia.

"Okay. Let me know when you book flights, and I will be at the airport to pick you up."

"Okay, darling. I better go, otherwise, I will be late and Carolyn hates when I am late. Be good. Love you."

"Talk to you soon," I end the call before she can drill me about not saying those three little words back. I don't love Melody, never have. Never will. We happened by accident. I got drunk one night when I was competing her father's horses in Europe, and we slept together. It was my first mistake, crossing that line. I was unprofessional and one of the reasons I put a stop to drinking so much. I thought it would just be a one-time fuck, but Melody had other ideas. And let's just say those ideas included a relationship and a ring at some point in the future. I was weak back then, wanting to keep her father as an owner, and not in a good place in my life. I gave in when I shouldn't have. It made her dad happy. Made her happy. Fast forward six years and here I am. Still with Melody in a relationship that I never wanted. I guess the saying is true though.

Every action has a consequence.

And Melody was mine.

———

The next morning, I am sitting in my office when my cell rings. I glance at my phone to find Christian Maxwell's name on the screen. Hitting the accept button, I answer the call.

"Christian," I say by way of greeting.

"Good morning, Theo, I hope you are well. I spoke with Thalia last night about the trip to Europe to view the horse you mentioned."

"That is right, I do hope that it is okay for me to discuss these things with Thalia?"

"Of course. She is eighteen and quite capable of making decisions on her own." I swallow at the reminder that she is eighteen, therefore perfectly legal. "I was hoping I could make the trip, but it looks like I have business in Los Angeles to attend to. I do trust Thalia will be safe with you, Theo?" he questions. I don't miss the underlying message in his voice. Will she be safe with me? Of course, she will. Doesn't mean she will be safe *from* me. I freeze at my thoughts. Jesus, I need to get my shit together. Stay away from the girl. I clear my throat.

"Of course, Christian." He lets out a breath.

"Good, good. I will arrange for one of my jets to take you. Let me know where you will be flying into and the area you are staying. I will have my assistant book accommodations. I have also arranged for security to join Thalia. I discussed this with you when we first spoke, and I would feel better if my daughter had a security detail when she is travelling abroad. I know it is probably overkill but I don't want to take any chances with my baby girl's safety." I nod, even though he cannot see me.

"Makes sense, Christian. Although I think I am very much capable of taking care of and ensuring no harm comes to her." I chuckle, although I am a little annoyed that he would think otherwise.

"I don't doubt that, Theo. I just want to have everything

covered. This is the first time she will be travelling abroad without family, and I would like to know she is protected in every way. It has nothing to do with your capabilities, it is just a worried father making sure his baby girl will be okay."

"Yes, of course. I will be in touch with the details in the next twenty-four hours, once I have spoken with Thalia."

"Wonderful. Have a good day, Mr. Rhodes." Christian ends the call. I drop my cell on my desk and lean back in my leather chair. Maybe I should tell Christian he needs to find someone else to train his daughter. It's not that I think she will find better. Because she won't. I just worry my restraint will snap and I will end up doing something that will ruin me. I can already feel this pull between us. I already feel a possessiveness I cannot explain over her. A knock at my door drags me out of my thoughts.

"Come in." A second later, my door is pushed open and the girl that is currently occupying my mind steps in. "You should be on a horse," I snap because I want to push her far away. I want her to dislike me. She straightens her spine, squares her shoulders, and I just know she is going to fire off with that smart mouth.

"Lolly is saddled up and I will be getting on in a minute," she hisses. "I was coming to let you know, my father is making arrangements for our trip to Europe." She glares at me. Her gray eyes sparkle. She looks beautiful. I clear my throat.

"Yes, well, I just spoke with your father, myself. Please go and get on your horse so we can begin." She stares at me a long beat before nodding and turning on her heel. I let out a harsh breath.

Those few days away with her will be torture and a real test on my self-control.

————

"Sit up straight, heels down. Stop being so stiff. Relax, Thalia, the horse can feel it and responds to what you are feeling. Everything needs to be smoother. More fluidity." She takes a breath and relaxes as she schools the horse in the arena.

"Good girl, much better. Can you feel how Lolly has relaxed? Remember, you have a living breathing animal between your legs. They feel what you feel." I internally groan at the mention of between her legs, wanting to know what it would feel like. What she looks like. Christ. I shake the thoughts from my head and watch her for a couple more minutes. I can see the improvement already, now that she is listening to what I'm saying.

"Good, do you see the difference in the horses when you listen?" She shoots me a look that tells me she wants to hit me but instead, she nods. I stifle a laugh.

"Right, cool her down and then meet me in my office."

———

"So, Thalia, I can see the improvement in you today even in such a short space of time, although I would not be comfortable letting you compete any higher than one meter twenty right now." Her eyes widen, she opens her mouth to speak but I hold my hand up to stop her. "That being said, you have potential and I think with the right horse, the right training we can get you to where you want to be. We will fly to Europe to view this horse and if it is not the right fit, I will line some more up to view. I want to get you ready for a competition at Royal Palm Equestrian Centre at the end of August. I think then I can really see what I'm dealing with. After that, we have a couple more competitions—let's call them a warmup—and then come January, we start the Winter Equestrian Festival tour. That will really give you a chance to show me what you are made of and get your name out there. If you get good results, it could mean potentially making the nation's Cups teams next year. After Royal Palm, we will travel and set up a base in Europe. It is the best place to be, and we will have our pick of FEI competitions. There is also the Global Champions tour, which I am sure you are already aware that your fathers' company will be sponsoring next year?" She nods. "Again, if you get good results, you'll get your name out there. You have the means and backing to achieve what you want. It is just a matter of listening to me and trusting my judgement. If you do that, I see no reason why you won't make teams or get good results," I finish. Thalia flashes a tight smile.

"That is good to hear, Theo. For a minute there I thought you were going to tell me to leave. To give up horse riding because I am no good." I don't miss the sarcasm in her voice. It makes my cock hard. I am only grateful I am sitting behind my desk, and she can't see it. I smirk.

"Well, for a moment there I thought I would be telling you just that. But I can see you want to learn, and you have the ambition. So, I'm willing to spend my precious time teaching you." Her lip tips up in a slight snarl. For some reason I get off on getting a reaction out of her. "On another note, we need to arrange details with your father for the horse we will be trying out. I think next week will be a good time to go."

Thalia nods, before pushing out of her chair. "Is that all? I want to go and bathe my horses,"

I frown. "Thalia, you have grooms for that,"

"I know, but I want to do it myself. To you, I may just be another spoiled little rich girl playing My Little Ponies, but I am not afraid to get my hands dirty. I love my horses and I want to bathe them. I also want to be the best I can be which is why I ignore the way you speak to me. If you think you are going to keep goading me until I crack and leave, then you have another thing coming. Keep throwing shit at me, but I am not going anywhere. I am serious about this." And with that, she spins and makes her way to the door, exiting my office. My mouth gapes, and my cock turns to granite at her words.

Jesus, I think I underestimated her. Honestly, I thought she was exactly what she just said. But here she is, proving me wrong.

None of my other trainees would be out there bathing their horses. None of my other trainees would call me on my shit attitude either. I want to keep Thalia at a distance but her feisty and take no shit attitude is proving to be an aphrodisiac. Even if I cannot admit that I want her...my dick can. I have never been so hard in my life than when I am around this girl. I fall back in my chair with a groan.

Fucking Thalia Maxwell. Coming into my space and stirring everything up. I need to stay away. I need Melody to get her ass back so I can get my dick wet. I need Thalia to stop prancing around looking so damn sexy. She is not aware of the reactions she elicits in me, but I just need her to stop...being her.

I scrub a palm down my face, growling in frustration. Something tells me things are going to get a whole lot more interesting around here.

Chapter Five

THALIA

I spend the next few days working my horses and getting to know the staff and other trainees. I take my grooms out for dinner. Jess, Maria and Milo. They seem shocked that I do. I'm not sure why. I may be a Maxwell, have appeared in movies and modelling campaigns, but I am just a normal girl. And in the showjumping world, that is what I want to be. Normal. I don't want to be treated differently because of who my parents are.

"So, Thalia, how are you finding training so far?" Jess asks around a mouthful of her burger. I grin. I like Jess, she's cool.

"Yeah, it's good. Although Theo can be a bit of an ass." They all frown and I wonder what I said for them to have this reaction. I open my mouth to ask when Jess speaks.

"I don't get it. I mean, yeah, he has his off days like we all do. But from what I hear and what I have been told, he has never been outright rude to anyone. Tessa sings his praises; thinks he is amazing. But I have heard how he speaks to you and yeah, he is an ass." It's my turn to frown.

"I'm not going to lie. I have been at Rhodes Farms for a while now and I know I only muck out the stalls, but Theo has always seemed nice. Always treated us with respect no matter what our job roles are," Milo adds. I mull over this information before sighing.

"Maybe it's just me then. He obviously doesn't like me." Snorts sound and my eyes bounce between them.

"Honey, there is no way he doesn't not like you. Have you seen you? Maybe it's one of those situations like in school with a bully and he is picking on you because he does *like* you but not in a way he should." This is from Maria. I snort, although my cheeks heat at the thought.

"I don't think so. He has a girlfriend," I scoff. But deep down, I hope there is some truth in what they say. I hope Theo does like me. Because even though he is a complete dick, there is something that draws me to him.

———

"Well done, Thalia, that was very good. Now come around to the combination. I want you to sit up, keep your leg on and hit the right strides between each fence," Theo shouts out to me. I smile. I can't help it. I like it when he praises me. Though it isn't often, I have come to crave it. Seek his approval. What the hell is wrong with me? I shouldn't want to please this man, but I do. With every bone in my body, I do. I round the corner of the arena, doing as Theo says. Sit straight. Leg on. The first part, I take a stride out which doesn't help for the rest of them. I completely fuck it up and I await his wrath.

"What the fuck was that? I set it perfectly, expecting you to hit it right. Not jump the first part a stride out then fuck the rest up. Now go again," he snaps. I sigh. Pushing into a canter, I round the corner again, this time my head clear and focused on the combination as it should have been the first time. I clear it this time, the way Theo expected me to, and smile. I dare him to say something bad about it. I slow down to a trot, then a walk, glancing at him when he remains silent. His lips are pressed together in a hard line, but I don't miss the look of satisfaction in his eyes. I walk toward him, cocking a brow, silently asking him for his opinion. He lets out a harsh breath.

"Much better," he mumbles begrudgingly. "Cool him down. We are done for the day. Better to leave it on a good one, than keep trying and fuck it up again." I smirk, mock saluting him.

"Yes boss." His lips twitch but he doesn't smile. Just turns and stalks toward the barn.

I think I won that one.

I ride back to the barn; Maria appears and grabs the reins. I wave her off.

"It's okay, Maria, I want to groom him." She looks at me like I have two heads and I snort. It never ceases to amaze me that people just assume I am here to ride and not get into the nitty gritty of things.

I tie Zeus in the cross ties and remove his tack, taking it to the room where it is all stored. The smell of leather hits me as soon as I step inside, and I inhale. There is nothing like the smell of horse tack. I pop it on my assigned saddle and bridle racks. I make my way back to Zeus, where I wash him off then groom him. I spend a good fifteen minutes doing this and I don't miss all the confused looks sent my way from the staff. It's in that moment that I know the other students don't do this sort of thing. Carter walking over and speaking confirms it.

"You know, you pay someone else to do that for you." I look at him and smile. Carter is an attractive guy with his light brown hair and chestnut eyes. But you can tell he is privileged, rich, and would never lower himself to doing something as simple as grooming his horses. It's doing things like this that ground me. I enjoy it. It's my happy place.

"I am aware," I shrug. He steps toward me, reaching out to try and take the brush from my hands. I frown at him as he throws it to the side.

"Why don't you leave your groom to do that and let me take

you for dinner." I stare at him for a long beat before I chuckle and grab the brush he just took from me.

"I'm good thanks, Carter." Undeterred, he steps right up to me. His mouth drops to my ear, hot breath hitting me.

"Come on, princess. I want to get to know you. Let me take you out, have…" he trails off, heading snapping up when a voice booms across the barn.

"Thalia, can I see you in my office…NOW." Theo snaps the last word, making both me and Carter jump. Theo turns and, in a few steps, disappears into his office.

"Who pissed him off?" I glance to Carter, who is watching with confusion the space where Theo just stood.

"Probably me. I only have to breathe, and he gets angry." Carter chuckles, his eyes softening as he looks down at me. He jerks his head.

"Go on. You better go before he comes back out." I sigh before asking Maria to pop Zeus back in his stall and then I make my way to the office of doom. I step inside. Theo is watching his laptop intently, never once looking at me.

"Shut the door," he mutters, and I do as he says. I obviously did something to piss him off and I don't want to antagonize him further. I drop down in one of the seats facing him and wait for him to speak. It takes a long minute but eventually his blue eyes come to mine, the intensity in them makes my breath hitch.

"All arrangements have been made for us to travel to Europe next week. We fly Wednesday evening in your father's jet. Be here no later than 5.00 P.M." My brows furrow in confusion. I already know all this. My father told me. Instead of questioning him., I nod.

"That's great," I respond because I don't know what else to say. He eyes me, his lips twitching into a…smile?

"You did good today, well after you fucked up that one time, but I guess we all make mistakes. Especially when it comes to a live animal." I am utterly confused right now. How can he go from being so asshole like... to this? Complimenting me. Smiling at me. My lips curve into a grin on their own volition. I like this side of him.

"What are you smiling at?" he rasps, the sound going straight between my legs. My cheeks heat and I drop my eyes to my lap. "Thalia?" My gaze moves back to his, the heat in them has my heart pounding in my chest. I may not be experienced with men, but I know lust when I see it. Does he want me?

"Nothing. It's just nice to get a compliment." He grins bigger, the sight is heartbreaking. It should be illegal to be that good looking.

"I am not always an asshole, Thalia." His words are so soft, they wrap around me, caress my skin until goosebumps appear. What is this man doing to me?

"Debatable," I whisper, then clamp my mouth shut. He throws his head back and laughs. A real laugh. I feel like I have entered another dimension. I have only been here just over a week and Theo has never acted like this with me. He has been standoffish. Cold. This Theo, the one that smiles, laughs and compliments me, is one I can get on board with.

"Yeah, I guess. Anyway, you better get home. I'm sure you have schoolwork to catch up on." he states. I nod, pushing out of my chair with a shy smile. Stopping at the door, I turn to find his eyes still on me. My stomach dips. Never in my life have I wanted someone's eyes on me as much as I want his.

"Thank you," I whisper. With that, I leave his office.

Chapter Six

THEO

I don't know what I am playing at. I told myself to stay away from her but when I saw Carter fawning over her like she hung the fucking stars and the moon, I couldn't stop myself. My blood boiled and I saw red. I had to get her away from him. From there, it went from bad to worse. I softened toward her. I was nice. I need to keep up the asshole act, so she hates me. I can't have her making eyes at me like she just did. Like I am everything she needs. Everything she wants.

"Fuck," I mutter the curse in frustration. Maybe I should let her go. Tell her she will be better off training with someone else. But then, what if someone else gets his claws into her? I know how show jumpers are and even if I sent her to a female trainer, she would still be open to the male attention at competitions. And trust me, she will have all their attention. Before I got with Mel, I was the worst of them all. Always sleeping around. There were a few of us that would even make bets on who could bag the most women at competitions. Me being the competitive asshole I am, I always came out on top. I am not like that anymore. I haven't touched another woman since I have been with Mel and that's saying something, considering I don't even love her, and I have women throw themselves at me at every event I compete at. It's not a big ego. It's the truth. The women in this sport are just as horny as the men. Sometimes worse.

I can't have Thalia around that environment without me protecting her. I need to keep her away from that side of the show jumping world. The toxic fucked up sexualized part where anything goes.

And I mean anything.

From the outside, the world of show jumping is money, glitz, and glamor. But all that glitters is not gold, and dig deep enough, you find out the truth. The seediness. The corruption. The horniest people around. I shake my head. With those thoughts in mind, I know I won't be letting Thalia go anywhere else. She is staying with me, where I can keep an eye on her. Keep the vultures away because I know they will come. Not just because she is going to be the hottest piece of ass on the circuit but also because of her name. They will all be trying to lock down the beauty that is Thalia Maxwell. For selfish reasons too. They will be wanting to use her like I do Mel, hoping her family will invest in their next rides and get them to the next level.

Guilt floods my chest. I am no better. I keep Mel around because of the money her father plows into my career.

But I will keep Thalia safe.

Even if it's from myself.

————

I turn a circle on Eros after jumping the big oxer I have up in the arena. Eros is my top horse and the one who I went to the Olympics with last year. He is nearly 17 hands and gray in color. At only nine years old, he is so talented and has so much to give. Over the last few years, I have had many offers for him but have always convinced Mel's father it would be more beneficial to keep him. And it is.

For me.

Movement out the corner of my eye has me glancing over to the viewing area to find Thalia watching me with a smile tipping her lips. I pull to a walk and check my watch. It's past 4. She shouldn't be here. It's been a few days since my jealousy got the best of me and I called her into my office and it's a few days until we fly to Belgium. I stride toward her, studying her face. Her determination, eagerness to learn, never ceases to amaze me. If I am honest, I thought she would be like every other spoiled rich kid that trains with me. But no. She is different. The fact she is willing to groom and muck out her horses tells me that.

"Hey," I rasp.

"Hey, that was amazing," she breathes. The sound of her voice goes straight to my cock and makes it harden against the damn saddle. It's hard enough riding a horse with a dick between your legs, and I am not small by any means. But when you have someone like Thalia in front of you, it is ten times worse.

"Thanks. What are you doing here? Shouldn't you be doing schoolwork or something?" It's not really a question. Part of the agreement with her father about being here was on the condition that she studied online. It's important to him that she gets a college degree, and I can't blame him. A lot of people don't make a career in this sport, only as a hobby. An expensive one at that. The only difference with Thalia is her family is so rich, they have the means to get her to the top. Not that it matters either way. The girl has the world at her feet and the potential and determination to do whatever she wants.

"I finished all my work. I wanted to come and see the horses, then I saw you out here and wanted to watch. You can learn a lot from watching your idol." I smirk, blowing out a breath. Jesus. I am this girl's idol? The thought makes me rock hard.

"Thalia, you will make my ego bigger than it already is if you say shit like that." She smiles beautifully. The sight is so beautiful, I blink just so she doesn't blind me.

"You are. I have admired you ever since I saw you compete at the Global tour in New York. You were amazing. I knew then that you were the only person I wanted to train with. I followed your career, watched you on the live streams whenever you competed. There is something to be said about the way you come together with a horse; you make it look so effortless. So...mesmerizing," she breathes. My heart beats so hard in my chest I think it's about to jump out. Wow, I think I just fell in love.

Kidding.

Maybe.

If she carries on, I just might. I had no idea she felt like this. Shaking my head, I remember Mel and that I'm supposed to be staying away from Thalia like this. I clear my throat.

"Thank you, that is nice of you to say. You should get home. I have stuff to do." Her mouth drops open at the change in my tone, but she nods, pushing to a stand and leaves. I sit there for a few minutes, watching her. She thinks I am mesmerizing but it's her that takes that title. She has no idea what she does to me. What *I* want to do to her. I groan in frustration. This girl is dangerous. If I'm not careful, make one wrong move, I could lose everything I have worked so hard for.

So why does she feel like she is worth risking it all for?

Chapter Seven

THALIA

We pull up to the private airfield. Theo ignored me the whole journey, focusing solely on his cell. I would take offence, but the guy is so hot and cold with me, I can't bring myself to care about his little mood swings. The driver hops out of the SUV, followed by my security for the trip, Greg. He has worked for my family for years and my father insisted he accompany me since we're leaving the country. My door opens and I hop out without looking to see if Theo is following.

"Miss Maxwell," Frederic, one of my father's pilots, greets. "The jet is ready to go. It looks like it will be a smooth flight to Belgium and the flight time is expected to be a little over ten hours. Please board when you are ready, and we will get on our way."

"Thank you, Fred. We'll board right away." He nods before making his way to the jet. It's a relatively new purchase of my father's—apparently one private jet isn't enough—a Gulfstream G650ER and a little larger than the Bombardier Global 7500, his other aircraft. You may be wondering how I know all this. Well, let's just say I am a bit of an aviation geek and my father explained in full detail the models of aircrafts, what they do, and the differences between them.

"Nice jet," Theo lets out a low whistle dragging me out my thoughts. I glance at him; he looks so handsome right now in casual wear and a ball cap. My eyes drop to his torso, the way the plain white tee clings to his muscled arms and six pack.

Jesus. The man is sex on legs.

"Thalia?" Theo smirks, having caught me full on checking him out. I shake my head and start to board the plane.

"We need to board, the pilot is ready," I blurt. Theo snickers behind me as I climb the steps. I need to remind myself that he is my trainer, nothing more... But I feel this pull toward him, despite his asshole ways. I feel Theo hot on my heels, so close to me, his breath hitting my ear creating goose bumps.

"Eager to get to Europe Princess?" I don't miss the smile in his voice.

"Yes, the quicker we get there, the sooner we get back," I snap, taking a seat in one of the plush chairs towards the back. Theo looks around, before deciding on the seat opposite me.

"It doesn't work like that, Princess. I am not going to rush this viewing. We need to make sure it's right."

"Why are you calling me Princess all of a sudden?" I ask.

Theo smirks, motioning around at the inside of the jet with his hands. "Do you not see this? I mean, I train rich kids; I have a rich *girlfriend*," he enunciates the word, whether to remind me or himself. I'm not sure. "But not on this level. Daddy did well for his princess."

"Stop calling me that," I hiss. "My father works hard for what he has achieved. You shouldn't shame people for that."

He eyes me for a long minute before speaking. "Oh, I'm not shaming anyone. He has done well. I'm referring to some research I did a few days ago. It's common knowledge that you are Daddy's princess. The *good* girl. The *well-behaved* sibling." He flashes me his straight white teeth and I open my mouth to respond but the blonde attendant speaks, stopping me.

"Miss Maxwell, my name is Lauren, and I will be looking after you this flight. Can I get you a drink?" Her gaze briefly shifts to Theo, and I don't miss the way her eyes light up.

I nod. "Thank you, Lauren, can I get a still water please?"

"And for you sir?" She turns to face Theo fully. I can't see her face but whatever is on it makes him smirk.

"A whiskey on the rocks would be great, Lauren." He flashes her a smile that makes my pussy clench and Lauren blushes before she scurries off to make our drinks. I inwardly groan.

Fuck.

This is going to be a long trip.

———

We land in Belgium around ten hours later, just like Fred said. After Lauren handed me my water, I excused myself and made my way to the private cabin at the back of the jet. It has a double bed, and I wanted a decent sleep. I also wanted to get away from Theo. Things feel weird between us. Like we were playing some sort of game, and it was a case of who was going to give in first. I don't want to play anything with him. I just want him to train me. I just want to ride my horses.

I make my way off the jet to the waiting SUV. Theo is back to ignoring me and glued to his cell. I don't have much experience around men but if they are all like this then screw them. I will stay a virgin forever. I don't want or need their shit or mood swings.

"Miss Maxwell, I am Elias. I will be your driver for the duration of your trip." The tall man standing by the SUV greets in a Dutch accent. I flash him a smile.

"Good morning, Elias. This is Theo and Greg." I point to the two men. Elias shakes both of their hands before loading my bags into the vehicle. I get inside, rubbing my arms to keep warm. It's much colder in Belgium than it is in Florida.

The back door opens, revealing a grinning Theo. I resist a groan. He is so beautiful, it hurts. "Cold, Princess?" he teases. I roll my eyes but otherwise ignore him and switch my cell on so I can let my father know we've arrived. I pull up his details and hit call on his name. It only rings three times before he answers.

"Hello sweetheart, have you landed?" I nod even though he can't see me.

"Yes, Daddy. We have met with the driver and will be leaving shortly for the barn."

"That's good. Please keep me updated and let me know how things go. Theo informed me that if this horse is not the right fit, he has another lined up in the UK, so the trip could be a bit longer if that happens." I glance at Theo, whose lips are tipped up in a smirk as he stares at his cell.

"Okay, I will call you later. Love you, Daddy,"

"Love you too sweetheart, be careful." He ends the call. I shove my cell in my purse and lean back on the leather seat, letting out a harsh breath.

"Something wrong, Princess?" I roll my head to look at Theo, narrowing my eyes on his smug face.

"No, *Theo*, everything is great." I flash him a saccharine smile. His lips twitch and he shakes his head before focusing back on his cell.

———

We pull up to the impressive white brick barn. Theo steps out of the vehicle and greets a tall man who strides toward us.

"Lois, good to see you."

"Good to see you too, Theo," Lois drawls in a thick Dutch accent. It's much stronger than Elias's. I climb out of the vehicle when Greg opens my door, and make my way around to the two men who are now laughing. Lois stills when he spots me, his eyes zeroing in on me as a smirk crosses his face. Theo, who has his back to me, glances over his shoulder at what has caught his friend's attention. When he sees it's me, his jaw clenches. He spins his whole body to face me.

"Lois, this is Thalia, *my* student," he introduces me and if I am not mistaken there is a hint of possessiveness in his voice. Lois closes the distance between us and takes my hand in his, shaking it as his eyes rake over me. He isn't a bad looking guy and looks to be around the same age as Theo. But it still makes me feel self conscious, the way he is looking at me.

"Nice to meet you, Thalia, it's not every day we have such a beautiful woman at our stables." I blush, tugging my hand out of his when he holds it a bit longer than what is deemed appropriate. A hand clamps down on my shoulder. My gaze snaps up, finding Theo now hovering over me, but his eyes are on Lois.

"Don't, Lois. She is not like the women you are used to," Theo grits, his voice low, intimidating. Lois flashes him a grin.

"Of course, Theo. I was just being friendly. If I cannot appreciate such a beauty, then it is a crime," he chuckles out as I stand here wondering what the hell is going on. "Come, come. The horse is ready to be saddled up." He spins on his heel and strides back to the barn. I glance up at Theo who seems to be frozen.

"Theo?" I whisper, making his eyes dart to mine. He shakes his head as if he is ridding himself of a thought.

"Let's go, Thalia," he says harshly and strides in the direction Lois went. I glance over at Greg, who is watching me with narrowed eyes.

"Are you coming?" I ask with a raised brow. He shakes his head and pushes off the SUV.

"You need to be careful around all these men, Thalia. You are an attractive young woman that can easily be taken advantage of." My eyebrows furrow in confusion.

"What do you mean?" I look up at Greg as we walk toward the barn. He shakes his head and sighs.

"Just be careful." I frown, wondering what's wrong with all these men today. Maybe it's lack of sleep?

We step into the barn with movement everywhere and around twenty stalls all filled with horses. Spotting Lois and Theo by a dark gray horse, I make my way over. Lois's eyes land on me and they sparkle with what looks a lot like mischief?

"Ah, Thalia. This is Roman, also known as Romantiek. It means romance in English." Lois flashes me a smile before continuing. "He is currently the number one horse in Europe and has competed on the Dutch Nations Cup teams with me. He is a very good horse." I nod, glancing at Roman. I have seen videos Theo showed me of him competing. They do not do him justice; he is even more beautiful in real life. He seems like a good quality horse and built for show jumping.

"Why are you selling him?" I murmur.

"Because the owners want to sell. Although, they are in no rush and want him to go to the right rider. If I had the money they are asking for, I would buy him myself," Lois drawls.

"Can we get him saddled up?" Theo interrupts, impatience clear in his voice. Lois nods.

"Anki, get Roman tacked up." Lois clicks his fingers at a blonde girl, who nods and scurries away. I assume to get the tack required for Roman.

Ten minutes later, I have my helmet in hand and watch as Theo schools the big, beautiful gray. He wanted to ride him first to make sure he was okay. I stare, enthralled. He makes it look effortless as he jumps the huge fences. It is seeing him now that reminds me why I want to train with him despite his behavior toward me. The guy is fucking talented on a horse and the best of the best in the sport. He comes to a stop, smirking arrogantly. I roll my eyes; the guy's ego knows no bounds. I even contributed to it when I said what I did the other day about him being my idol. I make a mental note not to say such things. His head doesn't need inflating any further. He hops off, rounds Roman, and jerks his head.

"I will give you a lift up." My heart rate picks up. I just know it's because Theo is about to touch me, even if it is innocently. I shift to the side of Roman and lift my leg. Theo's fingers wrap around my boot clad calf, and I feel a shot of electricity shoot through my body. "Thalia?" Theo questions when I don't move. I clear my throat.

"Sorry, let's go on three." I glance at him, and he nods, counting to three. When he hits the number, I jump as he lifts me and land in the saddle.

"You, okay?" I glance at him and nod. "Let me adjust the length of your stirrups, they are a bit long." He fiddles with the stirrup leathers, adjusting the length on both sides. "Okay, let's start. Just get a feel of him and then we'll go from there." I nod and squeeze Roman into a walk. He feels comfortable and I can already tell he is well schooled. A few minutes later, I push him into a trot and then a canter. He feels like an armchair. Comfortable, nice long strides, a lovely rhythm and good outline. After I've schooled him for around fifteen minutes, Theo calls out to me.

"How does he feel, Thalia? You look like you are enjoying him."

I smile. "He feels really good. Comfortable." Theo nods.

"Come down to the upright. Sit up, keep your leg on and hands soft."

I trot away from Theo and then push into a canter again. I circle the arena once and then come down to the upright that is about three feet high. Kicking at the last minute, I take off about a stride out.

"Don't move your legs, Thalia, he was coming down to the fence nicely until you kicked him. I don't want to see your legs move at all. If they do, I will strap them down," Theo barks. My cheeks heat. I know I should not have done that, but nerves took over at the last second. I need to remember Roman is an experienced horse. I set off again and this time, sit still only applying a little pressure with my legs. I clear the fence in a perfect stride and smile only for it to drop when Theo shouts.

"Just because you hit the stride doesn't mean it was good. Your posture is all over the place and your hands are hard, soften them and for god's sake, sit up straight or I will stick a board down the back of your shirt."

———

I finish an hour later. Theo certainly put me through my paces with Roman and I feel exhausted. I hop off and hand him over to the blonde girl who saddled him up—I think her name is Anki—and turn to face a waiting Theo and Lois.

Lois says, "What did you think, Thalia? He is a good horse, yes? *You* looked good up there." I don't miss the flirtatious tone of his voice, or the way Theo stiffens. I smile.

"Yes, he is lovely and has so much talent. The fences I jumped today are the biggest I have ever done. What were they, one meter sixty?" I ask, because I'm just so happy that I got to jump such a high course. It's an achievement for me and something I will have to get used to when I step up a level. The highest I have competed on is both Zeus and Lolly who are around one meter twenty-five, which is still big but not Global Champions tour heights.

"Yes, at least. He is more than capable of competing at the level you want and has the record to prove it." I open my mouth to speak but Theo talks, stopping me.

"Can you give us a minute, Lois?" It's not really a question but more of an order. Lois smirks but saunters off toward the barn. Theo faces me with a grimace on his arrogant but beautiful face. "Lois was being polite; you didn't look good. In fact, I have seen learner riders do a better job. You were missing strides. You were tense. Lucky for you, Roman bailed you out." My mouth drops open at Theo's words. For a minute I am completely gob-smacked. I know he can be a dick, but this is too much. I was not that bad. I straighten my spine and narrow my eyes at him.

"I am sorry if I'm not quite up to your amazing standard, Theo. It was my first time on a new horse. I was nervous. There is no need to be an asshole about it," I hiss. I swear his lips twitch with a smile, but I am too angry to look close enough. Theo sighs.

"At this point, for what you want to do and achieve, you should be able to get on just about any horse and be able to ride them how they deserve. We will come back tomorrow and if you can't show me that you can ride him properly then I think we should look at you training elsewhere. I don't have time to waste on someone who isn't even average." Again, my mouth gapes and my eyes widen. This fucking asshole thinks he can belittle me and then tell me he won't train me if I don't prove myself. I had an off day. I was nervous riding a new horse. But tomorrow, I will prove him wrong. I will show him that I am more than capable. I have been riding for years. I may not be the best, but I know I have talent. Maybe not to Theo Rhodes's standards. But if I didn't, I wouldn't have been able to compete at the level I have. Normally, I would say fuck him but he is literally the best in the world. If I want to do this, I need Theo. And I *will* prove him wrong.

With this new determination, I flash him a sweet smile and make my way back to the SUV.

I was a bit harsh. She didn't deserve my wrath but for some reason, I want to push her buttons. I want her to fight me. And she does. The more I push, the more she pushes back. It shows her strength. I don't know why I am being like this with her.

That's a lie, I do.

It's because I want her, but I know I can't have her.

Being around her is torture. My dick is constantly hard and I feel like I am on a constant high. I feel like I'm losing my damn mind.

Watching Lois eyeing her up like she was everything he ever wanted brought out the animalistic side in me that seems to be reserved for her. I wanted to rip the fucker's head off. I have known Lois for years and his reputation with women is well known. At every competition he is seen with a different woman and at last year's Global Champion tour, he was caught in a stall with three naked women. One of them being a high-profile German socialite. It was all over the press, embarrassing not only the sport but the families of the women involved. But that's Lois, he does not care. He likes to have fun and never takes things too seriously. I used to be the same. But I grew up.

I want him to stay far the fuck away from Thalia Maxwell.

No, not want.

Need.

I won't be held responsible for my actions if he doesn't keep the fuck away. I know for sure he will go after her hard now but as long as she is with me, I will not let that happen.

I glance at my watch to check the time 6:54 P.M. I am meeting Thalia and her security in the hotel restaurant for dinner at 7:30 P.M, so I have time to call Melody and inform her I'm in Europe. I am dreading this call; I know she will want to hop on a flight to Belgium which is why I've put if off so late.

I don't want her here.

I grab my cell and hit dial on her number. It only rings twice before she picks up.

"Darling, I was just talking about you," she purrs, her words a little slurred and I know she's been drinking even though it is just before 6:00 P.M in the UK.

"Melody, I hope it was all nice things?"

She giggles, the sound in the background dies so I assume she has moved to a quieter room. "Of course. You're calling early, is everything okay?"

I clear my throat. "Actually, I just wanted to let you know that I am in Belgium with a client. We leave for the states early tomorrow morning. It was a quick trip which is why I didn't tell you." The line goes quiet for a long minute. I pull my cell from my ear to check the line is still connected and then she speaks.

"You are in Europe, and you didn't tell me?" she hisses, but I don't miss the hurt.

"It was an impromptu trip with a client, Mel. For work. If I was here for longer than a day, I would have told you. And anyway, you are coming back to the States next week, are you not?"

"That is not the point, Theo, I am your girlfriend. What are you hiding? Who are you there with?" she grits, accusation clear in her tone.

"I'm not hiding anything. I am here with a client, to see a horse. It was a last-minute trip."

"Who are you there with?" she snaps.

I sigh, scrubbing a palm down my face. Although there is nothing going on with me and Thalia, Melody will assume there is because she will see this as me hiding things from her.

"Thalia Maxwell and her security detail."

She huffs out a laugh. "No wonder you didn't inform me of your trip to Europe. She is a beautiful little thing, Theo. I bet you couldn't wait to get her all to yourself."

My blood boils at the insinuation. Yes, I have had thoughts about Thalia, and she also makes my cock harder than anyone I have ever been with before, but I have not crossed that line with her. I will *not* cross that line.

"That is enough, Melody. She is strictly business. If all goes well, this could be a big earner for me. Now stop with your dramatics. How much have you had to drink?" I ask, changing the subject.

Her voice drops to a whisper, "Don't bring drinking into this, I went for lunch with some girlfriends and had a few glasses of champagne. You came to Europe and didn't tell me. That hurts, Theo.".

"Melody, it isn't like that. I didn't set out to hurt you. It was a last-minute arrangement set up by Christian Maxwell," I lie. "If things had been different, I would have told you."

She lets out a harsh breath. "Okay. Just next time, let me know. I will be back in Florida next week. Daddy might come with me; said he wants to talk business." Great, just what I need, Arthur Whitworth visiting. He is even more demanding than his daughter.

"Sounds good. I better go, I have dinner arrangements."

"Bye baby, I will speak to you later." She ends the call. I release a breath. At least she didn't get into who I was having dinner with. That would have been another argument.

————

I spot Thalia alone at a table in the hotel restaurant. Normally, I would find a restaurant in the town but her daddy apparently only books five-star hotels and this hotel has one of the best restaurants in the whole of Belgium. I stand there studying her for a minute. She really is the most exquisite thing I have ever seen, with her long dark hair and her unusual gray eyes. But it's not just that. I like her determination, her feistiness, her ambition. It's a massive turn on.

She glances up and spots me, a shy smile crossing her face as she throws me a nervous wave. I briefly wonder where her security detail is. She shouldn't be left alone and not just because of her name but because every man in here is looking at her like she is their next meal.

I make my way over, pulling the chair out and dropping down in it.

"Where's Greg?" I ask.

One—because I would not have agreed to dinner if I had known it would have just been the two of us. It feels too intimate.

Two—because, like I said, she shouldn't be left alone. She jerks her head to a table to the right. I spot Greg nursing a beer.

"I asked for privacy so we could discuss some things,"

"What do you want to discuss that cannot be said in front of your bodyguard?" I cock a brow. She straightens her spine, squares her shoulders, juts out her chin and I know whatever she wants to discuss is going to be calling me out on my shit.

"Why do you treat me so badly? I have seen you with Marissa, Kiara, and Carter and you don't speak to them like you do me. Do you get off on putting me down? Making me feel like shit? Am I not good enough for your impossible standards? I give it my all and then some, Theo. I do not see any of the others mucking out their stalls, grooming their horses." Her eyes sparkle with challenge, making my dick harden in my pants. She looks sexy as hell all fired up.

I smirk like the asshole I am. "You need more work than my other clients, Thalia. If you can't handle the pressure..." I trail off with a shrug of my shoulders, the insinuation clear. Not that I would let her leave me. I need to protect her. She scowls.

"I am not leaving, Theo. If that is your plan, for whatever reason, then I am telling you now, it will not work. I want to be the best and that means learning from the best which is unfortunately your arrogant ass," she hisses.

My lips curve into a grin on their own volition. I can't help it; the girl does things to me. And it's getting harder to come up with reasons to stay away from her. I slow clap, again, like the asshole I am. Her eyebrows draw together, and she frowns.

"I am the best of the best. Now, I can only hope you will listen to me when I tell you to do something. I am pushing you, Thalia, because you need it. You want to be the best and in order to succeed, you need tough love. I understand you have probably never had that before in your young life, but I don't care. I will not treat you with kid gloves just because of your last name." She stares at me. What's going through her mind right now, I have no idea. Suddenly, she smirks, making my cock turn to granite and my chest to pound.

"Whatever you say, Theo. Keep throwing your shit at me. I can handle it. I spent years on movie sets and modelling campaigns. Trust me when I say, you are a teddy bear compared to some of the people I've dealt with." And with that, she pushes out of her chair and turns on her heels.

"Where are you going?" She pauses, glancing over her shoulder.

"To order room service. I am suddenly very tired. Night, Theo." She finishes and walks away. I am left with a slack jaw and a hard cock.

Fuck.

————

The next morning, I meet up with Thalia and Greg in the lobby. Thalia is quiet, engrossed in her cell while we wait for the driver. I watch her, jealous that her focus is on the phone and not me. When I feel eyes on me, I look up to find Greg shooting me what can only be described as a warning. I cock a brow, daring him to say something. He just shakes his head and turns away from me. He isn't stupid; he knows Thalia is attractive, knows what I am thinking when I look at her.

Not five minutes later, the driver pulls up. He jumps out the vehicle quickly and rushes towards the little princess to grab her bags. I wonder what it must have been like for her growing up. A team of people around her ready to do everything and anything she needed. Must have been suffocating. We all climb into the SUV and Elias drives us the ten-minute journey back to Lois's. The fucker better keep his words and his hands to himself today. I am not in the mood for his shit.

We pull up to the barn to find Lois waiting for us. I texted him before we left so he knew we were on our way. When the vehicle comes to a stop, I hop out and make my way over to him. He smirks knowingly.

"Ah, good morning, Theo. How are you today? Sleep well?" He cocks a suggestive brow.

"Very well, thank you Lois. Can you cut the shit today? No flirting with my client. It's unprofessional and we are here to, hopefully, make a deal." He studies me for a long beat. For what I am not sure. Finding whatever he was looking for he nods, his lips curving into a grin.

"You can't blame me, Theo; the girl is beautiful, more beautiful than I have ever seen. If you think for one minute you will be able to keep all the men away from her at competitions, then you are deluded. You know what it's like. They'll be like flies around shit once they get a look at her." Jealousy surges through me and my fists ball. He is right. I know he is. Doesn't mean I like it. It is going to be a nightmare. The sport is full of sex and sin. It's debauched. If they made a reality show based in the show jumping world, people would be shocked. Show jumpers are probably some of the horniest people around and most of the men would probably give their right arm just for a night with a girl like Thalia. Almost makes me not want to take her to any competitions, to put her off for as long as possible. Tell her she is not ready. But I can't do that. Christian Maxwell will have my head. I open my mouth to say something but stop when I feel Thalia step up to us.

"Hi, Lois," she greets. His eyes sparkle with lust. I want to throttle the bastard.

"Ah, Thalia, it is good to see you," he replies, taking her hand in his and kissing it. My blood boils. I want to rip his hand from hers. I don't want him to taint her. She exudes innocence and Lois is...not so innocent. I don't want him anywhere near her. Maybe it was a mistake bringing her here and putting her on his radar. I know he will not stop until he gets her in his bed. It's what he does. I have seen it. It will become a game to him. Like the hunter and his prey. A growl works its way up my throat before I can stop myself and they both glance at me. I clear my throat, scowling at Lois.

"Can we get the horse saddled up? We have a flight to catch," I grit out. Lois flashes me a smirk before turning and heading to the barn. I turn to Thalia, who is already watching me with curiosity in her eyes.

"Stay away from him. He is bad news," I say before stalking toward the barn.

———

Thalia finishes up and hops off Roman, handing him over to the waiting groom. I smile at her as she whips off her hat.

"You did well today. Much better. How did he feel?" She beams at me, no doubt happy with my praise.

"He felt amazing, Theo. I think it will be a really good partnership. And he has so much talent. I can feel it," she breathes, her voice raspy. I have a sudden urge to know what she would sound like with me buried deep inside her.

Shaking the thought away, I nod. "Yes, he does, and you rode him like he deserved today. We will discuss it more on the flight home about what you want to do next. But I agree, I think it will be a perfect partnership. I got a glimpse of what you could achieve together. You rode the best I have ever seen you ride today," I tell her honestly because I don't always want to put her down. "Let's say our goodbyes to Lois and make our way back to the airfield." A shy smile crosses her face, her eyes drop only to come back to me.

"Thank you, that means a lot coming from you. I am going to prove to you that I am not an amateur and that I do have what it takes to succeed in this sport." I watch her for a long beat. The sincerity in her eyes. The hope on her face. My chest tightens and I feel like such an asshole for how I've been treating her. Forgetting where I am and what I am doing, I step forward raising my hand to cup her cheek. Her eyes widen and she gasps, making me pause and bringing me back to my senses but not before I graze her soft flesh with my hand.

And my god, she is so fucking soft.

What the fuck am I doing?

I cannot touch her like that. I shake my head and clear my throat, before stepping away and making my way to Lois, all the while thinking about other parts of her body I want to touch.

Chapter Nine

THALIA

We sit on the jet waiting to take off. It is now 12:08 P.M in Belgium which means we should be landing in Florida just before 4:00 P.M. Hopefully, I can ride my two horses when I get back.

My mind drifts to Theo and the way he touched my cheek. It was not in a friendly way, it was intimate. Don't ask me how I know that, I just do. It was in a way you would touch a lover. I bring my hand to said cheek and touch it softly. I can almost still feel his touch. I smile. He may be an asshole, but something tells me there is more to him than I originally thought. Someone speaking Italian brings me out of my thoughts. I glance up to find Theo, cell to his ear, mouth moving with Italian words.

"Ciao Mamma, come stai?" I study him and his dark features. Dark hair. Blue eyes. An arrogant asshole behavior. How did I not spot this? Theo is Italian. I am half Italian; I should have seen it. I watch his eyes soften as he talks to his mother. It's strange seeing him like this. Soft. Caring. He is like a different person as he speaks to her. He ends the call, glancing at me. I blush as his eyes bore into mine and my skin prickles all over.

"You're Italian?" I blurt, just to break the awkwardness. He nods.

"On my mother's side. Although, she has been in the states now for nearly forty years. She met my father on a gap year in America and never went back." I smile, tucking a stray lock of hair behind my ear.

"My mama is Italian." He stares at me as if I told him aliens just landed and then smiles.

"I am well aware your mother is Italian as I am sure most of the world's population is," he says, sarcasm thick in his tone. My cheeks heat. So, we are back to asshole Theo. I am beginning to think he is bipolar with all these mood swings.

"I was just making conversation," I mumble, turning away from his intense stare and looking out the window. A couple of seconds later, footsteps sound and my head snaps to the sound to see Theo making his way to me. I glance at Greg who is engrossed in a newspaper. He drops down in the seat next to mine and takes my hand in his. Electricity courses through me, sending a pulse between my legs and making my heart hammer in my chest. Theo glances at Greg to make sure he isn't looking before turning to me.

"I don't mean to be an asshole; it just comes naturally," he smiles with a shrug. "I guess I am l more with you because I want to push you and every time I do, you come back fighting harder. You are a fighter, Thalia, and determined. And sometimes that means more than talent, because you can learn to ride better but determination is something you either do or do not have and you? You have it in spades." My heart soars, a smile tugs at my lips. Theo squeezes my hand. My eyes drop to our entwined hands, and I briefly wonder how it would feel to have him as mine. Theo clears his throat and releases me, making me feel cold without his warm touch. He leans back in his seat and my gaze drops when I notice a big bulge in his gray sweats. My eyes widen.

Theo is hard.

Did I do that to him?

"So, what do you want to do going forward with Roman? I

know you will need to speak with your father, as will I, but I think the horse is perfect for you and what you want to do," he murmurs, his voice husky and low. My eyes snap to his face. I don't want to talk about Roman right now. I want to talk about why Theo has an erection. But it's not like I can just come out and say it. I stare straight ahead, willing my eyes not to drop to what is clearly a very huge dick.

"Umm, yes. I would like for a deal to be done. I will speak to my father when we get back to Florida. If I am happy, he will be happy to go ahead." Theo chuckles beside me and I slowly move my gaze to his face. Safe territory. He looks at me; I cock a questioning brow. He shakes his head as amusement dances in his eyes.

"Daddy's princess, always getting what she wants." I scowl, ready to lay into him. He holds his hands up, stopping me. "I am not saying it in a derogatory way. You are lucky, you have such a supportive father, a rich father. There are so many talented riders, but they don't have the backing to get to the level they want. You need to make the most of it, use what is available to you. I think that, along with my training, we will get you to where you want to be." With that speech, I relax.

I know I am lucky, but it doesn't mean I am not going to work damn hard to get what I want.

———

"Thalia?" Someone calling my name drags me out of my sleep. I open my eyes to find my head on Theo's shoulder and a weight on top of my own. Glancing up, I find it's Theo. Theo with his head on mine. My pulse picks up at this intimate embrace. Greg stares at me, before his eyes move to the sleeping man beside me. My eyes widen and I quickly move my head, waking Theo in the process. His eyes snap open and he looks at me. His brows furrow in confusion before something I can't quite detect flashes in his eyes.

"We have landed," Greg says, breaking our spell before spinning and grabbing my bags. I grimace. How the hell did we even end up like that? I cannot even remember falling asleep. Theo reaches down, discreetly trying to shift the bulge between his legs. But I see it.

Again.

I push to a stand and move past him. I need to get away, put some space between us. Maybe our little heart to heart brought us closer somehow. But it should not have brought us *that* close. He has a girlfriend for Christ's sake. My father would flip if anything happened between us. I make my way down the stairs and toward the waiting SUV. Greg glances at me, accusation in his eyes.

"What?" I growl. He sighs, looking at me.

"You need to be careful, Thalia. I see the way he looks at you." I shift on my feet. The way he looks at me. Theo doesn't look at me like anything...does he?

Instead of questioning him further, I climb into the car. I am his student. He is my trainer. Nothing can ever happen. If I want to stay training with him, we can never cross that line.

Theo hops in the back seat next to me, glancing at me with a smile. My heart thunders in my chest. I have never seen him look so sexy. He wears gray sweats and a tight white tee that shows off every muscle. And damn, does he pull the look off. Better than anyone I have ever seen before. I swallow and avert my gaze.

"Everything okay?" he asks, softly drawing my attention back to him. I smile.

"Yes, I am just tired." He frowns before nodding.

"Do you want me to get the grooms to exercise your horses or do you want to ride?"

"I would like to; I was thinking of taking them for a trail ride."

"I will join you, show you the good trails. I will take one of your horses and you can take the other." Butterflies form in my stomach and I roll my lips between my teeth to stop myself beaming at him. I should not want to be alone with him like that.

But I do.

More than anything, I do.

———

Theo makes sure the horses are saddled up and ready to go when we get back to the barn. I freshen up in the barn restroom and change into my riding wear. Theo appears on the golf buggy ten minutes later having also changed. My mouth waters, I have never seen a man look so amazing in equestrian wear. The jodhpurs fit snugly around his muscular thighs, and they do nothing to hide the outline of his impressive dick.

The man is big.

I briefly wonder what it would feel like to have him inside me. If he would even fit. I would surely be sore for days if I was taken by a man like Theo. After all, I am still a virgin.

"Thalia?" My head snaps up at the sound of Theo's voice to find his lips pulled up in a smirk. He caught me ogling him. Again. My eyes widen and my cheeks heat as I stare at him. "I said, are you ready?" I nod, unable to speak because I am so embarrassed. He chuckles, shaking his head. "Come on."

We make our way to where Zeus and Lolly are standing, saddled up and waiting for us. I glance at Tessa, Jess, and Maria and don't miss the curious expressions on their faces. At what, I am not sure. She smiles at Theo before excusing herself. We mount and I follow Theo out the barn. He takes me toward the paddocks where I notice a trail to the left. I follow him down the trail for a good fifteen minutes. We ride in silence but only until the barn is no longer in sight. He pulls Zeus to a stop and waits for me to come up beside him. I peer at him; the setting Sun hits him from behind and he looks delicious.

"Come on, Piccola," he rasps, making my heart leap. Piccola? It means 'little one' in Italian. He knows full well I would know that being of Italian descent. Why would he call me by a pet name? I can't say I hate it. Because I don't. I step up to him, flashing him a shy smile. He grins. "You're very quiet today," he states. I swallow. My whole body is on fire from the way he is acting.

"Just taking in the views." He watches me for a long beat, and I squirm in my saddle. He opens his mouth to say something before stopping himself. I frown wondering what it could have been. I don't have the chance to ask as he starts walking again. Settling into the ride, I decide to ask him questions.

"How long have you been riding?" Theo glances at me, pursing his lips in thought.

"I think I rode a horse before I could walk. My mother was an avid equestrian but more cross country than show jumping. As soon as I was old enough to understand all the disciplines, I knew my heart was in jumping. My parents brought me my first pony when I was ten and I competed at local competitions. My father did not want horses to be my end game though. He owns a well-known PR company in Miami and was hoping I would follow in his footsteps. To say he was disappointed, when I decided I wanted a career in show jumping, would be an understatement. We don't have the best relationship because of it." He sighs before continuing, "When I finished high school, I moved to Europe to work and train with a Dutch rider, which is how I met Lois. I spent two years there, competing and making a name for myself. I started to pick up rides, started gaining attention and owners. I met Mel, set up my own base, a small stable yard in England, and focused on getting to where I wanted to be.

"Within a year, I had a string of horses and was competing and winning all over Europe. I made the US nations cup team year after year. My goal moved and I wanted to make the Olympic teams. At twenty-four years old, I did. We came away with a silver team medal and I won individual gold. I was the youngest ever American to make the US show jumping team and still am to this day. Four years later, I was picked again, and we won team gold and won individual gold." He smiles to himself remembering how he achieved his goals. He turns his face to me. "You see, Thalia, anything is possible if you have the determination to do it. I even went against my father's wishes and have achieved more than he ever thought possible," he adds and I smile.

"I would love to do the same," I sigh.

"I believe you have every chance of succeeding...with the right horses and trainer."

"Did you have a bang on your head when we went to Belgium? You are being awfully nice."

Theo smirks. "I can be nice." I chew on my lip as I watch him. His gaze drops to my mouth. His tongue darts out, running across his full bottom lip. Liquid lust shoots to my pussy and I suppress a shiver. What I would give to have him run that tongue over me. As if he heard my thoughts, his eyes snap to mine and narrow. I look away, fiddling with Lolly's mane. Theo speaks again, breaking the now awkward silence.

"When did you start riding?" he asks the same question I asked him. I smile and look at him to find his eyes already on me.

"Not until six years ago. A friend asked me to go and watch her compete in a competition at The New York Equestrian Centre. Let's just say, I was hooked. I begged my parents for riding lessons which they allowed, and the rest is history. I started competing a year later with my own horses. When I started winning and proving myself, my father brought me more competitive horses. Meghan Quinn—my trainer in New York—insisted if I wanted to be the best, I would need better horses. She took me to view them, much like you did with Roman, and my father bought Lolly and Zeus." I jerk my head toward both horses before continuing. "Meghan has not accomplished what you have but she is good at what she does, and I learned a lot.

But you are the best, which is why I convinced my father to send me here."

"I know Meghan. She competed in high level competitions but never at the level I have competed." I don't miss the smugness in Theo's voice. I resist an eye-roll. "How come you never followed in your mother's footsteps?" he asks, changing the subject. I twist my lips in thought. People always ask me this question.

"Hmm, I mean, I have done acting and modelling but like you, my heart is with show jumping. It's what I want to do. I am not saying I will never act or model again but jumping is what I want to do." Theo watches me, his eyes sparkling with what looks a lot like...lust?

"Good answer. I can see you have passion, feel it in your words. You can go far with that attitude, Thalia," he murmurs, his eyes boring into mine. His words do something to me. I cannot stop myself from reaching out to him. Why? I don't know. His eyes widen before, he takes my outstretched hand and squeezes.

"Come on, let's get back." I die a little inside at his words. I could spend forever out here with him. Just the two of us. But then I remember, there is no us. He has Melody. What the hell am I doing, allowing myself to get caught up in this man? I need to put a stop to whatever feelings I am having. I clear my throat and flash him a forced smile.

"Yes, let's."

Chapter Ten

THEO

It has been a few weeks since Belgium and the trail ride. Something changed between us that evening, I can feel it. Thalia has been doing well with her training and her new horse, Roman, is arriving at the farm today. Christian eventually came to a deal with Lois to purchase the horse. It was a high price, but a good price nonetheless. It was in the seven figures and made headlines in all the Equestrian magazines but if he wants his little girl to be the best, then he must put his hands in his pocket.

Melody delayed her trip and will be arriving next week. I don't mind. In fact, it suits me just fine. I can only imagine the drama she will bring when she arrives in Florida. Thalia's big brother is in town. I thought her father was protective, but Evan Maxwell is next level. He looks at me like he knows exactly what I am thinking about his baby sister. Honestly, if he knew just what goes through my mind, he would want to kill me. And I wouldn't even blame him. The thoughts I am having about her, I have no business having.

As much as I tell myself to stay away, to not think of her in that way, I cannot stop. She brings something out in me that I have never experienced before. And she makes my cock harder than I have ever been in my life.

I shake my head, bringing me back to the now and the way the object of my obsession is slouched in the saddle.

"Sit up, Thalia, I thought we were past this. It is basic riding skills. Maybe you should take pilates or yoga classes to improve your posture because you currently look like a bag of shit," I shout. Her eyes snap to mine, brows furrowed in confusion. I know why she is confused. It's because I have been nice the last few weeks.

She sits up straighter, listening to what I say even though I can tell she wants to run that smart mouth of hers. I inwardly groan. I wish she would run that smart mouth all the way around my cock. As if she can hear my thoughts, she glances over at me. I clear my throat.

"That is better, can you not feel the difference when you listen to me?" She nods and carries on with what she is doing. Out of my peripheral, I spot Carter entering the arena, his eyes laser focused on Thalia. My blood boils, fists ball. This asshole is about to get himself kicked out of my training program. I don't even care about losing the two thousand dollars his parents pay me every week. He has gotten bolder, touching her, making her laugh.

I hate it.

I want to kill him.

I know it is irrational of me, but the fucker is pissing me off with his youth, his single status, his smug face and his perfect douchey brown hair.

He strides over to Thalia, who is now cooling off Zeus—with a grin. He says something to make her blush. I love it when she blushes. I want her to blush only for me. Having had enough of this fucker, I shout over.

"Carter, warm up. Thalia, give Zeus to Maria and meet me in my office," I snap, leaving no room for argument. I spin on my heel and stride away. I don't know what I am going to say to her when I get her alone; I just know I have to get her away from Carter.

Making my way into my office and dropping down in my chair, I clench my jaw. I should not feel like this over Thalia, this...possessiveness. But I do. I have never been like this with Mel. In fact, I would love it if she would go and find someone else to fuck and fawn over.

A gentle knock on the door has me clearing my throat. I would know who it is even if I hadn't asked her to meet me here. My body is aware of her whenever she is around. Every nerve ending inside me awakens when she is close.

"Come in." The door opens revealing who I knew it would be. She smiles, making my whole body come alive with need and my dick harden. I shift in my seat and because she has this effect on me—an effect I do not want—I scowl at her as she drops down in a chair.

"What the fuck was that?" I growl. Her eyebrows furrow and she glances behind her as if I am talking to somebody else. When she finds only the two of us in here her gaze comes back to me.

"What was what?" she asks softly.

"Don't be coy, Thalia. With Carter." Her eyes widen, mouth drops open and I can't even blame her. I am being irrational. Crazy. Her cute little button nose scrunches up and she straightens her shoulders. I brace myself for her response, knowing she is about to lay into me.

"I have no idea what you are talking about, Theo. Carter is a friend but like I have said before, if I want to date him, I will. You have no control over what I do outside of my time training with you and you certainly have no control over my dating life. What the hell is wrong with you? You have a damn girlfriend, or did you forget that?" she hisses, pushing out of her chair and throwing daggers at me with those perfect gray eyes. My cock turns to stone. I love it when she gets feisty.

She spins on her heels and strides to my door, but before she can make it, I am out of my seat, rushing after her. She grabs the handle; my palm pushes down on the door before she can open it. She spins to face me, glaring before lust flashes in those unique orbs of hers. Her chest heaves as she stares up at me. My eyes drop there on their own volition. I watch as her nipples harden against her thin tank top and my cock weeps.

"Theo?" she whispers, making my eyes snap to hers. Before I can stop myself, my lips crash down on hers in a bruising, needy kiss. She gasps, her lips parting allowing me entrance to her sweet mouth.

Jesus.

She tastes like heaven.

She tastes like *mine*.

I am not even thinking about the repercussions of this idiotic decision. At this moment, all I care about is her lips on mine. I need it like I need air to breathe. Her hands hit my chest and she gently pushes against me, breaking the spell I am under.

"Theo?" she whispers again. I stare down at her, my tongue darting out and running against my bottom lip.

"That was better than I could have ever imagined," I rasp. Her eyes widen, her own tongue darting out. I track it like my life depends on it. I want to feel that soft pink flesh on my cock, in my mouth, and all over my body.

"What was that, Theo? You..." she trails off, taking a breath. "You have a girlfriend."

"I am aware, Thalia," I bite, because what I have with Mel is not real. Well, not on my behalf anyway. She frowns. I push away from her, running a hand through my hair. "I want you. I know it's wrong, but I can't help it. I tried to stop myself, but I can't fight it anymore. There is something between us. I know you feel it too," I murmur softly, my eyes pinned on her waiting for her to admit it back.

Wanting her to admit it.

Her gaze drops to the floor, she wrings her hands together. "I feel it too, Theo. But we can't. What about Mel?" I sigh in relief at her words. I knew it wasn't all in my head. I step up to her, grabbing her hands and tugging her into me. I drop a kiss on her forehead.

"Let me worry about that. Just because something looks a certain way from the outside doesn't mean it's the truth. You should know that better than anyone, what with being in the spotlight," I tell her cryptically, because what I have with Mel is not what people think.

She glances up at me and I see the questions in her eyes but not wanting to go there right now, I press my lips to hers. She melts into me, wrapping her arms around my shoulders. My hard cock presses against her thigh and I wish we didn't have any clothes between us. I don't know how long we kiss for, I can stay like this forever, my tongue in her warm mouth, lips against hers. A knock at the door has us jumping apart. Thalia's eyes widen. I jerk my head to the chair, silently telling her to sit down as I make my way to my own seat and sit down.

"Come in." The door opens and in steps Evan Maxwell, his eyes narrowed on me before moving to his sister. His features soften as he strides toward her.

"I was looking for you. Are you ready to go?" He glances at me briefly. Thalia clears her throat.

"Yes, I just finished up. Did you already go to your meeting?" Thalia asks.

"Yes, I made it quick. I wanted to take you for lunch before I go back to New York." She beams at her brother and an irrational pang of jealousy slithers through me.

I want all her smiles.

She pushes out of her chair, looking to me. "Thank you for today, Theo. Can you let me know when Roman arrives? I would like to come and see him." I nod.

"Of course. Have a nice lunch." She smiles before they turn and leave. I let out a harsh breath.

What the fuck did I just do?

Chapter Eleven

THALIA

"What were you talking about with Mr. Rhodes?" I can hear my brother's voice, but I am not taking in what he is saying. All I can focus on is the way Theo's lips felt on mine. The way my whole body came alive. The fire that stirred in my belly when his hot mouth pressed against mine. I inwardly sigh. I want more of that.

Something has been shifting between us, but I thought it was all one sided. I thought it was all in my head, that it was a silly little crush on somebody I look up to, aspire to be like.

I guess not.

Theo wants me. He said so himself. The thought makes a pulse start between my legs and my whole-body shiver.

"Thalia?" my brother says. My gaze moves to Evan, who is watching me with a confused look on his face.

"Hmm?" He lets out a frustrated breath, running a hand through his hair.

"What has gotten into you? Are you even listening to me?"

"Sorry, I have a lot on my mind." I straighten in my seat and flash him a smile. His eyes soften and he smiles back at me. I love my brother...even if he can be more overprotective than my father. I know it is because I am the baby of the family. My sister is a little wild and will never be controlled so they project their protectiveness onto me.

"I said what were you and Mr. Rhodes talking about?"

"Oh, he wanted to go over the details of my new horse arriving." He eyes me for a long beat. Something passes in his eyes that I can't quite decipher before it vanishes. He clears his throat.

"How are you enjoying your training? It looks like a good set up. The farm, I mean."

"It's great, exactly what I wanted. All I want is to show jump, Evan. Not model, not act, not work for Dad's company. Just show jumping and being around my horses. To be the best, I must learn from the best and that is Theo." If Evan's frown is anything to go by, I don't think he misses the hero worship in my voice when I mention Theo's name. He purses his lips, like he is debating what to say next. Seemingly making his decision, he speaks.

"He is a good-looking man, Thalia—too old for you but still attractive—and you are a beautiful young woman. I don't want him to take advantage. You are innocent, naïve. We only have ourselves to blame. You are the baby of the family, and we all coddle you, but I just want to make you aware. Greg mentioned he might have seen Theo look at you in a certain way?" My pulse speeds up at the insinuation but I keep my face blank before rolling my eyes.

"Jesus, Evan, I train with him, nothing more. He has a girl-friend..." I trail off when Evan pins me with a look.

"That does not mean anything, Thalia, and it certainly does not stop anyone." I glare back at him.

"Greg overreacted; you know how he gets. It was all innocent and he is causing trouble for no reason. If Dad stops my training because of what Greg is saying, I will never forgive him," I growl. Evan studies my face, as if he is searching for truth in my words. Once he finds what he is looking for, he relaxes some.

"He didn't mention it to Dad, just me. I won't let him ruin this for you, baby sis...But you need to promise that if Theo is ever inappropriate, you will let me know." It's not a question, but I feel the need to answer anyway. If Evan knew that only seconds before he opened that door Theo had me pinned against it, kissing me... he would lose his shit and I would be on the jet back to New York with him. I reach out, grabbing his hand and giving him a reassuring squeeze.

"Of course, I will. You are being silly though. Theo has been nothing but professional," I chuckle, playing this whole conversation off. Evan lets out a harsh breath before the server comes and takes our food order. When she leaves, I look back to Evan wanting to talk about anything but Theo.

"So, tell me about your vacation?" He grins before going into a long conversation about the Maldives and his current girlfriend, Valentina Delgado, model extraordinaire. I listen intently, just thankful the attention is off me.

————

The next day, my stomach is in bits with nerves. I am eager to see Theo and talk about what happened yesterday. He messaged me to let me know Roman had arrived, but it was late, so I decided not to go over. I climb out of my SUV and head straight for the stables wanting to say morning to Zeus and Lolly and see Roman. He is as beautiful as I remember. I can't wait to get going with him.

Next, I make my way to Theo's office. I want to discuss what we are doing with Roman today; I assume he will need a few days to get settled, which is fine. I also want to go on a trail ride today and am hoping Theo will join me. I tap on the oak door and wait for his voice. It comes a few seconds later.

"Come in." I push open the door, only for my pulse to speed up when I see him. The man is a god amongst men. He is unbelievably attractive. His eyes narrow in on me, making my cheeks heat as I remember what we did yesterday. I step inside and close the door, giving us the privacy we need. "Thalia, what can I do for you?" His voice is bored, like I am an annoying fly he wants to swat. So different from the need in it yesterday. I frown as I drop down in the chair.

"Would you like to go for a trail ride? You said to give my horses an easier day today. And I know Roman will need a few days to settle." His eyes bore into mine; I squirm in my seat at his intense gaze.

"No, I would not like to go on a trail ride. I'm busy. Take one of your grooms," he bites out. I flinch at his harsh tone and wonder what could have happened between the kiss and now for him to act like such an asshole again.

He kissed me.

He made the first move.

Not the other way around.

"Okay, I will do that. I wanted to ask about..." I trail off suddenly feeling embarrassed and like a little girl.

"About what, Thalia? Spit it out." Jesus, the man is such a fucking asshole. Over his shit attitude, I straighten my spine and pin him with a look.

"About that kiss yesterday. What was *that,* Theo?" I hiss. He stares at me like he is looking straight through me. I don't like it. He sighs, running a hand through his dark hair.

"It was nothing. It should not have happened. I have a...girl-friend. It will not happen again. It was a mistake." Something a lot like jealousy courses through me and I want to cry. How can he be so cold? I thought things had changed between us. I will not give him the satisfaction of seeing me upset though, so I school my features and push out of my chair.

"Good talk, asshole," I growl, before storming out of there.

———

After my trail ride with Jessica, I bathe my horses. Jessica and Maria insisted it's something they should be doing but I want to do it myself. People may see me as just a little rich girl, but I want to be involved in all aspects of my horses. Otherwise, what is the point?

Once Zeus and Lolly are bathed, I put them in their stalls and head over to check on Roman. I open the stall door and his head whips up and he stares at me. "Hey boy," I say softly. He snorts before taking another mouthful of hay. I smile and make my way over to him. My hand lands on his neck, his gray coat is soft as I stroke my hand up and down. He looks at me again as if to say, "*What are you doing?*" I chuckle.

"I am Thalia, your new mommy. I cannot wait to get going with you. I think we are going to be a great team," I murmur against him. I am so lost in my own world that I don't hear the deep voice at first.

"Nice horse." Spinning, I come face to face with Carter, who is standing against the stall wall, arms crossed against his muscular chest and a sensual smirk tipping his lips. I grin.

"Yes, he is." Carter pushes off the wall and stalks toward me. My breath hitches at the heat in his eyes and I step back, hitting Roman's body in the process. Carter stops right in front of me, staring down like he wants to devour me whole.

"Go to dinner with me?" he rasps. My mouth parts and eyes widen. I thought Carter understood we are just friends. Clearly, I missed something and Carter has other ideas. He is an attractive guy, and any girl would be lucky to have him, but my head seems to be stuck on a certain asshole trainer of mine. On the other hand, Theo was dismissive toward me this morning and said we would not happen again. So why shouldn't I go out with Carter? With that in mind, I make my decision.

"Sure." I don't have much experience with guys, having been to a private all-girls school, and I think it's about time I started getting experience. Carter smirks down at me, like the cat that caught the canary.

"You will not regret it, Thalia. I think we could be perfect together. Both rich. Both hot," he murmurs, his hand reaching out and tucking a lock of my hair behind my ear. I want to vomit at that. It's not about being rich or good looking. It should be about what we have in common, and something tells me, we don't have a lot. I open my mouth to speak when the hairs on the back of my neck stand on end. I feel him before I see him and then hear his voice booming throughout the barn.

"Thalia, I need to speak with you in my office. Now." My eyes snap to Theo to find his burning with...rage? Jesus, he looks angry. I swallow and step away from Carter. We make our way out of Roman's stall when Carter decides to speak.

"Theo, any chance of you giving me a jump on Tia before I have to leave?" Theo glares at Carter. His jaw clenches so hard, I am surprised his teeth don't turn to dust.

"Go and get saddled up, I will be out in a minute," he grits before turning on his heel and stalking toward his office. I follow slowly after him, wondering what the hell I have done now.

I step over the threshold to find Theo pacing. Ignoring him, I start to make my way to a chair, when his voice stops me. "Shut the door," he grits, making me jump. I scurry to the door, closing it and then quickly drop down into a chair and wait for whatever he has to say. He stops pacing and pins me with a glare.

"What did I say about staying away from Carter?" he growls. I reel back.

"Who I speak to has nothing to do with you, Theo. And anyway, why are you so bothered? You said our kiss was a mistake," I smirk because I know he is jealous, even if he doesn't want to admit it.

"It was a mistake. You are here to train with me and ride your horses, not my dick." My eyes widen at the mention of his cock, and I can't help my gaze dropping south, only to come back to

Theo's when I notice the bulge in his pants. It's his turn to smirk, no doubt at my reaction.

"I-I-I," I stutter.

"You what, Thalia? Awww, does the sight of a cock scare you?" he taunts. I glare at him and straighten in my seat.

"No. I just don't understand you. I don't know what you want from me. You kiss me only to tell me it was a mistake. Then you get jealous when Carter comes around asking me out." He rounds his desk and drops down in front of me, his crotch level with my face. I blink several times then move my gaze to his face all the while chanting in my head not to look south. He lets out a harsh breath, running his hands through his thick hair. I want nothing more than to do it for him, feel his silky strands running through my fingers.

"I should not have kissed you. It was inappropriate on my part. It doesn't mean I don't want you...because I do. Something about you pulls me in. I want to taste every part of you." His eyes rake over me hungrily, his voice low, husky. "Things are complicated. I have a gir—I have Mel," he finishes, like he is trying to convince himself, not me. I push out of my seat, so we are nearly chest to chest. He sucks in a breath; I smile on the inside enjoying the reaction I get out of him.

"I never asked you to kiss me, Theo. Now if you will excuse me, I have a date to organize with Carter." I spin to walk away, but I don't even get a step before he is grabbing my wrist, spinning me and tugging me into him. His lips crash down on mine making my breath hitch in my throat. That same fire I have only ever experienced with him stirs in my stomach and every nerve ending comes alive. He kisses me like a starved man. Like he wants to swallow me whole. It is the best kiss I have ever had. I melt into him, never wanting it to end. But then it does and he pulls away, panting. My chest heaves as I look at him and I bite my bottom lip.

"Tell Carter no," he growls before exiting his office. I stand there in a daze for a long moment until a feminine voice breaks me out of it.

"Hey. Marissa and I were wondering if you wanted to get food tonight?" Kiara asks, her face scrunched up, no doubt at my disheveled appearance. She cocks a brow when I don't answer, and I finally find my voice.

"Sounds good," I smile before rushing out of Theo's office. I don't know what is happening between us. I should feel guilty about his girlfriend.

But I don't.

Call me selfish, but Theo is the one risking his relationship. And when he kisses me like he does, all I want is more. I never thought about losing my virginity, but I want to.

To Theo.

I want to feel his cock inside me, tongue in my mouth, lips on mine, hands all over me...I shiver at the thought.

I want him.

His girlfriend be damned.

Chapter Twelve

THEO

It's been a week since I kissed Thalia and I can't get her off my mind. Everything about her just does it for me. I have such a visceral reaction toward her, I couldn't stop this thing between us if I wanted to.

I don't know what it is about her, but I seem to lose all self-control, and it only seems to be getting worse. The past week has been sly glances here, little touches there. I am desperate to have my lips on her again, but I am trying to do the right thing and stay away... even if every part of me screams to take her and make her mine.

I make my way down to the barn, it's past 5 and quiet in the yard, only the grooms finishing up. I make my way inside only to stop when I see Thalia mounting Roman. My brows furrow. Her horses went on the horse exerciser today, having a quieter day as they have a competition tomorrow.

"What are you doing?" I ask as I stroll toward her. Her head snaps up, her eyes locking on mine. She blushes and I bite back a groan. I love when her cheeks get that hue of pink in them. I wonder if her whole body would go that color, if I touched her in places I am not supposed to touch her.

"I know the horses have been exercised today, but I had a shit day and wanted to clear my head." I stare at her for a long beat before nodding.

"Wait, I will come with you," I say without thinking. I shouldn't be alone with this girl but clearly, I have no restraint. I saddle up myself, not wanting to disturb the groom's routine and hop on Beau, a horse owned by Melody's father. I am hoping that by taking him on a trail ride it will make me think of my girlfriend and keep my lips and hands away from Thalia. I step up beside her to find her on her cell.

"Yes, Mama, I miss you too." She is silent for a long beat, listening to whatever her famous mother is saying.

"Okay, that will be great. I can't wait to see you and Daddy. Speak to you soon." She ends the call, sliding her cell into her jodhpur pocket. I raise a questioning brow, silently asking her if everything is okay.

"It was my mama. My parents are visiting in a few weeks." I nod. I have not yet met her mother, but I know exactly who she is.

Elena Maxwell.

Movie star.

It is a well-known fact she took a chance and left Italy to make it big in Hollywood. She only had small parts in Italian films before that and it paid off. She is now one of the highest paid actresses in the world.

"That will be nice for you," I drawl as we make our way down the trail.

"Yes, I miss my parents."

"How did they meet?" I glance at her, and she smiles to herself as if she is remembering something personal.

"As you know, my mother is an actress. Well, when she was eighteen, she left Italy and came to America," she tells me what I already know. "Anyway, she didn't know if she would ever make it, but she didn't want to live with regret if she never tried. She only had a little bit of money saved from small parts in films and modelling jobs she did in Italy. When she arrived in Los Angeles, she knocked on every agent's door and within a day, she got herself one." Thalia chuckles. "Elena Loren—as she was back then—is the most determined person I know and would not take no for an answer. She started getting small parts here and there for a few years and then one day, she got a call for an audition. It was for a part that would earn her a few bucks but again, it was not the main role. They had already cast Amalia Cameron; she was huge at the time and was getting a lot of roles.

"When my mama auditioned, she told me she put her heart and soul into it, and gave it her all. Said she had a feeling this was the movie that was going to make her. She left after her audition and two days later, the director himself called her, which she thought was odd. He told her she hadn't gotten the part. She was gutted but not one to give up, she pleaded her case and he offered her the role Amalia Cameron was cast for." I stare at Thalia as she gets lost in the story, mesmerized by how beautiful she looks when the sun hits her olive skin just right. She shrugs.

"I don't know what happened, whether it was a scheduling conflict or what, but Mama was right. It was the movie that made her. At just twenty, she had her first Darling nomination. It's the awards every actor wants to attend and win." I nod, even though she isn't looking at me. The Darling awards are the most prestigious awards in movie history, and I know Elena Maxwell has won a few of them now.

"For award ceremonies, a lot of different designers want to dress the stars, want their products seen on big name celebrities. My father's company wanted Mama to wear their diamonds. He insisted on taking the jewels to her himself. Said he had the perfect pieces and only he could be the one to dress her with them. They met and the rest is history as they say." She glances over at me with a smile. My heart beats in my chest. The girl is unbelievably perfect. Although I am beginning to think she is a witch and has cast some sort of spell on me.

"They started dating shortly afterwards. A month into dating, my father proposed on his yacht on the Amalfi coast. He flew her there as a surprise, got her father's permission and put a ring on her finger. Two months after the engagement, she found out she was pregnant with my brother. Not wanting her to have a baby out of wedlock, they married in the same place they got engaged three months later." Thalia sighs dreamily, lost in her story before she looks at me. "No one thought it would last, yet here we are. They love each other so much. It's the kind of love people write about..." she trails off pinning me with a look that makes my chest tighten and my pulse kick up. "The kind of love that *I* want. In a world full of fake relationships whether for publicity or power, they were true to themselves and married for love," she finishes.

I swallow at the intensity in her eyes, she doesn't know how right she is. I am in a relationship I do not want to be in for monetary gain. For investment from her father. Before I can stop myself, I am grabbing her reins, pulling the horses to a stop. I tug her toward me, then my lips are crashing down on hers. She gasps, allowing me entrance to her sweet mouth. But it's over too soon when Beau jolts making us break apart. Maybe it's a sign? Maybe Beau knows full well I should not be doing this. I know I shouldn't. But I can't bring myself to care.

"Get off," I say in a voice I don't recognize. She blinks at me. I jump off Beau and step up to Thalia who is still on her horse, eyes wide, lips parted. I grip both sets of reins in one hand, so the horses cannot go anywhere, and reach up to grip her shirt collar in the other, dragging her face back down to me. It's in this moment, I am glad I am 6ft 3.

Her sweet, plump lips meld against mine perfectly and I never want it to end. I release her shirt, my hand dropping down to her thigh and running up to the place I want to touch the most—a place I am sure is heaven. She shivers against my touch, and I smirk into the kiss enjoying the way she reacts to me. She pulls away.

"Theo?" She sounds drunk on my kisses and looks disoriented. I have never seen anything so damn beautiful in my life.

"Hop off," I growl. I need to touch her properly, run my fingers over her sweet jodhpur clad cunt. She does as I ask, steadying herself as she stands in front of me. I push her against the tree with my free hand, still gripping the horses in the other. Her eyes widen and I smirk down at her before my lips meet hers in a bruising kiss. She arches into me and touches my rock-hard cock. She freezes for a second before moaning and grinding against me. I never knew someone grinding their hot pussy on me could feel so good.

I groan, my hand snaking down to her waist. I slip my hand into her jodhpurs, thankful that the stretchy material allows me easy entry. She freezes, breaking the kiss.

"Theo?" she whimpers as my thumb grazes her clit.

"I want to touch you. Is that okay?" I ask, stopping my ministrations.

She bites down on that full bottom lip, peering up at me through her long dark lashes. She takes a breath then nods. I grin as she wraps her arms around my neck and pulls my lips down to hers. I sigh into her mouth as I continue my descent only to nearly blow my load when I feel how wet she is.

"You are soaked, Piccola," I murmur against her mouth. She squirms against my hand, silently begging for more. I slip two fingers into her panties and run them down her slit. She gasps and grinds against my fingers. My thumb joins the party beneath her panties and rubs her clit as my middle finger finds her tight wet hole and pushes inside. She jerks against me.

"Theo," she mewls. I bite down on her bottom lip as her pussy clenches around my finger. She is so fucking tight; it feels like she might break it. I briefly wonder if she is a virgin. She can't be. She is eighteen and when she looks like she does...there is no way. My blood boils at the thought of her with someone else and I push another finger inside her almost punishingly. She moans, her lips peppering kisses all over my face. I pump my fingers, her head drops back against the tree, and she moans. I watch as her tits move with every breath she takes. The sight is otherworldly. Thalia Maxwell caught up in her passion while I finger fuck her to orgasm.

Fuck me.

"That's it, Piccola, come on my fingers," I croon. Her eyes snap open, and she cries out as she does just that. I smirk, dropping a kiss to her lips before pulling my hand out of her pants and jodhpurs. She watches me, her face pink as she catches her breath. I bring the fingers I just had inside her up to my mouth and suck, tasting her juices. Her eyes widen in shock.

"Mmm, so fucking sweet," I mutter. Thalia straightens, her face falling.

"What did we do? You have a-a girlfriend. A long-time girlfriend," she blurts, panic clear in her voice. I sigh and look back to the two horses. So much for Beau keeping me away from Thalia.

"Let me worry about that. You did nothing wrong. I wanted it." She snorts and my head snaps back to her.

"Nothing wrong? I know you have a girlfriend, and I still didn't say no. I am a bad person." Her eyes glaze over. I cup her face with my free hand, pressing my lips to her forehead.

"No, you are not. Stop worrying. If anything, I should have put a stop to it, but I wanted it. I want you," I tell her honestly. Her eyes soften slightly, and she lets out a breath.

"I want you too," she whispers, looking ashamed of her admission. I will not have that. Not able to stop myself, I kiss her again. When I finally pull away, I smile down at her.

"Come on, let's get back to the barn."

———

After the trail ride and finger fucking my eighteen-year-old trainee against a tree, I'm sitting in my home office, going through all the paperwork for tomorrow. It's Thalia's first competition and I need everything to be right. I need it all to go well. Especially with Roman.

I hear the front door open and frown glancing at the clock. It's past 10 and no one ever comes to my house apart from Melody, the cleaner, and my parents. It's at least a mile away from the stalls—all on the same site—but far enough away that I use a golf cart to get to the barn. I push out of my leather chair only to freeze when I hear her voice.

"Theodore, darling?" the thick British accent calls out.

Melody.

What the hell is she doing here? She told me she had pushed her flight back again. Something to do with a gala for her father. I step out of my office to find her in the foyer. Her blond hair falls in waves around her back, she's wearing yoga pants and a hoodie. Casual wear. The outfit she always travels in. I clear my throat.

"Melody? What are you doing here? I thought you were not getting in until next week?" She flashes me a grin and makes her way toward me. She throws her arms around me, her lips drop to mine. I kiss her back, but her mouth feels wrong. Hard. I have the sudden urge to push her away. Instead, Melody pulls back so I don't have to. Her eyes narrow, no doubt at the way I kissed her. She studies my face for a long beat and then smiles.

"I missed you so much, I decided to surprise you," she chirps, not noticing my irritation at her being here.

"You should have said something. I would have come and gotten you from the airport," I mutter.

"And where would be the fun in that silly? I wanted to surprise you," she repeats.

"It is a nice surprise," I lie. "But I am afraid you came at a busy time. I am at a competition all weekend, so will not be able to spend much time with you."

"That's okay, I can join you, baby. I missed you so much," she purrs as her lips travel along my jaw. Again, it feels all wrong. Her smell. Her taste...

"Let me go freshen up and I will meet you in our bedroom. I need a good fuck as I am sure you do."

"Not tonight, Mel. I am busy and tired." She stills, stepping away from me.

"Not tonight? It has been over two months, Theodore. Unless you have been fucking someone behind my back," she says accusingly, her eyes narrowing.

"Mel, do not start that shit," I growl. I know what I have been doing is wrong, but I haven't fucked Thalia...

Yet.

Melody smiles sweetly. Too sweet. "It's settled then. Meet me in the bedroom." She spins and makes her way up the stairs. I run a frustrated palm down my face. I don't want to fuck Mel. I should. But I don't. Not after the things that have happened with Thalia.

If I don't have sex with her, she will know something is up and investigate. Dig deeper. And the only thing that has changed around here since Mel left is Thalia. It won't take her long to put two and two together. I cannot have Mel going after her. No matter what.

With that in mind, I slowly make my way upstairs.

Chapter Thirteen

THALIA

By the time Theo and I got back to the stalls yesterday evening, I had texts and missed calls from Kiara and Marissa asking where I was. I missed dinner with them. It was worth it though. I don't feel bad because I did something so much better. I had time with Theo.

On our own.

And then he gave me the best orgasm of my life. No man has ever been where Theo went and the only orgasms I have ever had were ones I had given myself. If he made me feel like that with just his fingers, I can only imagine what it would feel like to have his dick inside me. I got a better feel of his size last night.

He is big.

Very big.

I know it would hurt but I don't care. I want nothing more than to feel him stretching me, bringing me pleasure. The thought makes my stomach clench and wetness pool in my panties. I should feel bad, and I do.

A little bit.

He has a girlfriend. But something tells me there is a lot more to their relationship than meets the eye. Theo has said some cryptic things and I can't help thinking that all is not as it seems.

And surely, if he loved her that much and was happy, then he would not be doing what he has done with me?

I pull up at the barn to find the grooms loading horses onto the horse trailers. I feel guilty I wasn't here to help but Theo insisted it is what the grooms are here for, and I shouldn't get to the barn until 7:30 A.M. like the rest of the students. I step up to Maria as she is leading Zeus out of the barn. He looks beautiful with his mane braided. I glance at his body; he has a thin navy show blanket on with my name in silver embroidery and white bandages on his legs.

"Morning, Thalia. Your horses are all ready to go," she informs me.

"Thank you, have you seen Theo?"

"He is in his office. But be warned, he does not seem in the best of moods," she says before loading Zeus on the trailer. I snort. When is Theo ever in a good mood? He has more mood swings than I do when it's my time of month. I make my way across the barn to Theo's office. His door is open when I get there, and he is tapping away on his laptop.

"Theo?" His head snaps up, his blue eyes locking on mine. Jesus, the man is beautiful. Butterflies fill my stomach and my cheeks heat.

"What can I do for you, Thalia?" I frown at his curt tone.

"I was wondering if I could ride with you to Royal Palm?" Royal Palm is the biggest equestrian center in America and is the host of the Winter Equestrian Festival which begins in January. Something I can't decipher passes in Theo's eyes before he clears his throat.

"I would prefer if you took your own vehicle or travel with one of the other trainees." My face falls. I know he catches it because his eyes soften briefly before they turn hard again. Maybe

I am a stupid and thought things would change after yesterday, but clearly not. I school my features and force a smile.

"Okay, no problem. I will go and see if Carter wants to travel with me." His eyes flash with anger but before he can say anything, I turn away and leave.

―――――

Carter pulls into Royal Palm in his flashy black Ferrari. It's a nice car but I have never been impressed by cars. Or material things for that matter.

"When are we going to go for that dinner you promised me?" he drawls, his hazel eyes sparkling. I wish I could like him the way I like Theo, but I just don't see him like that. I will go for dinner with him though. Just need to make sure he knows it is as friends.

"Let's not talk about that now. I just want to focus on today. I am so nervous," I tell him honestly. Because I am. The butterflies in my stomach are for different reasons now. I want everything to go well today. I want to impress Theo. Carter's eyes soften.

"Everything will be fine, Thalia. I have been watching you and you have improved so much from when you first got here." I smile before climbing out of the car. Carter steps up beside me.

"Come on, let's go to the clubhouse and wait for Theo," he says.

We make our way toward the big white building; I look around at my surroundings and can't help the smile that tips my lips. The place is amazing. It's different to the equestrian centers I competed at in New York. I stop, taking it all in. The atmosphere. The arena with the colorful jumps. The smell of horse that permeates the air. This is what I want and I want it more than anything.

"What's wrong?" Carter asks, dragging me out of my thoughts. I grin at him.

"Nothing, I just can't believe I am here. This place is amazing."

Carter shrugs. "Yeah, it is. I guess it doesn't impress me so much anymore because I have been coming here for a few years but I can see why you are in awe. It is not like any other center in America." Carter grabs my hand and tugs me toward the clubhouse to wait for Theo.

We don't have to wait long. I am sitting with Carter, Kiara, and Marissa when Theo appears. I feel him before I see him. My body has become so aware of the man, it is scary. I frown in confusion when the girls mention Melody's name, that is until I glance over my shoulder. My face falls and stomach twists.

Beside Theo and holding his hand in a tight grip, is none other than his girlfriend.

Melody Whitworth.

When did she get back? And why didn't Theo tell me? He had his fingers—the same fingers that are now holding his girlfriend's hand—inside me less than twenty fours ago. Theo glances at me. I see the apology in his eyes and something that looks a lot like regret. They step up to our table. Melody is even prettier in real life with her blond hair, chocolate eyes, and flawless skin. She is beautiful. I can see why Theo is with her. My chest tightens and a pang of jealousy hits me. A throat clears but I don't take my eyes off my bottle of water in front of me.

"Morning all. Carter, Kiara, and Marissa, you already know Mel. Thalia, this is my girlfriend, Melody," Theo drawls, his voice bored like he doesn't care that this is hurting me. I have no choice but to look at him and his damn girlfriend. I plaster on a fake smile and take Melody's outstretched hand.

"Hi," she chirps in her strong British accent. "I have been so excited to meet you ever since Theodore told me you would be training with him. I am a big fan of your mother. And wow, you are just the prettiest thing. Beautiful," she murmurs as she stares at me. My stomach dips. I feel like a complete bitch for what I have been doing with her boyfriend. I glance at him before my eyes go back to Melody.

"Thank you. It's lovely to meet you," I smile although I feel sick. I release her hand and look back to my bottle of water.

"Is everyone ready for today?" Theo's voice sounds again. I nod, though I am not aware if he sees it. "Good, you three are not riding until the third class. Thalia, come with me, we need to walk the course." I push out of my chair and face the happy couple.

"Can I come with you?" Melody purrs as she runs a talon down his chest.

"No, Mel. I am working, stay here. Have some brunch," he snaps, making her recoil. My eyes widen. I glance to the three at the table who are not taking any notice. Maybe it is a normal occurrence?

"Let's go, Thalia," he mutters, spinning on his heel and striding toward the entrance. I flash a smile at Melody and rush after him. Once outside, I speak.

"What the hell, Theo?" I whisper shout. He glances down at me and rolls his eyes.

"Relax. You knew I had a girlfriend and that didn't stop you," he says calmly and I want to kill him. Anger courses through me. Yes, I did, and it didn't stop me but that doesn't make this situation any better.

"Yes, I did know, Theo. But you could have told me she was back in town. Ever heard of the saying out of sight out of mind? Well, it is a bit like that, which is why I didn't feel as bad about what we were doing. Now she is here, gushing over my mother, gushing over me," I choke on the ball in my throat. We step into the grass arena, I pause briefly and look around, momentarily forgetting about the issue at hand.

"Come on, Thalia. I do not have all day," Theo barks and I want to throttle him.

"What do we do now?" I ask.

"We focus on you not making a fool out of yourself in this

arena today and walking the course." I narrow my eyes at him. Clearly asshole mode has been activated today.

"You are such a dick. I meant about your girlfriend being here," I hiss. Theo stops abruptly and stares down at me.

"We do nothing. My girlfriend has nothing to do with you. Clear your damn mind and concentrate on being the best you can be today and proving to me you are capable." I chew my bottom lip, taking in his words. His eyes dart to the movement and I almost smirk. The asshole wants me, whether Melody is here or not.

"Okay." His eyes move to mine and narrow.

"Okay?" he repeats. I nod.

"Yes, Theo, okay. I am here for one thing and that is to be the best. Not get caught up in some twisted game with you," I mumble and resume with my course walk once again. I may be young and naïve.

But I am not going to let Theo get the better of me.

———

"Are you ready? You know the course?" Theo asks as he checks my girth. I am on Lolly ready to jump the one-meter fifteen Jumper class.

"Yes," I grit for what feels like the twentieth time. He looks up at me under the peak of his ball cap. He looks so damn god-like; he makes my stomach clench. And then my stomach clenches for a different reason when I remember why I am pissed with him.

His girlfriend is here.

"Thalia Maxwell, can you make your way to the tunnel? You are next to go," a female voice sounds over the speaker.

"Okay, let's go," Theo mutters and makes his way toward the tunnel that leads to the arena entrance. I follow him, my eyes moving around the arena as I memorize my course. I am so lost in my own mind, I don't realize the last competitor has exited the ring.

"Go on, Thalia, what are you waiting for?" Theo hisses. Ignoring him, I kick Lolly and off we go. I salute the judges and squeeze into a canter. I do a small lap and then turn to fence one, a big black and yellow oxer. I remember what Theo taught me and sit up, keeping my hands soft and my legs applying a little pressure. We clear fence one and I smile. It feels good to be back at a competition. Fence five is a water jump with rustic poles. I can feel Lolly spooking as we near it, so I kick. I may look messy, but I would rather that than her refuse it. She clears it a stride out. I know Theo will call me out on it, but I don't care, I jumped it.

It goes by so quick and before I know it, I am coming to the last fence, a red and white combination. I set Lolly up perfectly as I approach it, she jumps the first and touches a pole. I try to put it out of my head and concentrate on the next two, we jump them clear and then we are finished. I smile. Even though we had four faults, I am happy with that. I pull up to a walk and make my way out of the arena.

"That was just four faults for Thalia Maxwell and Lollipop," the judge announces. I spot Theo at the entrance, the corner of his mouth quirks up into a half smile.

"How was that?" I ask.

"Not bad. You were out on the water jump but the fence down was not your fault. Lolly looked tired toward the end. We need to up her work, get her fitter." I nod and hop off when we stop at the trailers. Jess grabs the reins.

"Well done, honey,"

"Thanks, Jess." She takes Lolly and starts stripping her tack off before washing her down and loading her back on the trailer. Maria steps up to me with Zeus.

"Hop on, we don't have that many to go before you are in on Zeus," Theo mutters, his eyes on his cell. Maria legs me up and I head for the warmup area. Twenty minutes later, I am back in the arena. I have jumped five fences and am heading for number six, which is a colorful floral oxer with insects. I feel Zeus looking at it and he starts to slow. I kick him forward, but he doesn't go. He stops two strides out and dips to the side so quick, I fall, landing on my back. I lay there, the wind knocked out of me.

"Jesus," I croak out when I feel a shadow hovering over me.

"Are you okay?" Theo asks. I don't miss the panic in his voice. I look at him, embarrassment coloring my cheeks. It's a fall that could have easily been prevented had I been sitting straight and squeezing tight.

"Yes, I am fine," I push up to a seated position. Theo reaches out with a hand. I take it, and he pulls me up so he is eye level and searches my face.

"Are you sure? It looked like you hit the ground hard." I brush off my jodhpurs and look at him.

"I am fine, Theo." I start for the entrance where I can see Maria with Zeus.

"That was an elimination for Thalia Maxwell and Zeus," The judge announces. I grimace but carry on walking, Theo hot on my heels.

"If you had been tight in your seat, you would not have fallen," Theo says, telling me what I already know.

"I know," I grit. I glance at him, and he shakes his head at my attitude. I don't care. I am pissed with him, too.

"Put him on the trailer, Maria. Thalia only has five until she goes with Roman." Maria scurries off toward the trailer and Theo turns to me. His hands cup my shoulders, igniting every nerve ending inside me. I swallow as my cheeks heat. He smirks. The asshole knows the effect he has on me.

"Do you feel okay to ride Roman?" he asks. I roll my eyes.

"Yes, I feel fine." He nods.

"Good. Now remember to sit up and keep your leg on. This course size will be nothing for Roman." I agree it won't be. But he is still a new ride for me, and I need to be ready for anything. Especially after what just happened with Zeus. Jess appears with Roman and Theo legs me up. The feel of his hands on me makes a pulse start between my legs and my pussy clench. I shake my head. I need to focus on not falling off my new horse, not how Theo makes me feel.

———

"The winner of the one-meter fifteen jumper class is Thalia Maxwell and Romatiek," the judge announces as we wait for the results. Theo pulls me into a hug. I can't help but get caught up in his excitement.

"Well done, Thalia. I knew you could do it." I smile and pull away.

"Thank you. I know Roman is capable of so much more, but it feels good after my fall on Zeus. A confidence boost."

"He is, but this is your first show and you have only had him for just over a week. Be proud of yourself." I grin at him. All his assholeness—yes I made up the word—and training methods seem worth it at this moment.

Chapter Fourteen

THEO

I end up winning the six-year-old qualifier class on my young horse and the $2500 derby on one of my grand prix horses. I have one class left. The seven-year-old qualifier with Beau. I make my way to the pavilion where I know my trainees and Melody have been watching. I step through the door and the first thing I notice is Thalia and the way her beautiful face is lit up with a breath-taking smile. I see nothing or nobody else but her. She is like the Sun, an otherworldly being.

I am drawn to her like a moth to a flame.

I don't know how to stop it or even if I want to.

I stride toward them, my fists balling when I see Carter grab Thalia's hand. Mel notices me first and pushes out of her seat.

"Darling, congratulations. You were perfect." She kisses me deeply and out of the corner of my eye, I see Thalia grimace before averting her gaze. I pull away.

"Thank you,"

"Theodore, Carter mentioned he is leaving; do you mind if I go with him? I am tired from travelling yesterday and I want a nap."

"Of course, but didn't Thalia travel with Carter?" I respond.

Mel frowns before looking at my piccola. And she *is* mine, even if she thinks otherwise.

"I was going to stay and watch you in your last class, and ride back with you if that is okay?" Thalia rasps. I want nothing more than to be with her on my own, but I know it is not a good idea. I have no self-control when it comes to her. Now more than ever, I need to stay away while Mel is back. She is like a bloodhound.

"Did Kiara and Marissa leave?" I ask instead.

"Yes, they left after they finished competing," Carter confirms. I turn to face Mel, who is watching me intently. I smile, dropping a kiss to her mouth.

"You go with Carter. I can bring Thalia back." Mel grins, leaning into me and brushing her tits against my chest. I resist a grimace.

"Maybe we can have round two tonight... And if you win the next class, I will do that thing you like," she purrs quietly but I know Thalia heard because her face looks like she has eaten a lemon. I clear my throat and smile but don't respond to Mel's comment.

———

I win the seven-year-old class. I don't know whether to be happy about it or not. Obviously, it's a good result but I can't help but think about what Mel said. The grooms have loaded the horses on the trailer and are on the way back to the farm. I stroll into the clubhouse, ready to get Thalia and leave. As soon as I step through the entrance, I am ambushed by Dean Carruthers and Calvin Decker. Both show jumpers, both men I have partied with on the circuit.

"Theo, man, you kept that one quiet," Dean drawls, flashing a smirk at Calvin.

"What are you on about?" I bark, my eyes moving around the

room trying to locate the girl that seems to have invaded my mind without even knowing it.

"Thalia Maxwell," he says. I freeze, my gaze moving back to Dean. He cocks a brow. I cock my head, eyes zooming in on him. His smile is wide, and I want to punch him in his mouth.

"Man, she is the finest piece of ass I have ever seen. Hotter than her mother and that is saying something because I spent many of my teenage years jerking off to pictures of Elena Maxwell. I wouldn't mind trying the real thing with her offspring though. Is she single? Can you introduce me? I am going to make it my mission to fuck her before the year is out." Both the idiots chuckle, making my fists ball. I clench my jaw as my blood heats.

"That is prime pussy if ever I saw it," he adds. I see red and fist the collar of his shirt, leaning in until my nose touches his. His eyes widen, no doubt at my reaction. I used to be just like these two assholes. Spent many years chasing ass on the circuit with them. But not anymore.

"You stay the fuck away from her. She is not like the easy women you are used to. She is a good woman and way out of your league. If I hear that you have been sniffing around her, you will not like the consequences." I push him away from me, looking at him in disgust.

"Jesus, Rhodes, what the hell," Dean growls, brushing down his collar as Calvin stares at me in disbelief. Dean watches me for a beat before a knowing smirk tips his lips. I have a bad feeling about what he is going to say before he says it.

"Careful, Theo, anyone would think you are jealous. But that can't be right, you have Melody." He tsks, leaning in close as he lowers his voice. "If I want to fuck Thalia Maxwell, I will and there is nothing you can do about it," he taunts. I want to hit the fucker, grab Thalia, and fuck her in front of him so he knows who she belongs to.

"Come on, Cal, let's get out of here." They both saunter away but not before Dean throws me a challenging look. I take a calming breath, then not spotting Thalia inside I make my way to the deck.

Stepping outside, I spot her at a table on her cell talking animatedly. I glance around, noticing more than a handful of men with their eyes on her. My heart rate kicks up, chest tightening. This girl will be the death of me. Why couldn't she have been ugly?

I start toward her, all the while my eyes stay on her face. She is completely oblivious to the lustful gazes being thrown her way and for some reason, it makes me angry. I stop when I reach her. She still doesn't notice me, too lost in whoever she is talking to. I clench my jaw. If someone tried to kidnap her, she wouldn't stand a chance. She has no clue about what is going on around her.

"We are leaving," I say impatiently, not caring that she is on a call. Her head finally snaps up, her eyes landing on me. She frowns.

"Aria, I will call you later. Flove you," she rushes out before ending the call. I stare at her.

'Flove you'?

What the fuck is 'flove you'?

"What's wrong?" she asks, concern in her voice.

"Nothing is wrong. But you need to be more self-aware," I say without going into detail. Her little nose scrunches up in confusion and she has never looked so cute.

Christ.

I have never been more attracted to someone in my life.

"Let's go," I bark, turning on my heel and making my way to my SUV.

I climb inside, turning on the ignition. Thalia scrambles into the passenger seat and as soon as she closes the door, I peel out of the impressive palm tree lined drive. The air is thick, my whole being is aware of the girl next to me, but I don't speak and neither does she. That doesn't mean I miss the way her chest moves in quick succession with every breath she takes. Or the way she glances at me every couple of minutes. Five minutes out from the farm, she speaks.

"Well done today, Theo, it was impressive watching you," she says barely above a whisper. I smirk remembering what she overheard Mel say earlier. I don't know why, but I want to punish her for the attention she received today. I want to be an asshole. I know it's not her fault men were drooling over her but that does not stop me.

"Yeah, well, I had good incentive, if you recall?" Her head whips to me, eyes widen, like she cannot believe I just said that. She isn't alone. I can't believe I said it either.

"What the hell is wrong with you? Not even twenty-four hours ago, you had me against a tree. Kissing me. Your fing—" she trails off, her cheeks turning a delectable shade of red.

"My fingers, what?" I goad, wanting her to say the words. She remains quiet. So, I carry on. Because apparently, I am a massive asshole when it comes to her. "My fingers inside you. Finger fucking you, Thalia," I taunt. She sucks in a breath but ignores me until I pull to a stop by her car. She unbuckles her belt and hurries out of my SUV. Spinning to face me, she growls.

"Enjoy your evening with your girlfriend, Theo." And with that, she slams the door, hops in her car, and leaves. I scrub a palm down my face. What the hell is wrong with me? I shouldn't have acted like that toward her, but she seems to bring out this side of me. A jealous, possessive side.

I need to apologize.

Before I can think about what I am doing, I am barreling out of my driveway and toward Thalia's condo. I know where she lives. Fortunately, it is all over her paperwork and lucky for me, only around fifteen minutes from the barn. I can go and apologize to her and be back home before Melody starts asking questions.

Pulling into her building parking lot, I spot her getting out of her SUV. She looks sad. My chest tightens that I am the one that has put that look there. A girl like her should never be sad. I jump out and stride towards her.

"Thalia," I call out. Her head snaps over her shoulder, eyes landing on me and narrowing.

"Oh, you weren't enough of a dick toward me in the car, you just had to come and seek me out to be more of an asshole?" she shouts. I hold back a groan. I love her feisty attitude. It makes my dick hard. I step up to her, spinning her to face me. Luckily, we are hidden by the side of the building, and no one can see us. The sky darkens and it looks like it might rain but I am not letting her go inside until I explain.

"I'm sorry, okay? I should not have said that. I just..." I trail off.

"You just what, Theo?" she presses. I sigh.

"I have these feelings for you. I don't know what to do with them. I am also a taken man. The things we have done are wrong. But I cannot help myself when it comes to you," I admit.

"Theo..." she whispers, her big innocent eyes staring up at me. She licks her bottom lip and my resolve cracks.

My mouth claims hers.

I kiss her like I am trying to consume her, and I suppose I am.

I want to consume her.

Claim her.

But then there is Melody and all the money her father has invested in horses. Am I willing to risk all that because of an intense attraction I have for a girl I have no business touching?

The rain starts hammering down on us, but I don't care. Right now, all I care about is this girl in front of me. Her soft sounds, the way she feels, how I want to make her mine. She pulls away, her eyes hooded. She looks drunk on me and I love it. Want more of it. My dick strains in my pants. So hard, I am surprised it doesn't punch through the material and run straight to her. Wet hair sticks to her face and my gaze drops to her heaving chest.

Her white tank is now see-through from the rain; her pink nipples are hard and visible through the thin material.

I want her.

I want to be inside her.

I want her nipples in my mouth.

To touch every inch of her.

Now.

"Can we go upstairs? To talk," I rasp. I know it's wrong. I know I have someone at home waiting for me but I cannot bring myself to care or stop. Thalia nods and starts towards her building. I follow her, entering the impressive lobby. She greets the doorman and a woman behind a desk, then makes her way to the elevator. We step inside, the air thick and energy cracking, as we remain quiet. The elevator comes to a stop on the top floor, the penthouse. I am not surprised. Only the best for Thalia Maxwell, Daddy's princess. She pulls out a key card and opens the door. She steps into her apartment, motioning for me to do the same. I glance around at the modern interior. All open plan, sleek and expensive.

"What did you want to speak with me about?" she asks, dropping down on one of the barstools at the breakfast nook. I round the counter and brace my palms on the marble surface, caging her in. She gasps, her hot breath fanning my face. Instead of talking, I press my lips to hers, enjoying it when her body shivers against me. She is so responsive to me; it's making me obsessed.

"Theo," she breathes against my lips.

"Don't talk. Don't ruin this moment. I know this is wrong. I know there's Mel. But I want you. I want you so much, it hurts. It's why I act like an ass toward you. I've tried to push you away." She chuckles.

"I would hate to see how you act if you didn't like me." She sighs, "I should feel bad about Melody but I don't think I do. Does that make me a bad person?"

"No. It makes me a bad person. I am the one with the relationship. I should have never started this and put you in this position. But you bring out this side of me. The no self-control side," I smirk.

"So, what do we do?" she asks. I grin, grabbing her thighs, opening them so I can stand between her legs.

"For the moment, we carry on as we are." I pepper kisses along her jaw, but she pushes me away. I frown.

"I want to know what the situation is with you and Melody before I do this. You said all is not as it seems." I groan. I don't want to talk anymore.

I want to kiss her.

Touch her.

Taste her.

But she deserves some honesty from me. I am expecting her to basically be my dirty little secret. If this ever got out to the press, it would ruin their wholesome family image and no doubt Christian Maxwell would be gunning for me. He'd ruin me.

"Mel and I have a complicated relationship. Her father owns most of my horses. To be honest, I never really wanted a relationship with her but felt I had to when I got drunk and fucked her one night." Thalia winces at my crass words. "It's why I stopped drinking. I know it makes me weak staying with her but having her father's backing has brought me success I never imagined."

"So, you stay with her because you don't want to lose the horses?" There is no judgement in her tone, just interest. I blow out a breath. When she puts it like that, it makes me sound like a complete asshole.

"Like I said, it's complicated. Can we stop talking about that now, so I can kiss you?" She blushes. It makes her look more innocent than she normally does.

"This conversation isn't over, Theo; I want to know everything." I nod before tugging her toward me and claiming her mouth. The heat between her legs and the way she tastes makes my cock harden between us. I know she feels it when she gasps.

"Bedroom," I mumble against her lips. She points in the direction of a door off to the side of the living area. I don't waste any time. I pick her up and carry her toward it. I don't know what is going to happen next, but I do know I need to taste her pussy. It's a need like no other. Like if I don't taste her, I will die.

I kick the door open and quickly glance around. California king bed, walk in wardrobe, expensive nightstand. All decorated in neutral colors. My eyes move to the sliding doors that lead to a balcony and I briefly wonder if it is big enough for me to fuck her out there. Not tonight but at some point. I stride toward the bed and drop her down. She looks up at me with lust filled eyes. It makes my dick even harder, if that's possible. She lets out a breath and nibbles her lip. She suddenly looks...nervous.

"Everything okay? I can stop if you want," I murmur, climbing on the bed and up her beautiful body.

"I-I'm a..." she trails off, averting her gaze. I frown before it clicks. Is she a virgin? No way is she a virgin. But then I remember how tight she felt around my fingers and her blushes whenever we kiss.

"Are you a virgin?" I blurt.

She bites her full bottom lip and nods. My eyes widen as an animalistic need comes over me. A need to be the first man inside her, claiming her and making her mine. But I can't do that. Not now that I know just how innocent she is. I need to take things slow with her. I push off her. Worry flashes in her eyes and she reaches for me.

"Where are you going?"

"You being a virgin changes things. We need to take it slow."

"But I want this. I want you."

"I want you too. But I am not going to fuck you and take your virginity like this. You deserve better." She pushes up to a seating position and takes my hand.

"I want this. Please," she begs, snapping any restraint I had. I push her down and pounce on her. I unbutton her jodhpurs and shimmy them down her legs. The white material is like a second skin, sticking to every inch of her. I tear them from her body, leaving her in little white panties, her wet tank, and a bra.

Jesus. She looks so innocent.

Virginal.

Because she is.

I am an asshole for doing this, but nothing is going to stop me now. Remembering what Dean said and how Carter wants her. It all spurs me on. She is not theirs.

She is mine.

And now I am going to prove it.

I peel her wet tank from her body, quickly unhook her bra, and rip her panties from her. Her chest heaves as she lays naked before me. She tries to cover herself, but I stop her. I part her legs slightly to find her pussy glistening and wet. I groan. She has the most perfect pussy I have ever seen. Wanting to taste her, I dip down and swipe my tongue from her slit to her clit.

Christ. She tastes like heaven.

Like *mine*.

She writhes beneath me. "Theo, what are you doing? I haven't showered," she breathes.

"I don't care. I want to taste you." And I do. With a palm on her belly to hold her still and my tongue on her pussy, I eat her until she is coming all over my face. Her juices are like a nectar on my tongue.

I straighten and look down at her. Her eyes are closed, chest heaving as she comes down from her orgasm. She has never looked more beautiful than this moment. Her eyes snap open, locking on mine before travelling south to where my erection strains against my pants. Her gaze moves back to my face, and she swallows.

"Can I...can I taste you?" I nearly blow my load right then at her words. I should say no. But I want to see her lips wrapped around my cock more than I want oxygen right now. I make quick work of removing my clothes and position Thalia on the floor on her knees in front of me. She peers up at me from her long lashes. I groan. I have never in my life seen anything so sexy. I run my thumb along her lower lip and wrap my hand around the base of my cock, moving it to her mouth.

"You okay?" I ask as she swallows.

"Yeah. I have never seen one in real life, and you are so big. I am wondering how you will fit in my mouth." I chuckle.

"It will fit but if it gets too much, I will stop." She nods as she licks her lips. "Open," I command. Anticipation shoots through me when her mouth parts. I don't think I have ever wanted anything more in my life. Right here, right now, I would give up everything for this girl.

I move my cock inside her mouth and nearly shoot my load.

Hot.

Wet.

Fucking perfect.

Just like I knew it would be.

She bobs her head up and down my shaft before running her tongue slowly, teasingly, across the top.

"Hollow out your cheeks, suck harder and grip what you can't get in your mouth. Hard," I grit, trying not to blow my load like a teenage boy. I lift my hips, sliding further in. She gags as tears gather in her eyes, but does as I ask. She may be new to this but just having her lips on me makes it the best blowjob ever. She sucks harder, taking me further down her throat. And when she looks up at me, her eyes flashing with lust, my balls tighten and I find my release before I can stop myself. Her eyes widen but she takes every drop of my cum like a pro. It is so hot, my dick stays hard.

"Fuck," I pant.

"Was it okay?" she asks nervously, before wiping her mouth and averting her eyes. I grip her chin, tugging until her gaze meets mine.

"Better than okay," I murmur, dropping a kiss to her mouth.

"But you are still hard," she points out as my dick bobs between us.

"This is what you do to me. I am always hard around you."

She rises and straddles my lap. A confidence I have never seen from her before flashes in her eyes. She starts kissing me. My eyes widen in shock. It is the first time she has ever taken control and damn if it doesn't turn me on. She grinds herself in my lap, if she doesn't stop, I am going to fuck her. She reaches down and palms my dick before lifting herself as if she is going to put me inside her. No fucking way can I let that happen, it will hurt enough when I take her. But like this? It would really hurt. I stop her just as the tip slides through her wet folds. My eyes roll to the back of my head. I deserve a medal; it is no easy feat stopping this. I am about a second away from shoving myself inside her but then I take a breath and remember that she is a virgin.

"Not like this," I tell her when she frowns at me. I push off the bed, Thalia still in my lap, and lay her down before climbing on top of her. Her breath hitches as I nudge her legs apart with my knee. I should not be doing this. Should not have touched her in this way. And not just because I have a girlfriend but because her father will ruin me. But Thalia seems determined to do this now and who am I to stop her?

I run a finger down her pussy to make sure she is still wet.

She is.

She is fucking soaked.

I don't have a condom on me, and I doubt she has any. That alone should put an end to this madness but no. I want to feel her bare, feel every inch of her glorious pussy. I am clean. I've have never fucked Melody without protection. Even after all these years, I still wrap it up. Guess you could say I am worried she might trap me. With her, anything is possible. Which is why I've never trusted her enough to go without.

"Are you on birth control?" I ask, stopping any more thoughts of Mel. Thalia chews her bottom lip but nods. I frown wondering why she would be if she isn't sexually active but then she explains.

"My mother insisted when my parents agreed to send me here. They knew I wouldn't sleep around but they wanted me covered in case I met anyone." Makes sense. A teenage pregnancy would be a scandal in the Maxwell family. So would this. But I couldn't give a fuck about that right now.

I drop a kiss to her lips, then line my cock up to her entrance. My heart beats in my chest. Adrenaline courses through me. I am about to fuck Thalia Maxwell. Take her innocence. With that in mind, I start to push inside her only to stop when she winces.

"Are you okay?" I ask, worry evident in my voice. She takes a breath.

"Yeah. It just hurts a little." She shifts beneath me. I knew it would. She is so fucking tight, and I am not a small guy.

"It will only hurt to begin with. As soon as I am fully inside you and start moving, the pain should turn to pleasure. Can I keep going?" She nods. I push further in. I feel some resistance and my heart pounds. Once I tear through, she is mine. The thought excites me so much, that without meaning to, I thrust until I am fully seated inside her tight cunt which strangles the hell out of my dick.

Fuck me. I have never felt anything better in my life.

I still, dropping my head to kiss her. "I am going to start moving now. Tell me if it hurts and I will stop."

"Do it," she whisper moans making me snap. I slowly thrust in and out of her, all the while gritting my teeth, so I don't come. The feel of her and knowing I now own her virginity has an orgasm building before I am ready. Needing her to come, I reach down and play with her clit. Her face shifts to pleasure and I know the pain has subsided now. I move faster as I circle her little bundle of nerves. She tightens around me, gripping me like a fucking vise and it takes everything in me not to come. Her lips part in ecstasy, I know she is close. Thank fuck because I am seconds away. She cries out, screaming my name as she coats my dick in her juices. That thought and the way she is clenching me has me following her. I pump into her a couple more times, stilling when I shoot my seed inside her, marking her as mine.

I roll to the side of her and collapse on my back, so I don't squash her. Wrapping an arm around her, I pull her into my side and press my lips to her dark hair.

"How was that? I didn't hurt you too much did I?" I ask. She shakes her head and lets out a content sigh.

"It was amazing. Even better than I imagined my first time to be." I smile only for it to drop when my cell rings. I shoot up and hop off the bed. I know who it will be. Fishing it out of my pocket, Mel's name flashes on the screen.

"Shit, I need to go." I quickly pull on my clothes then turn to face Thalia. My heart clenches when I see the sad look on her face. I am a bastard; I just took the girl's virginity and now I am bolting. I stride to her adjoined bathroom, grab a cloth and wet it with warm water. I make my way back to Thalia, parting her thighs so I can clean her up. It's the least I can do after she gave me something so special. Something that has never belonged to me. She tries to clamp her legs shut.

"I just want to clean you up," I murmur. She blows out a breath and allows me to open her up. I gently clean away my come and her blood, now mixed together. I must be a masochist because the sight alone, seeing her blood, knowing it was me that put it there, makes me hard again. Finishing up, I drop the cloth in her wash basket before I lean in and kiss her.

"I am sorry. I will make it up to you. I promise. Rest, Piccola," I whisper against her mouth before turning on my heel and leaving her on the bed.

Alone.

I am disgusted with myself. She should be made to feel special after her first time, not like a whore that I just fucked and left. She deserves to be treasured, cuddled, spooned all damn night.

The realization of what I have done sets in. Not only did I cheat on Melody, again, I took something from Thalia I had no business taking. And if anyone found out, I would be ruined and not just by Christian Maxwell. I would lose everything I have spent years building.

Why couldn't I just leave her alone? It's like she has cast a spell over me. I cannot resist her. I pushed and pushed, when I should have stayed away. Crossed lines I never should have thought about crossing. I will hurt people I do not want to hurt. All because I am selfish. I wanted her so I made her mine.

Nothing or no one would have stopped me.

Chapter Fifteen

THALIA

The elation I felt from sleeping with Theo quickly turned to confusion, then anger. It has been two days since we had sex and he has gone radio silent. I have not seen him. Fortunately, my horses were having some rest days after the competition, and I am not scheduled for any lessons. Otherwise, I would have lost my shit completely.

I texted him, but he never replied. I turned up at the barn at random times, but he was never there. I am confused and really fucking pissed off. How dare he take my virginity then ignore me? I understand things are more difficult for him, but he could have at least messaged me.

On the third day, I pull up to the barn, angrier than I have ever been in my life. I am supposed to be having a lesson on each of my horses today and Theo better show his face. If not, he will leave me no choice but to go to the house. My cell rings on my handsfree, my mother's name popping up on the dash.

"Hey, Mama," I answer.

"Bambina, how are you?" I smile, hearing her voice.

"I am good, are you okay? Where are you in the world?" I

know she has been away filming in central America, but she could be anywhere now.

"I am actually in New York with your father. I wanted to let you know we will be flying in tomorrow to visit you. I have missed you so much. We will be staying for a week at the Miami house." I smile at the excitement in her voice. As much as my mother was absent because of work, she has always been a very loving mom and every second of her time off has always been spent with us. She even stopped taking parts at one point when we were younger just so she didn't miss us growing up.

"I cannot wait. I have missed you too and Papa."

"Your father said you won your competition at the weekend?" I nod even though she can't see me.

"Yes, I did. On my new horse. I can't wait to show you him and my progress. I think Daddy will be happy with what he is paying for." I feign a laugh even though I cringe at my words. If he found out he was paying for extracurricular activities like losing my virginity to my trainer, then he would have a heart attack. My mother chuckles.

"You know your father does not care about the money as long as you are happy, Bambina."

"I know, Mama. Anyway, I must go. I have a lesson in ten minutes."

"Okay. I love you. See you tomorrow."

"Love you too," I murmur before ending the call. I hop out of my SUV and make my way inside the barn. My heart jumps when I see the muscular back of Theo.

He is here.

As if he can sense me, he glances over his shoulder. For a minute, I forget I am pissed with him and smile only for it to drop when he scowls at me. Nerves course through me, I fidget where I stand.

"Come on, Thalia, I have a lot to do today. And I am not going to work around you. If you don't want a lesson, tell me and I will train someone who does," he snaps, pushing me into action. I scramble toward where I can see Maria standing with Zeus, smiling even though I want to cry. How can he be such an asshole after everything?

"Hey, honey. Don't worry, he has been in a bad mood all morning," Maria whispers for my ears only. I flash her a grateful smile before climbing on Zeus and making my way out to the arena. I warm up in walk trot and canter by the time Theo strolls out.

"Okay, I think we need to focus on your seating position. I also think that we need to get you jumping some of the more colorful fences we have here. I told you after your..." he pauses as if he is looking for the right words, "...half round at Royal Palm that I thought Zeus was being naughty and he was. But I also think we need to get you sitting tighter so you avoid falls like that. No matter how bad he was, you could have sat that refusal if you had a better seat. If you were squeezing tighter with your legs, like I have taught you, then you would not have fallen." I nod, only because he is right. That doesn't mean my blood isn't boiling. Because it is. How can he act so normal after everything?

"I will set up a course. Do some more warm up exercises, focus on your seat and legs," Theo says and I take a good look at him. He looks like he has the weight of the world on his shoulders. Black circles under his eyes and his hair look like he has run his hands through it one too many times. My body heats, liquid lust running between my legs when I remember my hands in his dark strands. As if he can read my thoughts, he shakes his head, walking away. I sigh and continue my warmup, doing exactly what he asked me to do.

————

"You were good today, Thalia. Focused. You seem to have taken on board my advice and have made a lot of progress since you first came here," Theo drawls. I can't help my lips tipping up in a smile at his compliment. We are sitting in his office after three hours of training with all my horses. "I think you need another horse that is at the same level as Roman. The more horsepower you have, the more results and exposure you get and the more chance you have at getting noticed by teams."

"But I have Zeus and Lolly." Theo groans, scrubbing a palm down his tired face.

"I know you do. But they are never going to be at the level Roman is. They are one-twenty-five meter horses at the most. Hell, Zeus got eliminated in the one-fifteen class. Stop fighting me on this and just listen for once. Believe it or not, I know a thing or two about horses." He flashes me an annoyed look. I chew my bottom lip and inwardly smile when Theo's gaze drops to the movement.

"Okay, I will speak with my father. He is coming to visit tomorrow." Theo's eyes snap to mine and he nods.

"I know. He called me and invited me to dinner tomorrow night." My eyes widen. What dinner? My mother didn't mention a dinner. Does that mean Theo will be attending with Melody? As if he can hear my thoughts, he clears his throat and speaks.

"Melody and I will be joining you for dinner. Your father wants to discuss some business." Panic courses through me. How can I sit at a table with her knowing what happened between Theo and me? "Keep it together, Thalia. Everything will be okay." Theo's soothing voice pierces through my panic, grounding me. I nod, but I still have questions.

"How will it be okay? We-we-we," I stutter before taking a calming breath. "We slept together," I hiss. Theo gives me a droll look.

"I am aware of what we did."

"Do you even care?" I ask, disbelief thick in my voice.

"Of course, I care."

"Where have you been? Why did you not reply to my messages?" My anger from earlier comes back full force. I ask him the questions I have wanted to ask for the last forty-eight hours. Theo sighs.

"I had some things to sort out. Melody freaked out, wanted to know where I was the other night. She has not stopped asking me questions. I cannot have her digging any deeper and finding out about us. So, I did what I had to do." The insinuation is clear. I feel sick.

"Did you sleep with her?" My voice cracks with emotion. I know it makes me look pathetic, but I don't care. Theo stares at me for so long, I don't think he is going to answer but he does, breaking me in the process.

"She is my *girlfriend,* Thalia. I did what couples do. What I *had* to do. To protect you." I open my mouth to speak when his door flies open. My head whips back and when I see who has disturbed us, jealousy courses through me. Jealousy I have no right to feel. Melody's eyes move from Theo to me. I don't miss the flicker of suspicion before she covers it and moves toward us.

"Thalia, how nice to see you again."

"Hi," I flash her a small smile, looking away when her eyes land on Theo.

"Darling, I just wanted to let you know I am going shopping and for lunch with some girlfriends." Theo stares at her, annoyance clear in his eyes and voice.

"You don't need my permission; you are not a child, Mel," he snaps. Her cheeks turn pink in embarrassment, lips forming a thin line before she plasters on a fake smile.

"I know that, silly, I just wanted to inform you of my plans."

"You did and now you can go. I am working. And next time, don't just walk into my office, you knock." Melody's eyes widen in shock at his words and my heart sinks for her. But there is also a part of me that is happy. Happy that he is treating her like this.

Does that make me a bitch?

Probably.

Schooling her features, she leans down and kisses him. His left

eye meets mine. I see the apology in it, but I look away. I don't
need to see this.

"See you later, darling," she chirps, shooting me a smile.

"Bye, Thalia," she throws out before leaving the office. I slump
in my chair feeling like a piece of shit for what I did and the
thoughts I have been having toward her.

"It's not what you think," Theo murmurs. I glance at him, not
even trying to hide the tears in my eyes. I push out of my chair
and spin toward the door. At the threshold, I stop and look over
my shoulder.

"It never is," I spit before leaving.

———

It's 9 P.M and I am restless. My mind is going a mile a minute
with thoughts of Theo. After my training, I came back to my
apartment and did some schoolwork. Then I worked out until my
body ached and sweat dripped from me. I made some food, called
my sister and my best friend from home, Esme, who I haven't
caught up with in a while to try and occupy myself.

But still, I am restless. Finally having enough of tossing and
turning, I shove the comforter off me and get out of bed. The
only thing that is going to relax me right now is being around my
horses. I pull on some yoga pants and a hooded sweatshirt. Grabbing my keys from the side table, I make my way to my car.

Twenty minutes later, I am pulling up to the barn. It's dark
now and I probably shouldn't be here, but it is the only thing that
will calm my racing mind. I stride toward the barn to find the
doors shut. I make quick work of opening them, hoping that I
don't disturb any of the staff that live on site. Finding a body
brush, I head for Lolly's stable. I have owned her the longest and
something about her always settles me. She seems to know when
I am upset and when I'm happy. I know being around her will
help me some. I enter the stall; she snorts when she spots me. I

drop the brush and cup her muzzle before placing a kiss on her nose.

"Hey girl, Mommy is in a funny mood tonight. I just wanted to see you," I whisper. As if she understands my words, she nuzzles into me. I smile and release her head. Pulling off her blanket and popping it to the side, I grab the brush and start grooming her. It may seem like a weird thing to do, but it is like a calming balm to me. The smells and the environment in general. I don't know how much time passes but I start to relax, all thoughts of Theo leaving my head. That is until a deep voice startles me.

"What are you doing?"

I yelp, dropping the brush and clutching my chest as I spin around. Theo leans against the stall, arms crossed against his chest, a bored look on his face. I don't miss the way the corner of his mouth twitches in amusement. How did he get in here without me hearing him?

"Jesus, Theo, creeper much?"

He pushes off the wall on stalks toward me like a lion ready to pounce on his prey. My whole body comes alive with need, even though I don't want it to have this effect on me. I swallow at the intense look on his face, stepping back until I hit Lolly's body. His arms go to either side of me, hands braced on my horse, as he cages me in.

"You are the one creeping around Thalia. Are you not?" he drawls. His face is so close to mine, his hot breath fans my face.

"Yes," I breathe, my heartbeat hammering in my chest at his proximity.

"What are you doing?" he repeats.

"I was on edge. I wanted to come and see my horses. How did you know I was here?"

He chuckles. "I have a security system in place and you set it off. You are lucky I didn't call the police. When I spotted you, I came down here to see what you were doing." He leans in closer, his nose nuzzling into my hair. He inhales deeply.

"Whattt are you doing?" I stammer as my stomach tightens and arousal pools between my legs.

"I love the smell of you," he groans as he strokes his nose up and down the side of my face. I gasp when I feel his cock harden between us. He pulls back with a smirk. Grabbing my hand, he places it on his hard length.

"This is what you do to me Thalia," he hisses. I pull my hand away. Not because I want to. But because he needs to know I am not going to be that girl. The type that comes running when he clicks his fingers. Our relationship—if you can even call it that—has all been on his terms. I need to grow a backbone and stand up to him.

"You have ignored me for two days, Theo. When I do see you, you act like nothing happened. Like you didn't take my virginity and then bail. Then when I do see you, you are an asshole and tell me you fucked your girlfriend," I snap. His eyes spark, lust flashing in them

"When you grow up, Piccola, you will understand that sometimes you must do things you don't want to do, for the greater good. Melody is my girlfriend. If I don't fuck her, she will know something is wrong. She already started asking questions about the other night. Just because I took your virginity, was the first man inside your pussy, does not mean you have a claim on me." My mouth drops open at the audacity of this man. The fucker just smirks and carries on. "That all being said, I like what is between us. The forbidden aspect of it gets me so fucking hard, I can't see straight. And you? I have never been harder than I was the other night. You can be angry all you want, but you know you want me as much as I want you," he growls.

Dipping down, he sucks my lower lip into his mouth. I want to deny the arrogant bastard. Tell him to leave me the hell alone. But I can't . Something about him draws me to him. Makes me want him more than I have wanted anyone. Maybe it makes me stupid. But when his lips are on mine and his body is against me?

I lose all my senses and the only thing that matters is him. Us. The way he makes me feel.

Lolly moves a step. I lose my footing and fall back. Theo's big hands grip my waist, steadying me. He spins me until my back hits the stall wall. Gripping my thighs, he lifts me. My legs wrap around his torso on their own accord, like they know they belong there.

But that's not right.

Theo is not mine and never will be.

He smashes his lips down on mine, making me gasp. He uses that to his advantage and plunges his tongue inside, making love to my mouth like he made love to my body. I moan and grind against his thick hard cock. Theo pulls away. I whimper at the loss of contact as he smirks. Gripping the waistband of my pants, he makes quick work of removing them and my panties. The cool Floridian air hits my warm, wet folds, making me squirm.

"Theo, what are you doing? We can't do this here; anyone could see us," I rush out, panic gripping me. He ignores me. Holding me with one hand, he pulls down his sweats. His dick springs free, bobbing between us. My mouth waters at the sight, remembering what it felt like to have him inside me.

"Shhh, this is going to be quick and hard. Can you be quiet?" I nibble my bottom lip, wondering how I went from losing my virginity three nights ago to having sex in a stall. My parents would freak out if they ever found out. My dad would lock me away, never to be seen again. Even knowing this, I don't put a stop to it. Theo glides his length through my pussy before lining up with my entrance. He pushes into me in one hard thrust. I cry out at the way he fills me. He covers my mouth with a palm only to remove it and replace it with his mouth. He moves in and out of me relentlessly, never stopping to give me a moment to adjust to him. I moan and he swallows the sound. Wanting to gain some control, I pull my lips away and taunt him.

"I wonder what my father would say if he knew he was paying

you to teach me to ride not only horses but your dick." His eyes flash and he stops for a second only to piston his hips and thrust into me harder. My eyes squeeze shut at the feeling; he is deeper than he has ever been. I open my eyes to find him smirking at me and I know he is going to be an asshole even before he opens his mouth.

"Maybe I should be charging him more. You are getting four lessons for the price of three. Not only my expertise on your horses for three hours a day but also my expertise in riding my cock. That shit doesn't come cheap, Piccola. I happen to be an excellent teacher in both forms of riding," he throws back with a wink. Asshole. I thought for sure, he would stop this once I mentioned my father. He reaches down, his thumb landing on my sensitive clit.

"I'm going to need you to come before I do. Your pussy is strangling my cock and you feel so fucking good. I don't think I can hold on much longer," he rasps against my mouth. He plays with my little bundle of nerves, and it only takes seconds before I feel an orgasm building. He swivels his hips, hitting a place inside that makes my orgasm tear through me so quickly I see stars. I cry out his name, the sound getting lost inside his hot mouth. My head falls back against the wall as Theo thrusts a couple more times before stilling and finding his own release. His forehead lands on my sweatshirt covered chest. He groans as his dick pulses inside me, filling me with his cum. We stay like that for a long minute, lost in our orgasms and each other. That is until a cell vibrates. Theo pulls out of me and tucks his cock back into his sweats. He gently pops me on my feet before grabbing his cell. I know who it is by the way his lips form a tight line and his face turns cold.

"I need to get back to the house," he murmurs. I hear the regret in his voice, but don't look at him. I pull my pants up and nod even though I want to cry. How can I be so stupid? Messing around with a taken man.

"Yeah, go. I am just going to put Lolly's blanket on and go home," I say in a cold voice I don't recognize. I start toward Lolly only for Theo to stop me with a hand on my arm. I glance over my shoulder. His mouth parts, ready to say something, but I stop him. I don't want to hear another one of his apologies.

"Don't," I grit. He squeezes his eyes shut as if he is in pain, before spinning on his heel and exiting the stall. I wait for his footsteps to fade before I let the first tear fall.

———

I walk into the fancy restaurant with my parents and their security detail. They landed this afternoon and after I exercised each of my horses, I drove over an hour to spend some time with them at their home in Miami. They will be staying there for the duration of their trip and even though it is a good drive from my apartment and Theo's farm, they have promised they will spend every minute they can with me. My parents chose a restaurant halfway between Miami and Wellington but that's not because it makes it easier for Theo. It's because the owner is a friend of my family's.

"Christian, it has been too long my friend," Dashiel Rothman drawls, taking my dad's hand and pulling him in for a hug. He releases him, his eyes going to my mama and me. "Elena, you look as beautiful as ever. Luisa will be very disappointed she missed you. She is working a big modeling campaign." Luisa, Dashiel's wife, is my mama's best friend. They met when she came to the USA. He takes her hand, kissing both her cheeks. "Thalia, sweetheart. Look how grown up you are. Stunning." He kisses my cheek and I smile. My father speaks.

"Dash, thank you for accommodating us at such short notice." He waves him off.

"Nonsense, I would have cancelled other bookings if I needed to." They all chuckle as I stand here, nerves swimming in my stomach. I am dreading Theo and Melody's arrival. Dash leads us to a private dining area, and we take our seats. A server takes our drink orders and leaves us to wait for our other guests.

"Bambina, you look beautiful. That dress looks lovely with your skin tone," my mama coos. I glance down at my yellow cotton summer dress. She is right, it does. I also may have worn it for Theo.

"Thank you, Mama. How is filming going?" I ask, wanting to know about her latest movie. It is the perfect time to catch up with her while my father is in deep conversation with Dashiel.

"We just wrapped actually, which is why I managed to get this time with you. I am flying to Europe in two weeks to start promotion and the premier of *La Vie Est Belle*. There is already talk of a Darling award. It could be my sixth," she tells me excitedly.

"That's great, Mama." The server brings our drinks, cutting off conversation for a long minute. When he leaves, I open my mouth to speak when my mother's eyes go over my shoulder. I know who is here. I feel him.

With every part of my body and soul, I feel Theo Rhodes.

The air thickens, my pulse picks up and I take a breath waiting for him to appear in my line of sight. My father pushes out of his chair.

"Mr. Rhodes, thank you for joining us." Out of my peripherals, I see him clasp my dad's hand to shake.

"Thank you for inviting us. This is my girlfriend, Melody," Theo murmurs, but I hear it. My breath gets caught in my throat at the word girlfriend. My father greets Melody with a kiss to her cheek.

"Nice to meet you, Melody." I glance over just as Melody beams at my father then her eyes move to my mother. They flash with excitement. I remember what she told me about being a big fan. I resist an eye roll, because frankly, that would just be rude.

"This is my wife, Elena," my father looks at my mother with so much love and adoration, it makes my chest tighten. Their love is tangible. You feel it whenever you are around them. Theo takes my mama's outstretched hand and shakes it. I watch for any sign that he is excited to meet the great Elena Maxwell, but no. He keeps the same bored expression he always wears. I am brought out of my trance by Melody's high pitched British accent. I cringe.

"It is so nice to meet you, Elena. I am a big fan. I wanted to be just like you when I was a little girl." My mother smiles but I can tell it's forced. Melody can only be twelve years younger than my mama at most. Looking between them, I realize I am being kind because if I didn't know any better, I would say Melody looks older. My mother is all natural whereas Melody has inflated lips, a botoxed face and too much make up. It's aged her.

"It is always nice to meet a fan." I grimace at my mother referring to Melody as a fan. Everyone takes their seats and much to my annoyance, Theo sits next to me.

"Thalia, you look lovely," Melody chirps from Theo's other side. I flash her a smile.

"Thank you. You do too." She beams at me before her attention moves to the menu. I shift in my seat when I feel Theo's attention on me, his gaze assessing. Intense. I glance at him. His eyes drop to my exposed collar bone, he licks his full lips making me clench my thighs. He smirks as if he knows full well what he is doing to me. I need to divert his attention from me, fast, before anyone picks up on our tension.

"Hi, Theo," I mutter before looking away from him. Jesus. He is going to give us away if he keeps looking at me like that. He clears his throat as if he just remembered we are not alone.

"Thalia," he rasps before turning his attention to my father who is thankfully looking at a menu with my mother and misses that awkwardness.

After everyone has ordered and the server has brought a bottle of wine for the table my father speaks.

"So, Theo. How is my princess getting on? I know she won her competition on the new horse but how is her riding progressing? You have been working with her for nearly two months now, what is your assessment?" Theo pops his glass of water on the table.

"I have to say, Christian, the improvement in Thalia since she began with me is tenfold. She has been really impressing me with her determination and her willingness to learn. As long as we keep going the way we are then I have no doubt she will have great results at the Winter tour, which is our first major competition." My mouth drops open, eyes widening at his words. He has never said anything this nice to me before. He always puts me down, makes me feel like shit, like I am not good enough. I glance at my parents who are both beaming with pride.

"That is very good to hear," my dad drawls.

"However," Theo starts and my shoulders sag. I was waiting for the other shoe to drop. "I spoke with Thalia yesterday, and I think she needs another horse that is competing at the same level as Roman. Lolly and Zeus both have their limits and will not go any further than what they are currently competing in. Show jumping is a money sport and to be the best, you must have the best. There are so many talented riders in this game that never make it because they don't have the financial backing.

"That is not a problem here. You already told me you are willing to spend the money to get your daughter to where she wants to be. And I think by adding another horse that is top level, it will get her there quicker. She has improved vastly since we started and there is no doubt in my mind that she does have talent, but we still have a long way to go in getting good results and her name out there. It will not happen with just one top class horse." I let out a breath I didn't realize I was holding and look at my father. He stares at Theo for a long beat before nodding.

"I trust your judgement, Theo. And I am willing to do what it takes for Thalia to succeed. Do you know of any horses for sale that she can view?" my father asks, taking a sip of his whiskey.

"I will put the word out there that I am actively looking and ready to buy. There are many horses that might not be available right now, but everything is for sale at the right price, right?"

My father chuckles. "That is right, Mr. Rhodes, everything has a price."

Everyone falls into easy conversation, except me who stays mainly silent. Dashiel leaves us to go and take care of some business, so it is just the five of us. I feel awkward and guilty with Melody so close. Fortunately, she excuses herself to the restroom, giving me a few minutes to breathe.

"Bambina. Did Dash mention Parker is moving to Miami?"

I shake my head. "No, he did not." Parker is Dash's son and my brother's best friend. At twenty-four, he is six years older than me, but we all grew up together.

"He said he no longer has your cell number, so I passed it on to him. He has always had a soft spot for you, that one. Maybe you could catch up with him when he comes to town."

"No, he does not. He always had a thing for Aria." My cheeks heat when I feel an intense gaze burning a hole in the side of my face.

My mother flashes me a knowing smile. "It was never Aria, sweetheart. He has been head over heels for you for years. A blind man could see it. But you were always too young. You were Evans's baby sister. And your father would have killed him if he had gone near you." My mother chuckles, dropping a kiss to my father's cheek. "Maybe you should give him a chance now. How lovely would that be, to bring our families together like that?" I mull over her words. Yeah, Parker Rothman is hot, and any girl would be lucky to have him. But I have never seen him in that way. I open my mouth to speak, when I am startled by a big hand clamping down around my thigh and squeezing possessively.

It's a warning.

Silently telling me not to even consider going out with Parker. I don't move, afraid if I look at Theo it will give away what he is doing. He releases his grip some and runs slow circles on my bare skin, moving higher and higher under my dress and closer to my sex. I try to clamp my thighs together, but he grips me harder, running a finger down my pantie covered pussy. I resist the urge to moan. Or cry. How the fuck can he do this to me when my parents are sitting only feet away? Trying to ignore him, I turn my attention back to my mama and decide I am going to fuck with Theo. I clear my throat.

"You are right, Mama; I should catch up with Parker. I haven't seen him in a while." My mother beams, happy with my answer. Anger radiates from the man next to me as he squeezes my thigh several times. His way of telling me this isn't over. I will be punished for my insubordination. I bite back a smile.

Melody comes back to the table and thankfully, Theo removes his hand from my thigh. Just from that little contact, I am soaked. I dread to think what I would have been like if he carried on his ministrations.

"Thalia, sweetheart," my father says, bringing my attention to him. I know from the tone of his voice that I am not going to like what he says. "We will be leaving Greg here with you as your security detail." My eyes widen and I start to object. Greg is perceptive. He already mentioned something to my brother. He will sniff it out if I so much as look at Theo in the wrong way. Thoughts race through my mind like how the hell will me and Theo be able to have sex if Greg is following me but then I remind myself that I need to stay away from him and that this could be a good thing. It could be just what I need to stop this madness with Theo.

"It is non-negotiable. What with awards season coming up and all the publicity surrounding Maxwells, with the designs we are doing for the Swedish royal wedding, our family is a target right now. I will not risk you being used by some chancer trying to make a quick buck by using you for ransom. If you don't agree then you will leave me no choice but to bring you back to New York" I frown. That can't happen.

"But how does anyone know where I am? I live in the middle

of nowhere in Florida. I am not in the spotlight, Daddy; I haven't done any films or modelling for a while now."

"I know, and they didn't until you placed in your competition at the weekend. It was in some of the equestrian magazines and my head of security advised me it would be best for you to have a security detail just in case. This is not up for discussion. Greg will live in the condo beneath your penthouse. You know we want you to have your independence sweetheart, but I will just not risk your safety. Evan and Aria have the same. We are not singling you out." His eyes soften as he watches me. I nod. If there is one thing my father cares about more than anything in the world, it is his family. He will do everything in his power to stop anything from happening to us.

"If it would be easier, Thalia can move in with Melody and me. We have plenty of space and security." My head whips to Theo when he speaks. Is he seriously suggesting that I move in with him and his girlfriend after everything that has happened with us?

Is he crazy?

Is he imagining a sister wife situation?

Monday night with Melody. Tuesday night with me and so on.

I don't think so.

My father clears his throat. "While that is a very kind offer, Theo. I would much prefer my daughter to have her own space and Greg." My mother takes my hand, drawing my attention to her.

"It won't be forever, Bambina. We just want you safe. And like your father says, your sister and brother have been assigned the same. It is not just because you are his favorite." Her eyes twinkle in amusement. I smirk, knowing she is playing with my dad.

"Elena, baby, I do not have favorites." My mother scoffs with a smile and shakes her head. I bite down a chuckle. I love the play-fulness between my parents and one day hope to have the same.

"Although maybe Thalia has them beat by a little bit." He

holds his thumb and pointer finger centimeters apart as if to prove his point. "But that is only because she is my good girl and she doesn't cause scandals like her siblings," he winks at me. I chuckle remembering what my father is talking about. Evan, caught in a threesome on the open deck of a yacht in Ibiza, and Aria when she got papped leaving a club drunk, very underage. Guilt courses through me when I remember that I am not the good girl my father thinks.

In fact, I am pretty sure what I have been up to is worse than what my brother and sister have ever done. It would kill my father if he found out I have been sleeping with a man twelve years my senior. A man who is very much taken. As if he knows where my thoughts have gone, I feel Theo's gaze boring into me. Instead of looking at him, I smile toward my parents. If it gives my parents peace of mind to leave Greg, then I can do that. The alternative is not something I even want to think about. No way am I going back to New York. Not when I am finally making progress.

"Okay, Greg can stay," I concede making my parents smile.

Chapter Sixteen

THEO

It has been a few days since our dinner with the Maxwells and I feel out of sorts. Maybe it's because I haven't had Thalia's tight pussy since that night in the stall. Maybe it's because of the talk about her dating this Parker guy. Or maybe it's because she now has a shadow following her everywhere, making it impossible to even get a minute with her let alone enough time to fuck her.

It's competition day. Her parents are still in Miami and will be watching her. I need everything to be perfect. I need to get my head in the game and off Thalia's tight cunt.

But it's harder than you think.

Thalia has become like a drug to me and if I don't get my next fix soon, I fear I might do something stupid. Like fuck her in front of her parents.

Melody and I pull up to Royal Palm. She has not stopped talking my ear off about how she is going to do everything in her power to be best friends with Elena Maxwell. And I have just about had enough.

"The Maxwells are business, Mel. You need to stay away from them and not get too friendly," I snap. Her eyes widen before narrowing on me.

"What is wrong with you lately? You have been off since I got back from the UK." I don't miss the accusation in her voice.

"Nothing is wrong. I am just stressed and you are not helping with fangirling over Elena Maxwell. You have never been like this with any other of my students and you are going to stop being like it with the Maxwells. This is my business, and I will not let your crazy obsession with the woman ruin it."

"A business you would not have if it wasn't for my father investing in you," she spits. I was waiting for her to throw her father into it. Melody always does when she thinks she is losing control. I spin to face her in my seat.

"The agreements I have with your father have nothing to do with you. You forget your place Mel but don't worry, I will remind you. Yes, your father owns most of my top horses, but I don't need him or his money. I can find another ten investors before you can even blink. So do not threaten me because you will not like the consequences. You forget that you use me as much as I have used you and your father's money. If that goes," I pin her with a look, "so does this arm you hang from, parading around like the first lady of show jumping." I glance down to my arm, driving the point home. Melody forgets that she likes to be seen with me. That she likes the opportunities that come with being seen on my arm, as the girlfriend of Theo Rhodes. She schools her features and plasters on a smile.

"Noted, darling. I will keep any conversation with the Maxwells strictly professional. In the meantime, can you think about the conversation we had?" My eyes widen that she is even bringing this up right now.

Marriage.

She wants me to marry her.

It will never happen so long as I have air in my lungs. I give her a pointed look.

"We talked about this. I don't want to marry you." She pouts, thinking she looks cute, but she doesn't. She looks like a duck with her inflated lips. It's weird how I am only now noticing all these things since my piccola came along. They never bothered me before but they definitely do now.

"Theodore, think about it. It makes sense. It's the next step. It is what everyone expects of us. My father included." Ah, there she goes again with her father and the underlying threat. I know he expects it. Doesn't mean it is going to happen though. I might have considered it three months ago but not now with Thalia coming into my life.

"Come on, I have work to do."

———

"Well done, Thalia. Brilliant riding today," I tell her as she comes out of the ring after placing first in the one-meter-thirty class on Roman. We stepped it up a level today. She didn't disappoint. She is still not at the level the horse is used to but bigger than what Thalia has ever done. She smiles down at me. A real smile that makes my chest tighten.

Christ. This girl will be the death of me. I swear it.

"Thank you, he felt amazing." I nod, taking the reins so I can help her down. We hand him over to Jessica and start toward where her parents are sitting. They are in a private area surrounded by their security since Elena was getting harassed in the clubhouse. You can tell how much Christian loves his wife. As soon as he saw she was uncomfortable, he arranged a quiet balcony.

"Honestly, it was so much better. Even from last weekend. The improvement in you is amazing," I praise, making her stop and look up at me as if I have grown two heads. I am not surprised, normally I am chewing her out about her riding, making her feel not good enough.

"Wow, did you hit your head?" she asks. I chuckle.

"No, I just thought you deserved to know the truth and the

truth is you rode brilliantly. You should be proud of yourself." She looks down to the asphalt, nibbling that full bottom lip I love so much. I want nothing more than to nibble it myself. Suck it into my mouth and taste her. It takes every bit of restraint to stop myself. Her gaze moves back to me.

"Thanks, Theo. That means a lot coming from you." I nod and we carry on to her parents. Pushing through the doors of the balcony, her father rises with a big smile on his face.

"Sweetheart, you did amazing. You looked so good out there." He pulls her into a hug and a slither of unwarranted jealousy courses through me. It is irrational—he is her father—but I don't want anyone touching her but me. He passes her over to Elena who coos softly spoken words into her hair. It's interesting watching them. You would think a family like this—rich, famous —the parents wouldn't have time for their children but it's clear to see how much they both love their daughter. Christian shakes my hand.

"Theo, I want to say thank you for all you have done. She looked amazing out there."

"I can't take all the credit; I can only teach what I know. It is Thalia that is determined and willing to learn. She is proving that every day she shows up, takes my criticism, and learns from it." Christian nods, his eyes filled with adoration for his daughter.

"I want you to make it a top priority to find her another horse. I may not know much about these animals, but it is clear to see Lolly and Zeus are not up to the same standard as Roman."

"Of course. It will be my first call of business on Monday morning. I have already put the word out."

"Join us for lunch?" he asks, taking his seat.

"I would love to, but I must find Mel. I am competing with my own horses soon."

"Ah, then, we look forward to watching you." I nod before glancing at Thalia who already has her eyes on me. She blushes and looks away, making my cock harden in my jodhpurs.

I smirk.

Tonight, she will be mine.

Greg and her parents be damned.

───────

Me: Can you get away from your shadow and come to the barn? 9:00 P.M?

It only takes a minute to get a reply.

Thalia: What for?

Me: I need to see you.

Thalia: It is a bad idea. We need to stay away from each other...in that way.

Me: Staying away from each other is a bad idea. Come to the barn at 9:00 P.M. Please.

I hate saying please. I have never begged anyone in my damn life. Guess this girl is the exception for many things.

Thalia: I will try.

And now here I wait, In the dark shadows of the barn. I don't even know if she will show. But I need to see her, to feel her lips against my own. To make her mine all over again. It doesn't make sense. This need I have for her but it's there. I have tried to control it, but it's like a wildfire.

Untamable.

Unstoppable.

And I am tired of fighting it.

The barn door quietly opening stops my thoughts. I peek around the stall, smiling when I see the beauty that has totally consumed me step in. She looks nervous as her eyes dart around; she chews that damn bottom lip of hers making me groan. She moves toward my office, no doubt thinking I am in there. When she steps in line to where I am hidden in the shadows, I reach out, wrapping one arm around her waist and one around her mouth to muffle her scream. I tug her into me, making sure to avoid her flailing arms and legs. My cock turns to granite as I hold her in my arms.

"Calm down, Piccola, it's me," I whisper in her ear. She instantly relaxes and I release her. She spins to face me, her gray eyes filled with anger.

"Jesus, Theo, are you trying to give me a heart attack?" she hisses. I wrap my arms around her waist, pulling her flush against my body. Dropping my lips to her ear, I grin when she shivers.

"Now why would I do that? I am having way too much fun with you to kill you off," I rasp. She pulls away.

"You know, you really give me whiplash. I cannot keep up with your hot and cold." I frown, but I know exactly what she is saying. I have been a complete bastard to her only to turn around and show her how much I want her. I know it confuses her. It confuses me. I go back and forth with myself about doing the right thing and ending this. Hell, I shouldn't have even started it. But now? I am in too deep to walk away.

I nuzzle into her neck, trying to avoid eye contact and answering the question but she pushes me away. She crosses her arms across her chest, pushing up those perfect tits. I lick my lips remembering what they felt like in my mouth. She clears her throat; my eyes snap to hers where she's glaring at me. I sigh, knowing she will not let me touch her until I speak.

"How can you be okay with this? Especially after dinner with my parents the other night. It was so awkward at that table, knowing I have slept with you. And Melody right there acting like you two are the perfect couple," she whisper shouts.

"You think I am okay with this? I'm not Thalia; I am disgusted with myself. Being with you? I am risking everything. But I cannot help how I feel. I cannot stop wanting you," I growl, taking a step toward her and pulling her into me. "I tried to not want you. But this thing..." I trail off. She eyes me, silently asking me to continue with what I was going to say. "This thing between us is too strong, too big to ignore. I know you feel it too. I am man enough to admit I have no power when it comes to us. I am not strong enough to resist you. I don't *want* to resist you." Her eyes soften and lips part. She drops her head to my chest and sighs.

"I am not strong enough to stay away from you either. I tried. I really did." I let out a relieved breath, slowly walking her back until she falls into the hay. I drop down on top of her and pepper kisses all over her face.

"My need for you overpowers any guilt I feel," she murmurs so quietly I almost miss it, but I don't. I gaze down at her, understanding exactly what she is saying.

"I feel the same." I smash my lips down on hers in a bruising kiss. It's a claiming. I want her to know exactly who she belongs to. I quickly rid her of her yoga pants and tank. Then remove my own gray sweats and white tee in record time. The need to be inside her is overwhelming. I reach down to check if she is ready, groaning when I find her already soaked.

She gets off on this sneaking around as much as I do, even if she won't admit it.

I line myself up with her entrance and push inside her. I grit my teeth; she is so fucking tight. Her eyes flutter closed as she wraps her long-tanned legs around my waist. I lift her hips so I can get in deeper. So deep that she will feel me for days. She gasps. There is still so much I want to teach her. I can't wait. I thrust into her. Slowly at first enjoying the feel of her tight, wet, silky pussy around me.

"Faster, Theo," she whimpers. I grin.

My piccola likes it fast and hard.

I pick up my speed, circling my hips as I drive inside her wet heat. She claws at my back. I know it is going to leave a mark, but I can't bring myself to care. Not when I am so caught up in this. In her. Sometimes, I think I want to get caught. I want the world to know Thalia Maxwell is mine. That she belongs to me. My balls tighten as the familiar feeling of an orgasm builds and I pull out. Thalia's eyes pop open and land on me.

"What are you doing?" she asks. Without answering, I shift and drop down, running my tongue up her perfect cunt. She rocks her hips against my face as I latch onto her clit and shove two fingers inside her. Making sure they are properly lubed up, I remove them and walk them to her tight little hole. She freezes. I look up to find her questioning eyes wide and on me.

"You will enjoy it, I promise. I will only put one finger in. But soon, when I think you are ready, I am going to fuck you here with my cock." I don't give her a chance to answer. I know she will like this, and I want to give her pleasure like she has never felt before. I work my finger inside her ass, gently stretching her. Jesus. She strangles my finger. I can't even begin to imagine what she will feel like wrapped around my cock. She stiffens.

"Just relax. It will hurt more if you tense up." She takes a breath and nods, relaxing as a much as she can. Once my finger is fully seated, I use my free hand to work her pussy with two fingers and suction her clit with my mouth. I work her slowly, but it only takes minutes before I feel her pussy and ass clamping down on me.

"Theo, I'm going to come," she whispers, her voice breathy. I thrust my fingers in both holes and suck her clit harder. That sets her off. Her hand covers her mouth as she comes apart. My good girl knows she must be quiet. I withdraw my fingers, quickly climb up her body, and thrust into her with my cock. She whimpers at the intrusion.

"Open your eyes. Look at me," I demand. Her eyes flicker open and land on me. I bring the fingers that were in her pussy to my mouth and suck her cream off. Her eyes darken with lust. I smirk as I feel another orgasm barreling through her. It happens so quick, her pussy clenches around me, sucking my own release from me. I smash my lips to hers, knowing I need to swallow both our cries. Seconds later, we are coming apart together. I roar into her mouth as I fill her with my hot cum. Collapsing, I make sure to brace myself on my elbows so I don't put my weight on her.

"Jesus. I don't think I have ever come so hard." Thalia smiles up at me, pleased with my words.

"I know I am new to all this but that was the most intense orgasm I have ever had. Especially when you had your fingers in my..." she trails off, her cheeks pinking. I smirk, dropping a kiss to her mouth.

"In your ass, Piccola,"

"Yeah."

"Did you like it?"

She nods. "Yes. It hurt at first, but I enjoyed it once I relaxed."

"I told you. Stick with me baby, there is so much more I can teach you." She rolls her eyes and pushes me off her. Sitting up, she looks around for her clothes. Finally locating them, she grabs them and puts them on as I do the same. I should get back. I told Melody I was coming to check on one of the horses I thought had colic. I don't need her coming down here because I was longer than she expected.

"I better go before Greg finds out I am gone." I pull her in and kiss her like she is the air I need.

"I will see you tomorrow. Let's go on a trail ride?"

"Okay, but I don't have long. I am spending the day with my parents before they leave." I nod.

"Get here early. Like 7:30 A.M and we will go before my other students wake up to train."

———

I walk in the front door to find Melody pulling on some sneakers.

"What are you doing?" I ask. She pins me with a glare.

"Where were you? You have been gone for over an hour. It does not take that long to check on a horse, Theo." I don't miss the suspicion in her voice.

"Why are you questioning me, Mel? You have been acting crazy since you've been back," I snap. She reels back as if I have slapped her.

"Acting crazy? *You* have been acting strange since I got back. You disappear. You don't want sex. What is going on, Theo?" I scrub a palm down my face in exasperation.

"Nothing is going on. And we have had sex since you've been back here." She scoffs.

"Barely, you never initiate it. You used to want to fuck all the time..." she trails off and nibbles her lip. She is right, I did.

And I still do.

Just not with her.

For some reason, I feel like I am betraying Thalia by being intimate with Mel. Which is stupid. She is not my girlfriend. Mel is...well, she is something and I am betraying her every time I touch Thalia, yet the guilt doesn't hit me. She stares at me, waiting for an explanation. One I cannot give her.

"I'm going to bed." Her face falls at my words but instead of comforting her like I should, I start for the stairs. I need to wash the scent of Thalia from me before Mel gets too close.

Chapter Seventeen

THALIA

Greg and I pull up to the barn. He officially started as my personal security detail and moved into the condo beneath me the day after my father told me. As much as I hate having a babysitter, I don't want to be shipped back to New York, so I deal with it.

"You can stay in the car, Greg. I won't be long; I am just going to take Roman on a trail ride and I am sure you don't want to follow on foot." He eyes me for a long beat before nodding.

"Good job I brought some reading material then," he grumbles, grabbing the Wellington Daily paper from the back seat. I snicker.

"Enjoy," I chirp, hopping out of the SUV. I start toward the barn. A shiver runs up my spine and my body heats remembering last night in the hay with Theo. The sex was amazing. I want to do it again and again. I want Theo as mine. Whatever expectations I had about sex before Theo took my virginity, he has exceeded all of them.

"Ah, you're here," his deep voice snaps me out of my thoughts. I glance up at him. My cheeks heat when I find his intense gaze already on me.

"Yes," I breathe. He smirks before spinning around and walking toward Roman and Topper, one of Theo's horses, where they are ready and waiting. I make quick work of finding my helmet and getting on. We start toward the trail—a place that has become ours. When we are far enough from the barn, Theo says, "How are you feeling?" I frown at his words, not understanding why he is asking me that. "After last night? I was a bit rough with you," he explains. I blush and clear my throat.

"I feel good. You didn't hurt me." His eyes search my face for any hint that I am lying. He won't find it though. I enjoyed last night.

"And your shadow didn't notice you were gone?" I chuckle at the name he has given Greg.

"No, Greg has no idea I left last night." He nods. He seems off this morning, like he is lost inside his head.

"Is everything okay? Did I do something wrong?" His eyes snap back to me and soften. He lets out a harsh breath.

"You didn't do anything wrong, Thalia; you could never do anything wrong. You are perfect," he whispers the last word, but I hear it. Wanting to change the subject and get him talking, I speak.

"So, when are we going on another trip to Europe for horse shopping?" He grins. And it's the sort of grin that could melt panties.

"I have not found a horse suitable yet. But when I do, we will make plans straight away for a viewing. It will be nice to have you to myself for a few days..." he pauses and then scowls as if remembering something. "I forgot about your shadow for a second there. But what he doesn't know won't hurt him and as soon as he goes to his room...I will be coming to yours. It will be nice to hold you for the whole night and not just a quick fuck," he muses to himself before coming to a stop at *the tree*. I call it *the tree* because it is where Theo first finger fucked me. He glances over at me. I squirm in my saddle. His eyes flash as they move over my body.

"We shouldn't but I can't help myself when it comes to you. Hop off."

"Theo, we can't. What if someone else rides down here?" He jumps off Topper and pins me with a look that says *get your ass off that horse now.* I sigh and slide off Roman. He grabs me with his free hand and tugs me into his hard body. His lips drop to my ear, making me shiver when his hot breath hits me.

"I only want to kiss you," he murmurs before nibbling the soft flesh on my ear lobe. My pussy pulses as liquid lust soaks my panties. There are no words to explain the effect this man has on me, and something tells me it is a once in a lifetime thing. I will never feel this way with anyone but him. His mouth drops to mine. He runs his tongue across the seam of my lips, silently asking me to open for him.

I do.

Of course, I do.

He groans his approval at my submission and makes love to my mouth in a way only he knows how. I am so lost in the kiss; in Theo, that I don't hear his name being called. But then I hear it. As clear as day, I hear it. As does Theo. We both freeze. He tears his mouth from mine.

"Shit," he hisses, moving away from me. I spin to see if I can see the owner of the voice but see nothing because of the grass hill that blocks us from sight.

"Get on the floor," he barks. I frown, not understanding what he is asking. "It's Mel. You need to get on the floor to make it seem like you fell." I nod and quickly drop to the floor. Minutes later she appears, just as Theo is pulling me to a stand.

"What's going on?" she asks. I don't miss the hint of suspicion in her voice as her eyes narrow on us.

"Thalia's horse spooked. She wasn't sitting in the saddle tightly enough and fell." Pity flashes in her eyes. I hate it but would rather have that than the suspicion.

"Are you okay?" she asks and I nod.

"Yes, I should have been concentrating more." She smiles before her gaze moves to Theo.

"Why didn't you say you were going on a trail ride? I would have come with you." Theo clears his throat.

"It was a last minute thing and Thalia turned up just as I was leaving."

"Well, I found you now. So how far are we riding?" she asks excitedly. Something a lot like guilt hits me in the stomach.

"I am not sure, as far as we feel I guess," Theo shrugs. Mel beams at him and I feel awkward. Not wanting to go on a romantic trail ride with them, I speak.

"Umm, actually, I will leave you two to it." Mel frowns at me in confusion. "I need to get back. I forgot I was meeting my parents. It's their last day in Miami." I climb back on Roman, and Theo climbs on Topper. Mel steps up beside him. My stomach turns. They look like the perfect beautiful couple. She leans in and kisses him.

"Guess it's just us two then," she purrs seductively. I look away, not wanting to see the lust on her face. Theo pulls away.

"See you tomorrow, Thalia. Make sure you are on time for your first lesson." I nod as he turns to Mel. "Come on, let's go," he snaps. I watch them both as they walk away. Maybe Mel nearly catching us is a sign that we should stop whatever it is we are doing. Maybe this is the wakeup call I needed. With those thoughts in mind, I make my way back to the barn. Feeling empty. Feeling like I just lost him.

After spending the day with my parents, Greg drives us back to Wellington. I feel exhausted and if I am honest, upset at the way Theo dismissed me earlier as if I was nothing. As if we hadn't just nearly been caught.

"Everything okay?" Greg asks, glancing at me from the driver's seat.

"Yes, just tired." He nods before focusing back on the road. I need to say as little as possible to him. He is like a dog with a bone and if he gets one inkling about Theo, he will latch on to it until he finds out the truth. He already has his suspicions. He's already said something to my brother. I don't need him saying anything to my father.

Not twenty minutes later at just past 9:00 P.M, we pull up to our apartment building. I hop out of the car, and we make our way into the building. Once in the elevator, Greg speaks again.

"If you need anything, *anything* at all, you know where I am. Yeah?" I freeze at the tone of Greg's voice. Does he know I left the apartment last night? I plaster a smile on my face and look at him.

"I know, Greg. I really am just tired. Really. It's nothing a good night's sleep won't fix." He eyes me for a long beat before nodding. Thankfully, the elevator doors open, ending any further conversation. I rush toward my apartment before Greg can say anymore.

"See you in the morning. Can we leave for the farm at 8:00 A.M?"

"Of course, Thalia," he replies. I smile before entering my condo.

I quickly shower, pull on some sleep shorts and a tank, then slide into my California king bed. I sigh. My bed is so comfortable, even more so than my one back home in New York. Grabbing my cell, I scroll to my sister's name and hit call on Facetime. It rings for around five times. I start to think she won't answer, that maybe she is at a party or some social event. Then the call connects, and Aria appears on the screen, wet hair and a towel wrapped around her.

"Little sister," she chirps in greeting.

"Did I disturb your shower?"

She chuckles. "No, I was just getting out when I heard my cell.

What's up? Did the parents tell you about the new security measure?"

I snort. "Tell me? Yes, and they left Greg with me. Something tells me it was the reason for their trip."

She snickers, as she drops down into the wingback chair in the corner of her bedroom. Although she is attending NYU, she decided to live at our family home, not wanting to be in dorms. Aria has always been one for luxury.

"I have Bishop," she rolls her eyes. I know exactly what she is going to say. My sister has had a thing for the newest member of my father's security team since he started around three months ago. "He is so hot Thalia, like seriously. I want him so bad, but he will not break." She whines and I can't help the laugh that bubbles up. "Stop," she pouts, "a man has never not wanted me. It makes me want him more. He is like a challenge. One I have to win." She is right. My sister has never had trouble with the opposite sex. With her long dark hair and bright blue eyes that match our mother's, she is beautiful. I am sure he will break.

Eventually.

"Daddy could have at least given me Bronx. Old. Moody. Someone I don't want to climb like a tree but no. He gives me one of the hottest men I have ever seen." She is not wrong. Bishop is everything you could imagine in a hot bodyguard. Sandy blonde hair, chiseled jaw, bright green eyes, and a body that looks like it has been sculpted by an artist. He is gorgeous and the youngest member of staff at just twenty-eight. But he is also very off limits. My father would kill him if anything happened. I think of Theo and what my father would do if he found out.

Yep. He would kill him for touching his baby girl.

"I have made it a priority to get him while he is my personal bodyguard. I am going to do so many things to make him squirm. By the time I am through, he will be begging for me." I chuckle, knowing full well she will follow through with her words. "So, what else is happening?" she asks, changing the subject.

"Same old. I won a few of my competitions, so I am happy with that. When are you coming to visit?"

"Well done, I knew you had it in you. Umm, I was going to fly down Halloween weekend. Did they tell you Parker is moving to Miami?" I nod. "Well, he is opening a club that weekend and I thought we could check it out?"

"Yeah, Mama seems to think he has a thing for me."

Aria cocks a brow. "He does have a thing for you. And now that you are perfectly legal, he can act on it. Parker is hot, Thalia." I know he is and if Theo had not come into the picture, I could see myself with someone like Parker. It's a moot point though. Because Theo did come into the picture and all I see is him.

Unfortunately.

"I am not interested in Parker or anyone else for that matter. I want to focus on my riding."

"You need to lose your virginity sometime, Sis, and who better than one of the country's most eligible bachelors?" My cheeks heat at her words. If only she knew that I already gave that away, to a taken man no less.

"Don't worry about that," I say. She studies my face for a long beat. I squirm, panicking that she can hear the meaning behind my words. She lets out a breath.

"Okay, but we will be having this discussion when I come and see you. Get some days off. I will send you the details. And FYI, we will be staying in Miami. I already cleared it with Dad to stay at the house." We talk for another ten minutes and end the call with promises of talking in the next few days. I grab my Kindle from my nightstand flicking through until I find one of my favorite books. I am so lost in the story, the angst, I don't hear the knocking at my door until it gets louder. Dropping my device, I check the time on my cell. It's past 10:30 P.M. Maybe Greg has an emergency?

I grab my robe, quickly shuffling it on and make my way to the door. I rip it open only to freeze when I see who is standing on the other side.

Theo.

His eyes rake over my body hungrily. I try to suppress a shiver, not wanting him to see the effect he has on me.

"What are you doing here? Greg could see you," I hiss. He smiles and steps inside like he owns the place. I close the door and spin to face him.

"Mel went out with some girlfriends. I wanted to see you." He steps into me but I put a hand on his hard chest, stopping him. He glances at my hand and frowns before covering it with a cocky brow. "Come on, Piccola, I need to feel you. You are like a damn drug; one hit and I am fucking obsessed." I cross my arms over my chest and pin him with a look.

"I am not going to be used as your sidepiece, Theo. I am worth more than that. I *deserve* more than that." He sighs, running his hand through his inky hair.

"I know you do. Things with Mel are complicated. Her father has a lot of money invested in me. In the horses. I am at the top of the sport and cannot afford to lose them." I mull over his words. Basically, he is saying his horses are worth more than me? I understand...to a point. This is an expensive sport and although Theo has money, he still needs good investors.

"That's fine, Theo. But don't come here thinking I am just going to spread my legs every time you ask." I spin and walk toward my couch. Dropping down, my gaze meets his. He looks tortured. Unsure. So unlike the Theo I am used to. "Look, I get it. I really do. But maybe we should take a step back? We were nearly caught today." His eyes widen. He closes the distance between us in two long strides and drops down to his haunches in front of me.

"You don't get it. I want you, Thalia. More than I have ever wanted anyone. You need to give me time though. I need time to find other investors. Someone who is willing to invest in me without me having to whore myself out." I gasp at his words. Is that what he and Melody are? Is he with her for the money?

As if he senses my thoughts, he explains. "I met Melody when I was based in the UK for a couple of years. I was doing everything to get my name out there, to get to the top with the horses I had but they weren't good enough. We weren't not top level. But I did what I could and got results. My father never wanted me to go into horses as a career, wanted me to follow in his footsteps, but it's not what I wanted. Because of that, I have no backing from him even though he has the money. So, I did what I had to do.

"Melody took a shine to me and started training with me. I knew she wasn't serious about the sport, but she was serious about getting me and I used that to my advantage. I fucked up, got drunk one night, and fucked her. After that, I couldn't walk away because her father would have pulled his money. Six years later, I am still in a relationship I don't want just because I want to stay at the top. Yes, I have money from endorsements, teaching, and selling horses but it's not the sort of money to buy the kind of horses I want and to keep my home. Melody was a business opportunity I could not turn down. Do I love her? No. Do I care for her? Sure. But you? You are all I see. I know I should not have these kinds of feelings for you. Know I should have left you alone...but I can't. I want you. I have never felt like this about anyone before."

"Why are you telling me this?" I whisper.

"Because I need you to understand. I don't want Mel. It's you that I think about before I go to sleep. You I want to hold. You whom I want to wake up with." My breath hitches at his words and before I can stop myself, I am smashing my lips on his.

Call me stupid.

Call me naïve.

I probably am.

But I feel exactly how he feels. His arms snake around my

waist and he lifts me. Never breaking the kiss, he strides to my bedroom. He drops me on the bed and stares down at me with lust filled eyes.

"Strip," he demands as his hand goes to the button on his jeans. I slowly take my clothes off all the while Theo's eyes never leave mine. When he removes his black boxer briefs, my eyes widen as his cock springs free. I lick my lips. I don't think I will ever get used to the sight of his magnificent dick. My mouth waters at the sight. I hear a throat clear. My eyes snap to his, to find a smirk on his face.

"Like what you see?" he teases. I roll my eyes as he climbs on the bed and over my body. His lips catch mine in a punishing kiss. I moan and roll my hips against his hard length. He reaches down, running a finger through my wet folds.

"Christ, you are fucking soaked," he groans as he pushes two fingers inside me. I clench around him, pulling him in deeper. Sensing what I need, he moves down my body. His lips wrap around my clit, and he curls his finger inside me, hitting the spot that makes me see stars. It's only seconds before I am screaming out his name and coming all over his fingers. I pant, trying to catch my breath but he doesn't give me a chance. He thrusts into me in one quick move, making my back arch and my breath catch in my throat.

"Fuck. I don't think I will ever get over how fucking tight you are," he grits as he starts to move. He doesn't need to tell me; I can feel him. Feel every inch of his perfect cock as he fucks me. Stretches me.

"Theo," I moan as he pounds inside me. He stares down at me; something flashes in his eyes, but he quickly shakes it away. He reaches down, rubbing my sensitive clit. Another orgasm rips through me. I throw my head back in ecstasy as I claw at his back.

"Theo," I cry his name like it's a prayer. He stills, releasing his hot seed inside me.

"Jesus, I needed that." He groans as he drops down next to me. He wraps his arms around me, pulls me into his side, spooning and holding me, like we are a real couple. He has never been like this with me after sex and for some reason, it makes my chest tighten. He nuzzles into my hair, breathing me in. Such a small thing to do but it makes me fall for him deeper than I already am and that scares me. It only takes minutes until his breathing evens out; I glance over my shoulder to find his thick lips slightly parted and a look of contentment I have never seen from him before.

I shift in his arms until I am facing him. He looks younger somehow. Almost angelic. I reach up and trace his face with my pointer finger. The man is beautiful. Thick black lashes frame chiseled cheekbones and a jaw so sharp it could cut glass. I drop a kiss to his perfect lips before snuggling into him. It doesn't take long for sleep to pull me under. Not a care in the world, as I lay in this man's arm wishing that we could do this every night.

I wake the next morning to find my bed empty and the spot Theo had fallen asleep in cold. I frown. What time did he leave and why didn't he let me know? I thought we had turned a corner last night, what with him opening up to me. But again, he has made me feel like a cheap fuck.

I sigh and grab my cell to check the time, 6:48 A.M. I have time to use the building's pool before Greg takes me to the barn. I push out of bed, quickly find a swimsuit, pull it on, then make my way down to the basement where the gym and pool are.

After swimming for thirty minutes, I rush back to my apartment. Quickly showering and drying off, I dress in my riding gear, make bagels and coffee before Greg knocks on my door. Which should be any second. On que, the knock sounds. I smile to myself as I pull it open, making Greg frown.

"Did you have a good sleep?" he asks by way of greeting.

"Yes. I went for a swim and made us bagels and coffee. All with," I glance at my watch, "two minutes to spare." Greg chuckles and shakes his head.

"You know I would have waited had you been running late, Thalia." I grin and turn, heading to the breakfast counter where I have left our breakfast and coffee.

"Can you come and grab the coffee and I will take the bagels?" I ask, glancing over my shoulder. Greg nods and strides over to me. He picks up the two travel coffees and I grab the bagels, my cell, and keys. We make our way down in the elevator, then hop in the SUV. The journey, much like last night, is silent. I sip my coffee and eat my bagel while my mind races with thoughts of Theo. I am angry at him. I know I don't have the right to be. He obviously needed to get home and I can't even begin to imagine the questions that would have been asked had he stayed the whole night...but it hurts that he just left without saying goodbye.

Fucked me and left me. Again.

We pull up to the barn and my stomach dips with nerves. I take a breath and hop out of the car. Better to rip the band aid off, get it over with.

I step into the barn to a flurry of movement. Grooms mucking out stalls and tacking up horses.

"Hey, Thalia," a deep voice says behind me. I startle and clutch my chest. Carter chuckles. "Sorry, I didn't mean to scare you."

"It's okay. What's going on?" I wave my hand in the direction of all the activity.

"Not sure. Theo has called a meeting at 8:30 before training starts." I frown wondering what this is all about. Yes, the barn is normally busy with people doing all sorts of jobs, but this feels different. Carter throws his arm around my shoulders.

"Come on, let's go and find out what's happening."

Chapter Eighteen

THEO

I am so tired, I can't think straight. I snuck out of Thalia's bed at 2:00 in the morning. I didn't want to leave her. She looked beautiful sleeping. Like an angel with her dark hair cascading over her white pillow. It took every bit of restraint not to climb back in and fuck her again.

But I had to get back.

I woke to find several missed calls from Mel. I knew I would be in the shit. She must have been home and found me absent. I should never have let myself fall asleep but being with Thalia had brought me a calmness and contentment that I had never felt before and I couldn't help myself.

I got home to find Mel in tears and drunk. She ended up shouting and screaming at me for nearly three hours, begging me to tell her who I was fucking behind her back.

I denied it.

Of course, I did.

I eventually calmed her down. I told her I went for a last minute drink with an old school friend of mine who had been having trouble with his wife and I didn't tell her about it because I thought I would be a few hours at most.

Eventually, she bought my lie and went to bed but not without the threat that if I was screwing around behind her back, she would take everything from me. I laughed at her, played it off, but I knew her words weren't empty. She would.

Which is why this morning, I am playing into her hands and have called a meeting with my staff and students. To prove I am committed, I am taking her away for a few days to Miami. We will stay in a nice hotel, go for dinners and shop—something Mel loves. I know this will hurt Thalia, but until I can sort everything out, I need to do this. I need to keep my horses with me and that can only happen if I find a rich investor to buy Mel's father out.

I am a bastard. But sometimes in life, we must do things even when we don't want to. I am dreading the look on Thalia's face when she finds out. Something changed between us last night. I know she felt it too. I saw it when I fucked her, the look of love and adoration on her face. I am pretty sure the same look was on my own. To begin, it was just an insane attraction towards her. But now? Now I feel things for her that I have never felt for anyone. What started as just sex has quickly turned into something so much more. This thing with her is making me question everything and sometimes I just want to tell Mel it's done and to take the horses.

I can rebuild myself. Find new owners. Investors. But it will take time. I wasn't lying to Thalia when I said I was looking into it. I have been. I am just hoping something will come from it.

Sooner rather than later.

A knock at the door drags me out of my thoughts. I swallow.

"Come in." The door opens and Tessa steps inside followed by Marissa, Kiara, Carter, and Thalia. Sweat beads on my forehead as my eyes meet hers. Everyone takes a seat. Wanting to get it over with, I start.

"So, as you know, we have another competition this weekend which you are all more than prepared for. I just wanted to let you know, I will not be doing any training for the next couple of days as I will be away, so won't be joining you at Royal Palm."

They all stare at me as if I have lost my mind. I would never leave before a competition; they normally get intense training in the run up to it so I can see why they are shocked. "You will all be fine, and I trust you are all capable of competing without me there. Tess will make sure you are looked after." My eyes shift to Thalia, who is studying me intensely. Hurt flashes in her eyes making my chest tighten almost painfully. She knows who I am going away with even without me saying it out loud. Not for the first time, I ask myself why I don't just end things with Mel. I don't want her. I want the exquisite beauty in front of me.

"That will be all. If anyone has any questions, please ask now. If not, get back to what you were doing. Thalia, can you stay behind so we can discuss a potential horse I have found?" Her jaw clenches and I know she wants to tell me to fuck off, but she won't. Not in front of these people anyway. Everyone leaves, making the air turn thick. I feel the tension rolling off her, hitting every part of me.

"It's not what you think," I blurt the words I keep saying to her, whether to make myself believe them or her. I don't know. She snorts and pins me with a look I am sure would make any other person wither. But not me, she just looks like an adorable angry kitten.

"So, you keep saying, Theo. I don't care anyway. I am over you and your bullshit. Have a nice romantic couple of days with your *girlfriend*." She pushes out of her seat and starts toward the door. I am out of mine before I can stop myself, grabbing her and spinning her toward me.

"If you had not let me fall asleep last night, this would not be happening. I should never have stayed at yours. When I woke in the early hours to missed calls and messages from Mel, I knew I would be questioned. When I finally got back, I found her in tears and my office trashed. She begged me to tell her who I was fucking behind her back. It was on the tip of my tongue to just admit to us, to end things with her. But then I thought about you. I don't want her to come after you and I don't want your father to come after me. And he will if he finds out. He will destroy me more than Mel ever could. So, I told her I was out with a friend then I promised to make it up to her and take her away. It placated her some, but she still threatened to take everything away if she finds out I am lying," I finish. My chest heaves as if I have run miles. My heart jackhammers in my chest as I stare down at her. Her gray eyes darken. I know she is not going to accept my explanation. Even if, in my own way, I am protecting her. She pulls her arms out of my grip before turning and heading back to the door. Before opening it, she glances over her shoulder at me, fire dancing in her eyes.

"Like I said, enjoy your romantic break." And with that, she yanks open the door and walks out.

———

It's day two in Miami.

I go through the motions.

But I feel numb.

Lost.

I booked a nice hotel. We have been to expensive restaurants. Melody shopped until she could no more. I fucked her last night from behind. I couldn't look at her face.

It felt wrong.

Her taste.

Her smell.

The way she felt.

Guilt consumed me with every thrust. I hated myself for what I was doing. The only reason I came was because I pictured a gray eyed beauty. Which in turn, made me feel disgusted with myself. Not once have I felt guilt toward Mel over what I have been doing. But guilt, I felt it last night. So much guilt, it consumed me.

I feel like I am cheating on Thalia. Which is stupid considering we are not a couple. But with every kiss and every touch with Melody? My mind screams at me to stop, to end this farce. But I am a coward because I didn't stop it. I carried on like the selfish bastard I am.

If I were a better man, I would let Thalia go. She deserves so much more than being someone's dirty little secret and yet, I can't. The thought of her with anyone else makes me murderous. Which is completely hypocritical of me, but I don't care. Thalia Maxwell will never be anyone's but mine.

I am sitting in the hotel suite after another day of shopping, waiting for Mel to get ready for our dinner reservation. I scroll through social media on my cell only for my teeth to clench, blood to boil, when a picture pops up.

Carter and Thalia.

At what looks like a restaurant. I squeeze my phone so hard, I swear I hear it crack.

What the fuck?

Is it a date? Is she into *him* now? My mind races with all sorts of possibilities. I jump out of my chair, not able to sit still. Pacing the room, I stare at the picture. Carter's arm around *my* piccola as he gazes at her lovingly.

That should be me.

Me taking her for dinner.

Me showing the world she is mine.

Before I can stop myself or question what I am doing, I pull up our message thread. It's irrational, reckless, but I cannot seem to bring myself to care.

Me: What the fuck are you doing out with Carter?

I stare at my cell for what feels like hours, willing her to message me back. She never does. It enrages me further to the point where I nearly get in my SUV and drive to where they are.

"What are you doing?" Mel's voice invades my raging thoughts and I glance at her. She is in a tight dress putting an earring in. I straighten, trying to school my features, but it's no use. I am pissed.

"Nothing. I was waiting for you." She studies my face, concern on her own.

"You look stressed. Are you sure you are okay?" She starts toward me, wrapping her arms around me when she is within reach. I look down at her as she smiles and my stomach rolls.

Her face is wrong.

She is wrong.

I resist the urge to shove her away and plaster on a smile instead.

"Yeah, I'm fine. Let's go, otherwise we will miss our reservation." I start to pull out of her hold, but she grips me tighter, a seductive look crossing her face.

"Or we could forget dinner and stay here. I will even let you fuck my ass," she purrs, making my stomach turn even more. I move myself out of her grip and she frowns. I grip her chin between my fingers.

"Dinner first," I say, making a smile curve her lips.

————

I wake to Mel draped all over me, asserting her claim without even realizing it. We didn't have sex last night. I got her drunk enough that she passed out when we got back. I scrub a palm down my face as I remember why I have woken in such a bad mood.

The picture of Thalia and Carter.

My blood heats just thinking about it and the way she ignored my message. I know she read it. She just chose not to reply. I can't even blame her. I am an asshole of the worst kind. Currently, I am laying in a bed with another woman wrapped around me. Yet, I expect Thalia to be mine. My dirty little secret. She deserves better but I can't seem to let her go. I don't want to. I have never in my life been so drawn to a woman before.

She is all I see.

All I want.

I just have to prove it to her.

I peel Melody's thin arms from around me and make my way to the shower. I need her smell off me. I need this whole couple of days off of me. My skin itches with my sins. I need to get rid of this feeling.

Twenty minutes later, I am showered and changed. I stroll back into the bedroom to find Mel scrolling through her cell.

"Morning," I drawl. Her head snaps up. She smiles, dropping her cell on the nightstand, and pats the empty space beside her.

"Why don't you come back to bed? We still have a couple of hours before we check out. I was hoping for another round, as we didn't get to fuck last night." I cock my head and stare at her as she sits up. The comforter pools around her waist. Her fake tits on display do nothing for me even if she believes differently. She cups her breasts and squeezes, trying to entice me.

"Come on, Theo, I need you. My pussy is wet and ready for your big cock," she moans out as a hand drops and drifts towards her cunt. She shoves the blanket off and spreads her legs, letting me see just how wet she is. Still, my dick doesn't even twitch. Before Thalia, it would have. That little enchantress has fucking ruined me for anyone else. Melody runs a finger through her glistening folds before shoving two inside her. My gaze doesn't move as I watch her finger fuck herself.

"Do you like that, baby? Like watching my fingers in my pussy," she whimpers. I need to fucking tell her to stop, to put some clothes on but I know she will get suspicious if I do. She has done this before. I even filmed it. Then I fucked her hard like she asked. So, if I don't act on her little show, I know more questions will come.

Fuck, I want to scream at my fucking cowardice. My hypocrisy.

I tell myself I am going to show Thalia what she means by walking away from Mel and the horses. Yet here I am, debating whether to fuck her just so she doesn't start with her shit again.

Quickly deciding that I can't end things with Mel until I find other investors, I strip out of my clothes, stride to the bed, and shove my dick in her mouth so she can get it hard.

She does.

Just.

I flip her over, so I don't have to see her smug face, pull on a condom and plunge into her.

All the while feeling sick to my stomach.

———

We pull up to the farm just after 2 P.M. I quickly change into some riding gear, hop on my golf buggy, and head down to the barn. I know in my heart Thalia isn't here. It sounds stupid, but I feel her whenever she is close. My soul knows her. It calls to her on a level even I don't understand.

I saunter into the barn and notice Carter laughing away with Marissa. I grit my teeth, physically having to stop myself from going over there and shoving my fist in his smug face. He glances over when he spots me.

"Hey, Theo, did you have a good trip?" he asks. I nod.

"Yes, thank you. Well done for yesterday. Tessa told me Vince jumped well?" A smile curves his lips. Carter is one of those people who thinks he is much better than he actually is on a horse. If it wasn't for the huge amount of money his parents pay me to train the little fucker, I would have gotten rid of him by now. After last night's video, I am considering it.

"Yeah, first place in the one-meter-fifteen hunter class," he gloats. I smile before turning to Marissa.

"And Sammy had four faults?" She sighs.

"Yeah, I still think there are some things we need to work on. Like distances in the doubles and combinations."

"I will watch the footage Tessa sent and let you know. But you are right, it will not do any harm working on those things." I say my goodbyes and make my way to my office. I want to go on a trail ride, clear my head. But first, I need to speak to Thalia. I pull up her number, hitting dial as soon as I take a seat. It rings out a couple of times only to be cut off. I pull my cell from my ear and stare at it in shock. Did she just hit decline? I press call again only to get the same result. I growl in frustration. Christ, she is not going to make this easy for me and she shouldn't. I respect her for that.

Realizing she is not going to answer, I shoot her a text.

Me: You cannot avoid me forever, Piccola.

I smirk, knowing that my message will really make her angry. My cock hardens just thinking about the fire in her eyes she gets when she is mad.

Chapter Nineteen

THALIA

The absolute cheek of that asshole.

Thinking he has any say on who I go for dinner with. Then trying to call me now that he is no doubt back from his romantic trip.

How dare he!

He just spent two days away with Mel, doing God knows what and expects me to, what? Just wait around for him.

Hell no.

The thought of them together. Having sex. Kissing. It makes my stomach turn. I hate that I feel this way. I have no right to. Theo is hers, not mine. I wish I had never started this with him.

I sigh, flopping down on the couch. Grabbing the remote, I flick on Netflix, trying to find anything that will occupy my mind. I settle on a series called *Ginny and Georgia* and get comfy. It's not often I get a chance to just veg out like this but sometimes, you need it. I am on the go all the time. My body and mind never really have a chance to rest. I think it is only right that I take some time for myself.

Everything that has happened since I got here is all catching up on me. I like to think of myself as a strong person. I had to be with the industry I grew up in. But I am big enough to admit this thing with Theo is eating me up.

I want him.

Completely.

As mine.

An emotion I cannot explain slithers through me. I hate him and I love him. I hate that he has done this to me, made me crave him to the point I can't see anyone else. If only I liked Carter, my life would be so much simpler.

I enjoyed our dinner last night. It was nice. What Theo doesn't know is that Kiara and Marissa joined us. I won't tell him that, though. Asshole deserves to drown in his imagination as much as I am.

A knock on my door has me startling. I know who it is before I even check the peephole. His voice confirms it.

"I know you are there, Thalia. Let me in so we can talk." I freeze. I don't want to see him right now. Why can't he just leave me alone? Give me time to process everything. Was me not answering calls or texts a big enough hint that I don't want to talk to him or see him?

"Please. I am not leaving until you open this door." My breath hitches at the emotion in his voice but I will not break. I will not be that girl that he can just walk all over. Instead of going to the door and letting him in, I turn off the TV and pad to my bedroom, closing the door and popping in my air pods so I can't hear his pleas.

———

I fell asleep.

When I wake, the sky is dark. How the hell did that happen? I grab my cell to check the time. 9:08 P.M. I open my phone to see missed calls and messages from Theo, reminding me why I went to my room.

He turned up, begging to see me.

I jump out of my bed and rush toward the door. It's all quiet. I guess he left. So much for not leaving until he saw me. Anger courses through me that he didn't follow through with his words. I don't know why I am surprised. It's not like he is a man of honesty. I guess I just wanted him to fight for me. Prove something to me. What? I'm not sure.

I look through the peephole. Not seeing him, I pull the door open only to yelp when a large body falls back, landing on my floor. Theo looks up at me.

"Told you I wasn't leaving until I saw you," he smirks. I want to kick him, wipe that look off his face. I cross my arms over my chest.

"Get up, Theo, and go home to your *girlfriend*." He pushes up in one swift move and I can't help my eyes moving to his hard body. The thin gray tee he wears showcases every ab and muscle. I swallow, snapping my eyes to his when he clears his throat. I scowl at him. He steps toward me, further into my domain and my pulse races. I need him away from me before I do something stupid like forgive him.

"I just want to see you. I need to explain—" I hold my hand up to stop him.

"No need. You already explained in your office. I get it. You never promised me anything. We were just sex. It's my fault really. I was naïve. Got caught up in someone I never should have. We had to end sometime; we can't keep doing this. Not to Melody and not for my peace of mind." His eyes flash and he steps into me, backing me up until my back hits a wall.

"This is not over, Thalia," he grits. "It will never be over. You are mine. You were mine the moment you let me pop that sweet cherry of yours and you always will be. So, what the fuck were you doing out with Carter last night?" he growls. I reel back, shocked that he has the nerve to say this. He is such an arrogant asshole. But I can't deny the effect he has on my traitorous body. My skin is alive and my panties are wet. By the smug smirk on his face, he knows it. I push on his chest, trying to get some space from him.

"You have some nerve coming in here and saying that. You went away with your girlfriend. Your fucking girlfriend, Theo. How dare you waltz in here and say that," I snap but it doesn't deter him. Oh no, it does the opposite. He smiles down at me before running his nose up my cheek, making me shiver. His hot breath hits my ear. I wait for what he says next.

"I don't want Mel. I want you. I told you what happened. So why are you making this so difficult?" he croons into my ear, but I haven't finished. If what he says is true then did he fuck her when they were away?

"Did you fuck her?" He pulls back to look at me. My stomach turns. I feel sick. I know from the look in his eyes that he did before he even says it. He runs a hand through his inky strands and takes a breath.

"I didn't want to. But she would have questioned it if we didn't...have sex. I thought of you the whole time." Bile rises in my throat. I feel like my heart has been ripped out. I knew they would have sex but hearing it out loud hurts even more than I care to admit. I squeeze my eyes closed as if it can stop the pain. I feel his hand on my chin, but I don't want to look at him.

I can't.

His words have destroyed me. It's stupid really. I have no claim on him, but it hurts.

"Open your eyes, Thalia," he says softly. The tone is so at odds with the Theo I know. My eyes snap open. He holds me in place, dropping a kiss to the corner of my mouth. "It didn't mean anything, I swear." I laugh but it's humorless.

"Let me go. Do you not even care that you could be giving me an STD? You go from me to her to God knows who else. Your dick must be full of diseases," I spit. He sighs like I am an annoying child.

"I have never cheated on Mel...until you. There is no one else and I have never had sex without a condom, ever. Again, until you. I always use protection with Mel. I would never put you at risk."

"You expect me to believe you have never had sex with Mel without protection when you have been together, what? Six years? Jesus, you must think I am so stupid and maybe I am for ever getting involved with someone like you."

"I don't expect you to believe anything but it's the truth. Trust me, Mel has tried many times to get me to go bare. I never have. You are the only woman I have ever had sex with raw." My eyes widen at his words. I search his face, looking for a lie only to find nothing but honesty. Maybe he can be honest? I know it sounds stupid but for some reason, I believe he would never put me at risk like that. Suddenly feeling overwhelmed and very tired, I pull out of his grip.

"You should go. I am tired." He searches my face. Sensing that I am exhausted, that I need space, he nods and steps back but not before pressing his lips to my forehead.

"I will see you tomorrow. If you believe anything, believe my feelings for you run deeper than I ever thought possible," he whispers then spins on his heel and leaves.

———

It's been a week since Theo turned up at my apartment and we are still not back to how we were before he went away for those two days. He goes out of his way to try and talk to me, to get me on my own. All the while I avoid him. It's getting awkward now and I know other people are noticing the tension between us.

"That was very good, Thalia. Hand him over to Jessica and meet me in my office. We need to discuss the horse I have found for you to view." I nod at him and walk Roman out of the arena. Guess he found a way to get me on my own.

I stride to his office, taking a deep breath before I knock. His deep voice sounds.

"Come in." I push the door open. Not making eye contact, I pad toward a chair and drop down in it. Finally glancing at him, my breath hitches at the intensity in his eyes. He watches me for a long beat before leaning back in his chair and running his hand through his hair.

"I have found a horse in the UK that I think will be suitable. We need to act fast. I can speak to your father, but I thought you might like to do that just to speed things up?" I nod.

"I will speak to him today," I say, pushing out of my chair. His eyes flash.

"Sit down," he says. His voice is so low, almost threatening, leaving no room for argument. I don't hesitate to do as he asks.

"I have given you space, Piccola, but that ends today. I will not apologize for doing something that benefitted us both and eliminated any risk of Mel finding out about us. If you were an adult about this, you would understand why I do the things I do." My blood boils. I want to kill the asshole. But I know he wants my rage so instead, I plaster on a fake smile.

"I understand, Theo. I will talk with my father and let you know what he says." I push out of my chair again. This time he doesn't stop me. I don't miss his tortured sigh though. I resist the urge to turn around and look at him. I know if I do, I will run to him.

Tell him everything is okay.

Tell him I want him.

But I can't.

I won't be that woman that gets walked over by a man.

———

Two days later, we are in the UK. If I was having any thoughts about forgiving Theo, it changed the moment Melody stepped on the plane. Apparently, she is going home for a couple of weeks for some big event her father is hosting. I seethed when she boarded the jet. I made my excuses and went to the bedroom, staying there the whole flight so I didn't have to watch them all over each other.

"Come around to the oxer, Thalia. Sit up and keep your leg on," Theo barks as I canter around on the black horse with the four white socks. He is beautiful and stands around sixteen hands in height. His name is JC, competition name Justify. Ironic really, considering Theo keeps trying to justify his actions. I internally snort and focus back on the horse. I just know we are going to be a perfect match even with the limited time I have been riding him. I must give it to Theo, he knows what he is doing when it comes to horses. But I already knew that which is why I wanted to train with him so badly.

"Well done. Very good. Now jump the upright then come down to the double, then the water tray followed by the combination." I do as he asks and cannot help but smile at the height JC gives each fence. He is not going to touch a pole. When I finish, I pull to a walk and make my way over to Theo who is standing in the middle with Finn McDermott, the current rider.

"What did you think?" Theo asks with his hands on his hips. I smile. A genuine smile. The first I have given him in over a week.

"He feels amazing. He is like a spring, the way he clears each fence." Finn chuckles.

"Yes, he is. I think I have said the same to many people before," he drawls in his thick Irish accent. Theo turns to Finn.

"We will come back tomorrow before we fly home. Around 10 A.M?" Finn nods.

"Of course. I will make sure he is ready."

I hop off and Finn takes the reins before handing him off to the groom. Theo grabs my elbow and leads me to the waiting SUV. I want to snatch my arm out of his grip, but I also don't want to bring any attention to us. Greg hops out, frowning before his eyes narrow on where Theo has a hold of me. He shakes his head almost imperceptibly but doesn't say anything just opens the door. I hop inside followed by a fuming Theo. I feel his anger radiating from him. But I don't care. I am angry too. I grab my cell out of my purse and start scrolling through. I ignore the man beside me, who's staring at me so hard, he burns a hole in the side of my head. Not fifteen minutes later, we pull into the hotel parking lot. I jump out, making my way to the lobby, as Greg falls in step beside me. I just want to get to my room and away from Theo. We step into the elevator, a fuming Theo jumping in with us. Silence descends, the air turns thick but still, I keep quiet. Greg speaks, breaking the silence.

"Do you want to grab some dinner, Thalia?" I glance up at him and shake my head.

"No, thank you. I am just going to order room service and go to bed." He nods.

"Think I will do the same. If you change your mind, let me know." I smile as the elevator comes to a stop. I scramble out, not once looking at Theo even though I can tell he is begging me to. I pull out my keycard, quickly scan it against the door, and enter my room. Once the door shuts, I let out a breath I didn't realize I was holding.

I don't know how much longer I can put up with this tension.

————

I am relaxing on my bed, just about to order room service, when a knock sounds at my door. I know who it is. I can feel him from here. The pull between us. The connection we have.

Guessing he is probably wanting to talk horses, I push off my bed, pad to the door and pull it open. All the breath leaves my lungs at the sight of him. He is gorgeous. So gorgeous it hurts to look at the bastard.

"Hey,"

"Hi," I breathe.

"Can I come in?" I move from the door and wave my arm motioning for him to enter. He saunters inside and takes a seat on the chair at the desk. I take a breath, closing the door. Taking the few steps needed to my bed, I drop down. The room crackles with energy so thick, I nearly choke. I hate it. The tension, this chemistry between us. A chemistry I cannot, no, *do not* want to break. He stares at me for a long beat making me squirm before he speaks.

"When I said about this trip...I had no intention of bringing Mel with me or did I think she would want to. It was naïve on my part. It was also a last-minute thing with her father. She will not be joining us on the flight home." I groan. I'm so over his excuses, over him and Melody.

"Look, Theo, I don't want to talk about it. It's done. If I had known this is what you wanted to discuss, I would never have invited you in. I thought you wanted to discuss horses." He glares at me. Then his fist hits the desk making me jump.

"Goddamnit, Thalia. I want you to hear what I am saying. See that I am being truthful and genuine. I want you and I am going to prove it." He stands, closing the distance between us. He crouches so he is eye level and pins me with a look that sets my whole body on fire. "Have dinner with me?" My eyes widen at his words.

"What?"

"Let me take you on a date. A real date. You deserve more than being hidden. I know a nice little pub within walking distance. Let me take you to dinner?" he asks. The hope in his voice makes my chest tighten. I want to please him, make him happy. But I also need to protect myself and my own feelings. But before I can change my mind, I speak.

"Okay." I still. That's not what I meant to say but the way he is beaming at me, I can't take it back. This is proof I seriously have no control when it comes to this man.

We sit by an open fire in a quaint little English gastro pub not far from our hotel. It's beautiful with its oak beams and modern furnishings. Theo told me a well-known Michelin starred British chef owns it. With the mouthwatering food and excellent service, you can tell it is a high standard restaurant.

"What do you think? Is your chicken okay?" I finish chewing and answer.

"It's amazing. Best chicken I have ever eaten." He takes a sip of his wine and nods.

"I used to come here a lot when I was based in the UK. Got to know the owner and manager well. Whenever I come back, they always look after me." A slither of jealousy courses through me at the thought that he no doubt brought Melody here. Instead of asking, I plaster on a smile and take a sip of my wine—eighteen being the legal age limit to drink in the UK—and glance around the old building.

"I never brought Mel here," he says just above a whisper. My eyes snap to his. How did he even know I was thinking about that? "I know that is what you were thinking." I nearly choke on my wine. He is so in tune with me and what I am feeling, it's scary.

"How did you know that is what was going through my head?" He shrugs like it's not a big deal that he can read my mind.

"It may sound strange. But I feel what you feel. I feel so..." he trails off as if he is thinking of the right word, "connected to you. I have never felt like this before. With anyone." I stare at him, mulling over his words. I understand it because I feel it too. I sigh.

"I feel it too. I know when you are happy. Sad. Angry. I don't want to. We are too complicated, Theo. Too messy. We should stop...this. I feel out of control when it comes to you. Like I am free falling off a cliff and you are the only person that can catch me. The only person that I *want* to catch me." He smiles. Taking my hand in his, he gives it a gentle squeeze, silently telling me he knows exactly what I am saying. How I am feeling. We finish our dinner and head back to the hotel.

Theo takes my hand in the elevator and without even thinking about it, I launch myself at him, pressing my lips to his. We both groan as if this is what we have been waiting for. In some way, I guess we have. He cradles the back of my head like I am a precious gem before pulling away.

"Jesus, I have missed your lips," he growls. I take a step back when the elevator comes to a stop. We step out. Taking his hand, I rush toward my room. Quickly opening the door, I pull him inside. A desperation I have never felt rolls through me. I want him so badly it hurts. He spins me, caging me in against the door, his mouth dropping to mine. His big palms grip my jean clad thighs, and he lifts me. I feel his big erection immediately and grind against it. He groans, quickly spins and strides toward the bed. He drops me down on it, his eyes hungry, needy. He bends, making quick work of removing his and my clothes and before I know it, we are both naked and he is plunging into me. I cry out at the intrusion; he stills, letting me get used to him again. It's been a while.

"Sorry, I should have eaten your pussy to get you ready. I just couldn't wait any longer to be inside you," he pants. I nod and arch my back, taking him deeper. He stares down at me like I am all he sees. Like he...loves me? I shake my head; he can't love me.

Can he?

Instead of dwelling on it, I move my hips, silently telling him to move. He takes the hint, grabs my legs and lifts them over his shoulders as he thrusts into me repeatedly. This position is deeper. So deep and so good.

He reaches down and pinches my clit. I whimper. He smirks as he plays with my little bundle of nerves over and over until I am screaming out his name, creaming all over his cock. Theo follows me over the edge, stilling when he spills his seed inside me. He groans before dropping a kiss to my mouth, then rolls to the side so as not to squash me. He wraps his arms around me and pulls me close. So close, it is like we are one. It's not long before sleep takes me under but not before I hear Theo whisper, "I am keeping you."

Chapter Twenty

THEO

It has been a week since our trip to the UK. Things are back to how they were before I took Melody away. I see Thalia most nights now that Mel is out of the country. I can't get enough of her. I thought a couple of fucks, I would get her out of my system. But no. She has somehow wormed her way deep inside me and made herself at home. I'm not even mad about it. I want her there. She has brought out feelings in me, I never thought I would have. I was satisfied with Mel. Someone I could tolerate and was even attracted to. But I didn't love her. I didn't want love or need love. Mel worked out all these years because I got something out of her without having feelings involved.

My career.

Sure, I care for Mel. But I was never in danger of falling in love. It was a career move, one that benefited me greatly. But then Thalia came along, with her innocence, beauty, and this insane chemistry I have never felt before and messed everything up. She makes me question everything, makes me want things I have never wanted before.

I am so screwed.

Melody gets back today after some business with her father. I am dreading it. It means sneaking around again but I will make it work. I have to. I have some big decisions to make. It will mean losing everything I worked for but there is nothing or no one that will stop me from having Thalia.

I pull up to the airport to collect Mel. It's just past 4. I am already anxious about seeing my piccola tonight. I have this need to be with her. Around her. And it's no longer just about the sex, although that part of our relationship is amazing. She brings a contentment I have never felt just by having her with me. It's weird but I have decided to no longer fight it. She is sneaking out to the barn tonight and I am going to tell Mel I have a sick horse. Hopefully, she will be so jet lagged, she will be asleep by then anyway. I am scrolling through my cell when the passenger door opens. Melody glares at me.

"Theodore, you could at least have opened the door." I grimace at the sound of her voice and the use of my full name. I mask it quickly and hop out to grab her luggage. After loading it, we get on the road. There is only a couple of minutes of silence before Mel speaks.

"So how was your trip? Did Christian buy his princess another horse?" she asks. I don't miss the sarcasm in her voice. She is one to talk. Mel is her daddy's princess. I glance at her with a frown. I am sure we already spoke about this.

"Didn't we talk about this already?" I ask, my eyes back on the road. I hear her huff beside me.

"No, we didn't. I have barely heard from you since I have been away. *And* you told me not to come to Surrey because you were busy," she spits. The indignation in her tone is obvious.

"I'm sorry, Mel, but it was a business trip. It would have been pointless making the trip from London just to see me for a couple of hours." I feel her eyes bore into the side of my head. She makes a sound low in her throat before settling into her seat. The conversation is effectively over.

———

Once I get Mel settled in and spend some time with her, I sit in my home office going through some outstanding paperwork. Christian purchased JC, the horse we viewed, for Thalia. I need to sort out all the travel documents as he passed a five-stage vetting and x-rays yesterday. It seems like a lot but when you are laying down money in the top end of six figures, it is needed for insurance—and because you don't want a top-class horse to have any health issues or go lame as soon as you get it. It was the same process for Roman and is not unusual in the equestrian world especially for high end animals. A knock on the door draws my attention from my laptop. I find Mel with a seductive grin on her face.

"I am tired. I was going to go to bed for a few hours. Why don't you join me?" I run a palm down my face and let out a harsh breath.

"I have things to do, Mel. Why don't you go on up and I will join you later?" Her face drops for a second before she schools it into a forced smile.

"Okay. I will see you shortly," she purrs, then leaves my office. My stomach tightens in concern. Something seems off with her and I can't put my finger on it. Maybe it's me being paranoid because of what I am doing with Thalia, but I don't like this unsettling feeling that something is coming.

———

When the clock hits 8:50 P.M, I quickly check on Mel to find her asleep. She is in such a deep sleep, she doesn't even stir when I shower or move around our bedroom. Satisfied that she is probably jet lagged and exhausted from a busy week of socializing and she is not going to wake, I make my way to the barn. I quietly pull open the doors and head inside, stopping when I find Thalia already here. My heart skips a beat at the sight of her. She sits on a bale of hay, wearing yoga pants and a sweatshirt. But that's not what has me pausing. It's the way the moonlight streams in through the big windows and hits her, making her look like an angel.

Otherworldly.

She is so damn beautiful, it should be illegal.

It's in this moment that I know no horse is worth more than this girl. She pushes to a stand and makes her way toward me, snapping me out of my thoughts. When she is within reach, I grab her hips pulling her flush against me before smashing my lips to hers. She moans into my mouth; I want to consume every part of it.

I want to own her.

Make her mine in every way.

An animalistic, primal need washes over me. I want to impregnate her so she can never leave me, to tie us together forever. I want to watch her belly grow with my seed. My cock turns to stone at the thought of her pregnant with my baby.

Growling, I pull back and stare down at her. Her lips are swollen from my brutal kiss. Her cheeks pinken. Fuck. She is so sexy.

"Theo?"

"Come on," I drag her to an empty stall. We could be doing this in my office—it would be more comfortable—but there is something to be said about stall sex. It gets me hotter than I have ever been. I love holding Thalia in my arms while I fuck her against the wall as the cool air hit us. I know she loves it also, if how wet she gets is anything to go by. I open the door and pull her inside. I lean against the stall door, watching as her chest heaves and her pupils dilate with lust.

"Strip for me," I command. She watches me for a long beat before doing as I ask. I have never seen anything sexier in my life as I stare at her removing her clothes. She stands in just her panties. I cock a brow, pinning her with a look that says *all of it*. She sighs before gripping the waistband and sliding them down her long tan legs. Straightening, she tries to cover herself. A growl rumbles up my throat. I step toward her and cup her face.

"Never hide from me." She drops her arms from her perfect tits. I smirk, dropping my head to take one and then the other in my mouth, lapping at them like they are a juicy steak. She squirms and moans at my ministrations, but I am not finished yet. Releasing her with a pop, I straighten and circle her. She watches my every move, like I am a lion about to pounce.

I am.

I want to devour her.

Every perfect inch of her.

"Touch your pussy, tell me how wet you are for me," I rumble. Her breath hitches and she freezes. She can be shy when it comes to her sexuality, but I want to knock that out of her. I want to show her that it's okay to experiment and enjoy these things. "Don't make me ask again, Piccola. Touch your pussy." She mews like a little kitten before her hand moves down her body and runs through her folds. She pushes a finger inside her beautiful cunt. I stop in front of her, mesmerized by her finger pumping in and out.

I groan at the sounds her wet pussy makes, at the way her finger glistens with her arousal. Suddenly feeling very jealous of her finger, I grab her arm, stopping her. I bring her fingers up to my mouth and suck up all her juices. She watches me with parted lips and wide eyes. Dropping her hand, I quickly rid myself of my clothes. My cock jumps out of my boxer briefs, hard and ready, desperate to be inside her. I grab her, lifting her up my body and back us up against the back corner. Dropping a kiss to her lips, I run my length through her wet folds.

"I have been thinking about this all day, Piccola," I groan before lining myself up and thrusting into her tight wet heat. She moans as I bury myself to the hilt.

"Me too. It's becoming a problem. I cannot focus on anything but you."

"Good," I grit selfishly. I want all her attention. I know she should be thinking about her horses, but I am selfish enough to want everything. I pump in and out of her, working her good. I reach down, gathering up some of her wetness. I move my thumb to her tight ass as she tenses.

"Relax. Trust me." She takes a breath and nods. My heart clenches that she puts so much trust in me, allowing me to do these things with her. I slowly push into her puckered hole, groaning when I feel how tight she is. I wonder what she will feel like when I finally stick my cock in there. Pinning her against the wall with my body, I move my free hand to her clit and rub small circles. Her eyes squeeze shut and her pussy clamps down on me like a vise, nearly pulling my own release out of me. I know she is close. I feel it in the way she grips me. In the little sounds she makes. It never takes her long when we are in the barn. She gets off on the forbidden, the sneaking around aspect of our relationship like I do. Even if she won't admit it.

She whimpers, moans, and mewls against me. I drop my lips to hers to swallow every single sound. We don't need one of the staff coming in to see what the noise is. Her legs tighten around my waist as do her arms around my neck. Her cunt grips me so hard when she comes apart, she has me stilling and following her over the edge. Milking me of everything I have as she squeezes me and coats me in her juices. I pull my lips from hers, my thumb from her ass and stare at her as she goes limp in my arms. She is even more beautiful when she climaxes. Her eyes pop open. I go on instant alert when I see the worry in them instead of satiated bliss.

"What was that?" I frown and look around, seeing nothing.

"What was what?"

"That noise. I heard a noise." Her head whips around frantically. I grab her chin bringing her eyes to mine.

"Nothing, Piccola, you are just being paranoid. It was probably just one of the horses." She relaxes in my arms. I gently drop her on the floor before I grab her clothes.

"Yeah, you are probably right. I think all this sneaking around is getting to me."

"It's amazing you keep getting away from your apartment without your shadow finding out. He isn't a very good bodyguard, is he?" I tease instead of addressing her worries. She pulls her pants on and rolls her eyes.

"He trusts me to be where I say I am. And fortunately, I have a spare set of keys that he does not know about. If I didn't, I would not be here." She strides to the door when she is fully dressed and I follow her to the barn door. Before she can open it, I pull her in for another kiss, not ready to let her go just yet. I wish more than anything, we could be a normal couple. That I could go to sleep and wake up beside her everyday. She pulls away. "I need to go."

I nod before watching her jog to her SUV, my heart chasing after her.

————

When I get back to the house, I shower in the downstairs washroom and make my way upstairs half expecting Mel to be awake. But she is still asleep. I climb in the bed, making sure to keep enough distance between us, and stare up at the ceiling with a smile. I have never felt like I do when I am with Thalia. She is something I crave. A drug I never want to give up. I am consumed by her.

She is in my blood.

In my veins

In my soul.

In my heart.

Is this what love is? This all-consuming madness and obsession. The voice inside your head that tells you to fuck everything else and make her yours?

I don't know how or when it happened but somehow, I fell in love with her. My piccola embedded herself inside me, became a part of me without me even realizing what was happening.

There is good and bad that comes with our relationship just like any other relationship. The highs of what we are doing outweigh any of the lows, but having Thalia, being inside her, is everything to me. I never want it to end.

I know what I need to do and having her as mine will be worth it.

Chapter Twenty-One

THALIA

My sister arrived this morning, and although I have missed her...I want to kill her. She is flirting with Theo like her life depends on it. I have never felt such jealousy as I do right now, watching her. Restraining myself from saying something is the hardest thing I have ever had to do in my life.

"Come on, Aria, let's go" I snap, making both their eyes land on me. I know I am being irrational; I know Theo has no interest. But I can't stand it. It's silly really, considering he goes home to Melody every night. But he is mine.

Theo searches my face before smirking. Bastard knows I'm jealous. Aria stares at me like she doesn't know me. And maybe she doesn't. I would never have snapped at her like this before. She looks from me to Theo and back again. I can see her head trying to work everything out. If the grin now curving her lips is anything to go by, she just did.

"Yes, let's. We have a party to get to tonight. We need to get on the road." I glance at Theo. I never told him about tonight, didn't think I had to. But the way he is watching me...it was a mistake on my part.

"Party?" he asks calmly but I don't miss the tension in his voice. Aria turns to him.

"Yes. Our friend, Parker, invited us to the opening of his club tonight. It's going to be amazing. Parker is obsessed with Thalia so I know we will get the best treatment." Theo's jaw clenches. He pins me with a look that makes a shiver run up my spine and not in a good way.

"Well, have fun. And Thalia, make sure you are on time in the morning. I do not want to hang around for you because you are hungover," he spits. Out of my peripherals, I see Aria watching us. A curious look is in her eyes before it turns mischievous. My stomach sinks. I know what she is going to say before she even says it.

"Why don't you come with us? I am sure Parker wouldn't mind." A dark grin takes over Theo's face.

"I might just do that. Why don't you send me the details, Thalia? I will see if Melody would like to go." My eyes narrow. I want to kill him. He is using Melody to get back at me because of some misplaced anger. I hate it. We were in a good place. Well, as good as you can be when you are someone's mistress. But with a few words because of his unnecessary jealousy, we are back to square one.

"Yeah, sure," I mumble before grabbing my sister's arm and dragging her away.

———

"OH. MY. GOD. You totally had sex with your trainer," Aria screeches as soon as we are through the door of my penthouse. I squeeze my eyes closed. I never wanted to tell my sister about this but she is too perceptive. Saw something between us at the barn. I could deny it, but what would be the point? Aria is like a dog with a bone; she will not stop until she has answers. Opening my gaze, I find her smirking at me.

"And don't lie to me. I always know when you are lying." I groan. Of course she does.

"Yes, okay. It happened a few times. But he has a girlfriend so it's not like it is going anywhere. And Daddy would kill me if he found out. Not only because it would cause a scandal but also because Theo is thirty. That is twelve years older than me." Aria squeals like this is the best news she has ever heard.

"Daddy's little good girl, being very naughty. This is so fucking hot. *Theo* is fucking hot. I would go there too," she muses before her glittering gaze meets mine again. "What was it like? He took your V card, right?" I sigh, dropping down on my couch.

"Yeah. It was good. *Is* good. The sex is amazing. Obviously, I have no one to compare it with, but I can't imagine it being any better."

"Did you come? During your first time?"

"Yes."

She grins. "Lucky you. Most girl's first time is just a fumbling mess and is over in minutes. Seconds even. Like mine. I can't imagine that a man like Theo would not make it good for you though. I bet he made sure to look after you before his own needs." My cheeks heat at her words. My sister and I are close, but I have never spoken to her about sex. Never had to. I was a virgin before Theo. Aria has spoken to me about her experiences, though.

"I am playing with fire, Aria. I know I am. But I can't stop. I don't want to. I just want him. I think I love him," I admit out loud for the first time. I have strong feelings for Theo but the last couple of days I have thought about what my feelings actually mean. I cannot imagine I would risk something like this just for some hot sex. If I am being honest, I think I fell for him months ago. My sister pulls me into a hug and sighs.

"Of course you do. Trust you to fall for the first guy you get involved with. A man with a long-term girlfriend no less." Tears build in my eyes. I don't even attempt to stop them. The whole situation is a clusterfuck. Does it mean I will put a stop to it?

No.

Theo Rhodes is like my own brand of heroine; one hit and I am addicted. I don't even think therapy would stop my obsession with the man.

My sister eyes me with what looks a lot like pity. I hate it.

"Just take it for what it is, Baby Sis. It might work out...it might not. But in the meantime, let's get our asses to Miami. We have a party to attend."

———

The club is amazing. All high-end furnishings, sleek bar and my favorite: the VIP area. It's contemporary, with plush, comfortable booths that overlook the entire club. We haven't seen Parker yet, but I know he is around. It is only a matter of time before he makes his way over.

I messaged Theo the details, but he decided against it—something about Mel not feeling well—and told me not to be late tomorrow. I rolled my eyes and sent him a thumbs up emoji to which he replied:

Theo: And stay away from Parker.

I didn't reply to that one. He can stew in his own imagination, and deal with some of what I do daily. I have no intentions of doing anything with Parker. After my talk with Aria, I know for certain I am in love with Theo. And unlike him, I can't even look at somebody else, let alone be intimate with them.

"Isn't this great? I am so glad we are doing this, Thalia, even with Greg and Bishop watching our every move," my sister shouts over the music. As it's Halloween, around fifty percent of the patrons are in costumes. Not average get-ups either, they look sexy as hell. I look at the servers, bartenders, and hosts. They all look like models just off the runaway. The women in their black corsets, fishnet tights, and booty shorts. The men are all topless. All have bodies most women would drawl over and they wear little bow ties and black pants. Nothing else. I wouldn't expect any less from Parker though. If he wants to make a statement, he most certainly will.

"Yeah," I answer. Truth is, I would rather be back home…in bed with Theo. I feel guilty as I don't get to see my sister as often as I would like but the loud music and all these people are over-whelming. My sister rolls her eyes. She knows exactly how I feel about all this.

"Parker, darling," my sister drawls. I follow her line of sight to see him stepping up to us with a big grin in place.

"Aria and Thalia Maxwell. It's been too long." He pulls my sister in for a hug and then grabs me, holding me at arm's length as if to study me before pulling me in. His hot breath hits my ear.

"You get more beautiful every time I see you, Thalia," he purrs. I pull back with a shy smile.

"Thank you, Parker. This place is amazing. I have no doubt it will be a massive success."

"I will make sure of it. It's the first project my father has given me complete control over. I have no choice but to prove I can make it work." He motions for us to sit. Signaling our private server over, he orders a bottle of Cristal.

"So, how have you both been? I hear you are living in Welling-ton, Thalia?"

I nod.

"Yes, I am training with my horses with a top show jumper."

"Your father said. What about you Aria? You still at NYU?"

"Of course. Daddy is letting me design a limited-edition collection once I graduate. Although, I will admit, I already have some ideas." Parker and I chuckle. When my sister wants some-thing, she goes for it no matter what.

"And Evan seems loved up with the model?" he asks. I snort.

"You know what he is like. He will soon get bored."

"I did invite them both tonight. He declined due to meetings with big clients. He has definitely settled down and grown up. If it had been last year, he would have been here and blown them off."

"Yeah, I guess so. We all have to grow up sometime though, right?" Aria says, her eyes sliding to Bishop before coming back to Parker with a smile. I don't miss the longing in her gaze as she looks at her bodyguard. I wonder if anything has happened between them yet. I make a mental note to ask her when we get back to the house.

"Right, let's drink this champagne and then I will give you a tour." We all take a glass the server poured and toast Parker to his new venture.

Forty minutes later, Parker is holding my hand in his and showing me every inch of his club. Aria decided to stay in the booth, choosing to antagonize Bishop over a tour of the place. I must admit, every part of it is impressive, the attention to detail shows everywhere I look. Parker comes to a stop, making me run right into him. He wraps his arms around me and pulls me close. His eyes search my face. I don't miss the lust in them, but it makes me feel slightly uncomfortable. He smiles, dropping a kiss to my forehead.

"You are exquisite, Thalia," he murmurs against my skin. I open my mouth to say something but am stopped when a flash goes off. I blink to find a man with a big camera. He must be part of the press. I try to pull away, but Parker holds me closer.

"Mr. Rothman, can I get a picture? Who is your date? Is it serious?" he fires off, quickly. I glance up at Parker to find him smirking. He pulls me in closer and faces us toward the man.

"Ah, Tony, of course you can. This beautiful young lady is none other than Thalia Maxwell and yes, she is my date this evening." My eyes widen at his words and annoyance slithers through me. But being a professional when it comes to things like this, I plaster on a big smile and let the man take pictures. I will be sure to have words with Parker about this though. I feel like I have been ambushed.

"Perfect. And if I may say so, you make a gorgeous couple." And with that, he walks away.

"I have to agree with him," Parker says with a smug voice. I pull away from him and he frowns.

"I am going to get back to Aria." I spot Greg not five steps behind me. He nods, knowing exactly what I want.

"Of course. I have some people to see, then I will join you." He drops another kiss on my cheek and strides away.

———

I wake to my alarm beeping. I groan, grabbing my cell from the nightstand and hit the off button. I go over last night in my head.

Parker.

How handsy and possessive he was over me.

The pictures.

How he acted like we were a couple.

Aria and Bishop.

How they disappeared for a good half hour.

I have so many questions for my sister, but I am not about to ask them at 6 in the morning. I need to get back to Wellington. I told Greg I wanted to leave at 6:30 A.M, not wanting to get to the barn late and give Theo an excuse to shout at me. I only had two glasses of champagne last night, but my head feels heavy this morning. I feel like I am getting sick.

Hopping out of bed, I quickly shower, dress, and make my way downstairs but not before checking Aria, who is still fast asleep.

Alone.

I turn the Keurig on, make two coffees to go, grab some pastries, and head outside to find Greg waiting in the SUV. I smile as I make my way across the asphalt. I may not like having a constant shadow, but he is always at my beck and call, making sure I am getting to places on time. I pull open the door.

"I made you a coffee and grabbed you a pastry."

He hums.

"Thank you. We won't have to stop to get McDonald's breakfast then." I scrunch my nose up, making him laugh. He knows I hate fast food. "Joking. I would never take you there, kid," he chuckles before barreling out of the drive.

Over an hour later, we pull up to our apartment building. Greg stays in the car while I run up to get in my riding gear. I do it in record time and before I know it, we are on our way to the barn. Anticipation slithers through me. Did Theo see the pictures of Parker and me? I have no doubt they are all over social media and online gossip magazines. For some reason, I don't want him to see them. Not that I should feel guilty. Technically, I am a single woman who can do as she pleases. But still, I can't help the worry in my gut.

Hopping out of the SUV, I make my way into the barn greeting all the staff as I go, only to come to a stop when an angry voice calls my name.

"Thalia, can you come to my office?" It's not really a question.

Awareness prickles my skin and I swallow. Stepping inside, Theo shuts the door behind me making me jump. He glares down at me. I know whatever he is going to say has to do with last night.

Chapter Twenty-Two

THEO

I woke to several notifications on my cell. I had set up an alert online for any pictures or news about Thalia.

Call me crazy or a stalker.

Maybe I am.

Whatever.

I needed to see what she got up to last night. What I saw made my blood boil. I had nearly gotten in my car and raced down to that damn club, just to claim her in front of that asshole. In front of everyone.

Parker Rothman.

Rich, eligible, handsome bachelor.

And someone I could easily see Thalia with.

He looked at her like she was the only thing he could see. He looked mesmerized. I can't even blame him. She does the same to me. Still, I don't like it.

I am an asshole.

A hypocrite.

But I won't share her.

Not with anyone, specially entitled little fucks like him.

She is mine.

I feel out of control right now. Like if I don't stake my claim, then I am going to lose it completely. My blood's pumping. Cock's getting hard. I am going to show my piccola exactly who she belongs to.

Bracing my hands on the arms of the chair where she sits, I get right in her face. She juts her chin out in defiance. I want to dart my tongue out and lick it. But I restrain myself. Just.

"I woke to some interesting pictures this morning, Little One," my voice is low. Calm. I am trying to hold on to the last bit of control I have. She shrugs.

"Nothing happened. Parker is a friend."

I clench my jaw, getting so close to her now. Her breath fans my face, her sweet scent hits my nostrils. I inhale her smell to calm myself. Remind me that she is here.

With me.

Not him.

Not anybody else.

"Those pictures looked more than friendly, baby. It looked like you were a couple. The magazines stated as much." She scoffs. I want nothing more than to bend her over my knee and spank the attitude out of her.

"You are in no position to say anything, Theo. Where's your *girlfriend?*" she grits out. I chuckle but it's not a nice sound. Her breath hitches and chest heaves. The pulse point in her neck turns erratic. My cock turns rock hard and when her eyes drop. I know she sees it. I think we are both getting off on this push and pull.

"She doesn't matter," I croon, lifting a hand and running my thumb across her full bottom lip.

"What do you want from me, Theo?" Dropping my hand, I lean right in, brushing my lips against hers.

"I want you...and I want to not wake up to pictures of you wrapped around another man. You are *mine*. Do you realize how close I was to coming to that club? To doing something I wouldn't be able to take back? Like killing that asshole. I didn't like him touching you." Her eyes narrow on me as fire burns in them.

"You are such a hypocrite. You go to bed with Mel every night and I am expected to be your dirty little secret. Just to be happy with a few fucks in the barn? No matter how much I like you, I don't want to do this anymore. I deserve more." She pushes me away. I stumble, not prepared for it. Thalia stands and takes a few steps to the door only for me to grab her and spin her back to face me.

"Don't walk away from me," I growl. She drops her eyes, but I don't miss the tears in them. My heart clenches. I never took into consideration how hard this must be for her—what she is going through. I am her first sexual partner. First man she has been with. She is right. I am treating her like a dirty little secret. I need to make some big decisions. Either I let her go for good—the thought alone makes me feel sick—or end things with Mel. Our relationship has been nothing but a business arrangement. I went along with it for the benefits I knew I would get. Being with Mel, having the backing of her father, has given me opportunities that I would have spent years trying to find.

Being with the beauty in front of me has shown me that I want something more. That I do want love. I can't keep up the pretense with Mel any longer. Maybe if Thalia had never come along, I would have been happy carrying on with Melody. But no more. I grip her chin and raise it, so she has no choice but to look at me.

"I'm sorry. I know there are things I need to think about, and I will. I don't want to lose you," I whisper. A tear falls. I track it as it moves down her beautiful face before darting my tongue out and licking it.

"I never did anything with Parker. I can't even look at another man, Theo. Stupidly, all I see is you." My heart beats faster at her words.

"All I see is you, too. I know I have made a mess of things but please give me the chance to fix everything?" She sighs, planting her tiny hands on my chest. She pushes up on her tiptoes and drops a kiss to the corner of my mouth.

"Okay."

———

"That's it. Brilliant, Thalia. Now come around to the upright." I watch as she jumps Roman. I am impressed. She has improved so much since she came here, I can't help feeling a sense of pride. She has taken everything I said on board and proved to me she can do it. "You were on stride until you took a pull on the reins. Come to it again and keep your hands still. Trust in him. Trust in yourself." This time, she does as I say and hits the stride perfectly.

"Well done. That will do for today. Cool him down and then we will discuss JC's arrival. I was updated by the transporter not long ago. He is currently in Holland. He will be crated and loaded on the plane tomorrow if all goes well with the vet checks." She nods, while walking off Roman. I leave her to it and head inside to let Marissa know she is next to train. Just as I enter the barn, I hear a golf cart pull up. Glancing over my shoulder, I spot Mel dressed to the nines, full face of make-up and a scowl as she spots Thalia in the arena. That's weird. Normally, she is all over the poor girl. Like a fly around shit. She hops off the cart in her stupid heels. Spotting me, she smiles.

"Theodore, darling." She makes her way toward me.

"What do you want, Mel?" She narrows her eyes before wrapping her arms around me. Looking up at me, she flutters her lashes.

"Just wanted to see you. I barely do anymore. You are always busy. You don't touch me. Haven't touched me since our weekend in Miami." I shuck out of her arms and pin her with a look. Just then, Thalia walks past, her eyes bouncing between us. Mel looks at her, her face pinches like she has eaten something sour. She schools her features and plasters on a smile. I can tell it's fake. Forced.

"Oh hi, Thalia," she gives a small wave.

"Hi, Melody," she greets before disappearing into the barn.

"She really is a beautiful girl, isn't she?" I frown wondering where this is coming from. Not wanting to play into whatever game Mel is playing, I shrug.

"I guess. Although I haven't really noticed. She is business." The words taste horrible on my tongue, but I will not give Mel any ammo. She scoffs, running a talon down my chest.

"Don't pretend you haven't noticed, Theo. A blind man would. Anyway, enough about the spoiled little princess." I resist a scoff. Thalia may be richer than any of us, but Mel is more of a spoiled princess than she will ever be. "If you are too busy now, I want you in early tonight. I will arrange for a nice dinner and then I want a whole night of you in bed. My pussy misses you," she purrs. A while back, my dick would have jumped at her words but not anymore. He doesn't even twitch.

"Go, Mel. I have things to do," I growl before turning on my heel and leaving her there.

———

After finishing my lessons and sorting out Thalia's new horse arrival, I find myself in my SUV making my way to her apartment. It's a bad idea but I can't stop myself even if I wanted to. Although Mel asked me to be home early, I can't bring myself to care that I won't be. I need to reclaim Thalia after last night. After our argument. And nothing or no one will stop me.

Pulling up at her building, I grab my cell and dial her number. It rings out and I think it is going to go to voicemail when she answers.

"Theo?"

"Hey, I'm outside. Can I come up? Are you alone?"

"I am, but my sister is due to arrive back here at some point."

"Make sure your shadow is not hanging around. I am coming up." I end the call, not giving her any chance to deny me. Climbing out of the car, I make my way inside and straight to the elevator. Hitting the button, the doors open immediately. I step inside, pressing the penthouse button and lean against the wall. Things have changed between us; I feel it and I know Thalia feels it too. It's just a case of when I am going to set things in motion, end things with Mel and her father. Shaking the thoughts away, I step out when it comes to stop to find Thalia shifting on her feet in the hallway outside her door. She spots me, her eyes light up, and she rushes towards me.

"What the hell, Theo? I don't want Aria to turn up while you are here. Can whatever you have to say not wait?" she hisses, grabbing my arm and pulling me inside. I grab her hips and shove her against the closed door. Her eyes light up with lust. She licks that full bottom lip.

"I need you," I rasp before dropping my mouth to hers. I kiss her like she is the air I need to breathe. And maybe she is. She has become someone I cannot go a minute without thinking about. This never should have happened. But it did. And now I am so caught up in her, there is no way out. I don't want there to be.

I pull away and stare down at her face. She is so flawless, so ethereal, it hurts to look at her. Her brows furrow as she looks at me. "Theo? Don't tell me you came over just to kiss me?" I smirk. I want more than a kiss; I want inside her. To feel her pussy clench around me as she orgasms.

"No. I need to be inside you." It's almost a plea. Sensing that, she grabs my hand and leads me to her room. I strip her of her clothes in seconds, mine following suit just as quick. I push her down on the bed and crawl up her body.

"You are so beautiful," I whisper. Her cheeks turn a delectable shade of pink. I want to consume her. Every part of her. My tongue darts out and I run it up her neck, only stopping when I reach her ear.

"I want you so badly right now. All I can think about, *dream* about is having my cock inside your tight cunt." She squirms beneath me, her lips parting slightly. I reach down with a hand to find her already wet and wanting. I run a finger through her folds, before pushing two fingers inside her pussy. I am aware we don't have much time—the last thing I need is for her sister to find me here—so I yank my fingers out and plunge inside her wet heat, groaning when I am fully seated. It's only then when all my tension slips away. My brows furrow. I realize it's because of her.

She calms me.

Grounds me in ways I have never felt before.

She reaches up and traces my face with her fingers. The softness in her eyes makes my chest tighten.

"*You* are also beautiful," she murmurs. I drop my lips to hers and slowly move in and out of her. This time is different from any other time. It's slow. Deep. Connected. For the first time in my life, I am making love to a woman. And it has never felt better. The feelings I have for her are like no other. Our whole beings, our souls, are connected in a way I don't understand. I knew this would happen once I touched her. Which is why I fought it. Why I was such an asshole. But I don't want to fight it anymore. I just want *her*.

"Theo," she moans, wanting more. I reach down to rub on that little bundle of nerves that I know will set her off. Her lips part in ecstasy and eyes flutter closed. Seconds later, her pussy is spasming around me, milking me for all I am worth and setting my own climax off. I still inside her, filling her up with my seed, claiming her as mine. I pull out and roll to the side so as not to crush her. She turns to face me. I cup her face, dropping a kiss on the corner of her mouth, her temple, her forehead, her cheek. The words I want to say are on the tip of my tongue but before they are released, she speaks.

"That was nice. Different," she rasps tiredly. I wrap my arms around her and pull her close to me.

"That was making love," I reply. Her breath hitches. I know it's because of the L word. I cradle her head in my chest, so I can't see her face. I know what will be looking back at me. It's the same thing I am feeling. But in the last couple of seconds, I have decided I will not say those three little words even if I feel them. Not until I have sorted things out with Mel. Thalia deserves more than some false promises. I want to do right by her. I want us to be together. But I must make sure everything is in order before then.

"I should get going," I mutter into her hair. Her body tenses, making me feel like a complete bastard. But right now, there is no other way. She pulls back and searches my face before sighing.

"Yeah, Aria will be here soon." Nodding, I release her and push out of the bed, quickly pulling on my clothes. She watches my every move and for a minute, I feel like she is the hunter about to attack her prey. But she doesn't. She just lays there watching me. Finally dressed, I drop a kiss to her head.

"I will see you tomorrow," I murmur before leaving her alone.

It takes every ounce of willpower I have to walk away from her.

———

"Where the hell were you? I went down to the barn and you weren't there. Dinner arrived over an hour ago," Mel screeches as I step through the door. I grimace at the look on her face. I have never seen her so angry.

"I had some errands to run," I respond coolly. Her hand lands on her hip and she purses her lips.

"Errands? I told you this morning I was going to order us dinner. I wanted us to sit down together so we could talk. What could possibly be so important that it couldn't wait, Theo?"

I shrug. "It couldn't wait." She eyes me, her face reddening. Any minute, I think she is going to blow. She takes a breath, no doubt to calm herself.

"Well, you are here now. I want to discuss the next step for us. Marriage? Kids?" I blow out a harsh breath and shake my head.

"I am not discussing this now, Mel. You know I don't want those things." I don't add 'with you'. No need to antagonize her further.

"How dare you, Theo. I have waited for six years; it is the next step. Don't you think my father has invested enough money in your career that the least you can do is make an honest woman of his daughter? He expects marriage. I expect it. So, what the fuck is the problem?"

"No problem. You knew I didn't want those things when you begged to ride my dick. I told you what we were then. But you pushed and pushed until we were a couple. I was never going to change my mind. You just thought that you would get your own way, like you always do." Her eyes widen before a sinister smile crosses her face. She takes a step toward me.

"Remember my father made you, Theo. I can quite easily have it all taken away from you. If you don't take the next step, then I will make sure he does. Six years. I have been by your side for *six years*. Championing you. Worshipping you. It's the least I deserve. That and to be able to fuck you without a condom. What long term couple do you know still uses protection? What are you so scared of?" she hisses. I wasn't lying when I told Thalia she is the only woman I have ever gone bare with. I have always used protection with Mel, because I knew of her intentions. If I gave her an inch, she would have me locked down with four kids by now, making me tied to her forever. She knows this. I know this. Which is why I always wrap it up. I reach out, wrapping my fingers around her throat. Her eyes widen, but not in fear, lust swims in them.

"Threaten me all you want, Mel. I will not have you hold my

horses over my head and let you think that you can hold them against me to push me into something that I do not want. It is *me* that is the talented one. *Me* that has made a name for myself. If you are not happy, you know where the door is. But don't for one minute think that I will suffer if you take the horses. I am the biggest name in show jumping. I can easily find more investors that don't come with the stipulation of having to fuck their daughters," I growl, shoving her away from me. She smirks, making me still. It's not a nice smile. It's damn evil.

"You think you can get rid of me that easily, Theo?" she tsks, spinning and making her way toward the stairs. She glances over her shoulder. "Oh, you really do not know me." And with that, she winks and makes her way up the steps, cackling like she knows something that I don't. Her words feel and sound ominous.

I cannot help but feel something bad is coming.

Chapter Twenty-Three

THALIA

The next three weeks go by in a blur of competitions and training. My new horse arrived over two weeks ago and spent a few days getting settled before I started riding him. He was more impressive than I remembered. I will be taking him to his first show at the weekend. It will be my last one before we start the winter show jumping tour at Royal Palm in January. It's a major equestrian event that lasts for around four months. It is my time to show Theo what I am capable of, get my name out there and get some good results. I am hoping to make the nations cup teams for the USA next year and to do that, I will need to make high placings.

My father finally signed a deal to sponsor the Global tour for the next three years. This will all be released to the press in early January. It will now be known as Maxwell's Global tour and is a series of competitions for invited top riders, held at special locations and iconic landmarks all over the world.

Paris at the Eiffel Tower.

London at the Royal Chelsea Hospital.

Monaco at the Prince's Palace.

New York at the Statue of Liberty.

To name a few. This is another reason I need to be getting good results. I don't want to compete just because my father is the main sponsor. I want to be invited like everyone else—make it on my own merit, because I am good enough. Not because of my name.

"Relax, Thalia, you know horses are highly sensitive animals that immediately pick up every feeling of their rider. It's basic knowledge, yes? So why are you so tense you look like you are about to snap? You are passing your energy through to JC," Theo barks. I snap out of my thoughts and sigh. I don't know why I feel so stressed lately. Maybe it's the pressure to show people I can achieve what I set out to do. Maybe it's because I need to study for my finals? Maybe because I am in love with Theo...and he is still with Mel? Although, she has taken a trip back to Britain before Christmas which means I get to spend more time with him. He even stayed over a couple of times. Cooking me dinners. Watching bad TV. Like a proper couple. I don't want it to end.

"Sorry, I have a lot on my mind," I mumble. He eyes me for a beat and sighs. "Hand him to Jess, we are done for today." I want to argue but by the look on Theo's face, he is waiting for it. I let out a breath and finally acquiesce. Hopping off my horse, I pass him to a waiting Jess.

"Thanks," I smile.

"No problem," she chirps, walking away.

"Can you ditch your shadow tonight and come to mine?" Theo murmurs behind me, making me jump. I spin to face him, a small grin on my face.

"I can try. Greg still doesn't know I have spare keys," I chuckle, making Theo smile.

"Good, means you can get away. I have plans for you tonight." He winks before lowering his voice and leaning in, "I am going to fuck that tension out of you." My whole body comes alive in anticipation. And now all I can think about is tonight, his body on mine.

"I will be there," I whisper. Theo nods, his eyes shifting behind me as he takes a step back. I glance over my shoulder to find Carter riding into the arena, his eyes narrowed on us both.

"I am ready, Theo, if you are not too busy," he grits. I frown at his tone before focusing back on Theo.

"See you tonight," he whispers before sauntering to the middle of the arena.

———

Back at my apartment, I get some schoolwork finished and then decide to video call Aria. I want to know what's going on with her. What went on with her and Bishop in Miami. Pulling up her number, I hit dial. It rings out. After a few seconds, the call connects and her face appears. I smile.

"Hey sister, you miss me already?" she teases. I roll my eyes.

"I do, actually. I also want to know what's going on with you. You have been avoiding me since I asked about a certain BG." Her eyes widen, cheeks pinken, and I just know that something has happened between them.

"BG? Really Thalia?" she hisses. I chuckle.

"Well, I didn't want to say *bodyguard* in case you had company." It's her turn to roll her eyes and she sighs.

"No, Daddy is working, and Mama is on location filming. The BG, as you call him, is downstairs."

"Perfect time for you to tell me what happened then." Her eyes drop before coming back to me. She lets out a breath.

"We slept together in Miami," she blurts. My eyes widen even though I am not really that shocked. I knew my sister would wear him down.

"What?"

"Don't act surprised. You knew full well I did, which is why you have been harassing me. He hasn't mentioned it since. I think I was a pity fuck and now he is worried he is going to get fired."

"No way you were a pity fuck. Look at you, Aria. But I can see why he would be worried. Daddy would be so mad if he found out and Bishop would most definitely lose his job."

"Yeah, about as mad as he would be if he found out you are screwing a thirty-year-old with a girlfriend." She widens her eyes and tilts her head as if to get her point across. I stare at her for a long beat, mulling over her words. I know she is right; I just hate hearing it out loud. Her eyes soften. "Sorry, I am being a bitch. I really like him, Thalia, and now he won't even look at me. The sex was amazing. Better than I have ever had—not that I have had lots of sex but still. I think he did it because I wouldn't drop it and I was drunk. See, pity fuck."

"No, you were not. If it is any consolation, I think he likes you too. I saw the way he looked at you in Miami and it was not in the way Greg looks at me. It was more. He looked at you with adoration."

"Yeah, well, it doesn't matter. He has made it clear nothing will happen again." Hurt passes in her eyes making my chest hurt. Both of us are in such shit situations with the men we have fallen for. Quickly changing the subject, so I can cheer her up, we talk about holiday plans. We will be spending Thanksgiving in the Hamptons with the whole family and Christmas in New York. We always get tickets for The Rockettes on Christmas eve. We've done it since we were little; it's one of the things I look most forward to about the holidays. That and spending quality time with all my family. When I think about it, it makes me realize I miss New York. My parents, brother, and sister. After all that has happened the last few months, it will be nice to go home for a few days.

———

I manage to sneak out of my building without Greg seeing me and head over to Theo's. I pull into his private drive—which is separate from the barn entrance—and bring my SUV to a stop outside his front door. His door is pulled open before I even have a chance to get out and he rushes down the steps toward me, yanking my door open and tugging me out.

"Missed me?" I tease. He drops his head into my neck, taking a deep breath. I shiver when he presses a kiss to my bare skin.

"You have no idea." He grabs my hand and pulls me up the steps and into his home. I have been here a couple of times now and the place is impressive. It may not be as big as some of the homes my parents own but it's somewhere I could see myself living. The house is around five thousand square feet but homely. Then you have the barn, the arena, and the acreage that comes with it. I would love to have a place like this someday with a barn full of horses. Looking at the décor, the modern furnishings, I briefly wonder if it's Melody's doing. Did she decorate this home? Shaking the thoughts away, I look at Theo to find him already watching me. His gaze is heated. My stomach dips at the desire swimming in his eyes. Out of the times I have been here, we've had sex once.

In the spare room.

I refuse to fuck in the bed he shares with Mel. I know I am crossing boundaries already but that is one I won't cross.

"You are beautiful," he rasps, tucking a strand of hair behind my ear. My cheeks heat. I drop my eyes only to bring them back to him.

"What do you want to do?" I ask, unsure of what his plans are for us. I didn't eat this evening, hoping Theo would cook or order in.

"Come, I made lasagna. My mother's recipe, passed on from her mama. I thought you would appreciate some proper Italian food." At that moment, hearing those words, I fall for him a little more.

I make myself comfortable on a stool at the breakfast nook, while Theo sets out the food. It smells delicious and just like when my mama used to cook. He lays out a plate in front of me, and loads a portion of lasagna, salad, and some garlic bread. My mouth waters; I wish we could do this every day. I wish he was mine.

"Eat," he whispers. I glance at him before grabbing my fork and digging in. It is even better than it smells, the fresh ingredients and Italian flavors bursting on my tongue. Finishing my mouthful, I turn to him.

"Oh my God, Theo. You have been holding out on me. This is amazing." He smirks and takes his own bite. He nods, swallows.

"It is, if I do say so myself. I wanted to do something special for you. Go back to both our roots and cook you a proper Italian meal." My chest tightens at the thought he put into this. Leaning forward, I drop a kiss on his mouth.

"Thank you. I love it. Do you realize how much we actually have in common?"

He grins, dropping his floor to his plate and eyeing me. "No. Why don't you tell me?"

I drop my own fork, turning in the stool to face him. Bringing my fingers up, I list them off.

"Well, to start, we both have Italian heritage, Italian mothers. They both came to the US." I display a second finger as Theo watches me in amusement. "We both live for show jumping and horses." I twist my lips in thought, then grin when I think of another one, my eyes lighting up in excitement. I had never noticed it before. I snap my fingers. "Our names. They both begin with TH," I say excitedly, making Theo throw his head back in laughter. I can't help but get caught up in his happiness and laugh, myself.

"What?" I ask. He stops laughing and wipes his eyes. He reaches out, cups my neck, and pulls my face to his. His lips brush mine.

"You are just too cute, Piccola. Too damn cute." He presses his lips to mine for a chaste kiss before pulling back and picking up his fork. We finish the meal talking about Italy, horses, and our plans for next year.

———

"Oh God," I moan as Theo thrusts in and out of me. He has been denying me an orgasm for the last fifteen minutes. Every time I get close, he pulls out of me and smirks. I want to kill him.

"You feel so fucking good baby. I don't think I will ever get enough of you. Your tight pussy has ruined me for all other women, Thalia," he groans. Just the thought of him with another woman makes jealousy course through me. I push on his chest, annoyed. He grins down at me. Dropping his head, his lips meet my ear.

"Aww, don't worry, Piccola. I only want your pussy. No one else could satisfy me like you can. Trust me on that. I have tried enough." He pulls back to look at me. He looks confused by his words. I frown. Shaking his head, he snaps out of wherever he just went and presses a kiss to my mouth.

"Just means you cannot ever leave me. I want you forever," he whispers. My heart clenches. Butterflies fill my stomach. I never want to leave him. I wrap my arms around his neck.

"If you really mean that, then you will have to get rid of your *current* girlfriend." He narrows his eyes. We have not had a conversation about what we are. Where our relationship is going. But this is the first time he has alluded to it being more than sex. We need the conversation. It needs to happen. Not necessarily right now, while he is inside me, but soon.

"Let's not talk about that right now," he grunts, pivoting his hips and hitting me in my most sensitive spot. I mewl, arching my back, trying to draw him closer. He reaches down, circling my clit. My pussy contracts, making him groan. "That's it, baby, come on my cock. I want your cream all over me," he grits, picking up speed. The familiar feeling of an orgasm builds, igniting every part of my body.

Before I know it, I am falling over the edge, screaming his name. He works me through my release, thrusting slow and deep until he finds his own and fills me with his hot cum. He drops down on his elbows so as not to squash me and nuzzles his face in my neck.

"Watching you come is the sexiest thing I have ever seen. I could watch it all day," he rasps before rolling to his side and pulling me into him. I groan, knowing I need to get back. It's unlikely Greg will check in with me but there is still a small chance he will. I can't risk that.

"I need to go," I murmur. Theo tightens his arms around me. I chuckle, turning in his arms. "You need to let me go. I can't risk Greg finding me missing."

"Five more minutes," he grumbles. I sigh and relax in his arms. His eyes close, freeing his face of any tension. He looks younger than his thirty years of age somehow. I trace my thumb across his cheek. His eyes pop open, softening as they land on me. Something I can't quite decipher shines in them, making me swallow. He reaches up and traces my lips.

"I will come to you tomorrow night. I want to stay the whole night with you. Wake up with you," he rasps. I don't miss the vulnerability in his voice. Something has changed between us these last few weeks. It's no longer just sex. I feel connected to him on a cosmic level. As if he can read my thoughts, he kisses me softly before speaking. "You know that this is not just sex for me, don't you?"

I shrug. I know how I feel. My feelings are way more than just a fling. I have fallen for him. I never stood a chance really. It was always going to happen; I was just naïve enough to think I could separate my feelings from a physical relationship. I won't tell him that though. Not until I know where he stands. When I don't speak, he fills the silence. "It is, Thalia. So much more than just a

fling. I am going to prove it to you. You will see." I smile. I can't
help it. What he is saying is everything I want to hear. But I can't
get my hopes up. Not yet. I pull out of his arms, this time he
lets me.

"I better go."

Theo sighs, scrubbing a palm down his face.

"I really don't want you to, but I understand. Give me a sec, I
will walk you to your car."

———

The elevator comes to a stop. I step out, eyes focused on my cell
and replying to a message my mother sent. I pad toward my door,
only to freeze when a deep voice speaks.

"Where the hell have you been, Thalia?" My head snaps up,
eyes landing on Greg who is standing outside my door. He looks
so angry, angrier than I have ever seen him. I swallow. Blink. Shit,
he *is* here. I shift on my feet.

"I just went to the store; I needed some women's toiletries," I
blurt, hoping he won't question me further at the mention of me
possibly being on my period. Most men get funny about that sort
of stuff. I am just hoping he is one of them. He narrows his eyes,
huffing out a laugh as he shakes his head.

"You are lying. You were with him, weren't you? You think I
am stupid, Thalia? I see how you look at Theo. How he looks at
you. How long has it been going on?" My stomach drops. Sweat
breaks out across my forehead before I compose myself. I
straighten. Lifting my chin, I look him in the eye.

"I don't know what you are talking about. I went to the store.
I didn't want to disturb you for something so small."

"What do you take me for? I have known you since you were a
little girl. You are lying. And you know full well you are supposed
to get me when you leave this building. It is for your own safety. I
cannot protect you if you go off without telling me. What if

something happened? What would I tell your father? That man is making you selfish, Thalia. He has a girlfriend for Christ's sake and is how many years older than you? Ten? Twelve?" He shakes his head, disappointment in his eyes. "I thought you were smarter than that. You deserve better than him. Better than being someone's side piece. Someone like you deserves the world, not sneaking around when he summons you." Tears blur my vision. What Greg is saying is making everything real. My and Theo's situation. My father would never approve.

"You won't tell my dad, will you?" My shoulders drop. I just admitted, in not so many words, that Greg's assumptions are correct. He sighs.

"No, I won't. But I want you to end it. And I want you to stop sneaking off without me. Jesus, Thalia, if anything happened to you..." he trails off. He doesn't need to say anymore. I nod.

"I am sorry. I didn't mean to upset you. Or anyone for that matter," I say.

He strides towards me, only stopping when he reaches the elevator.

"Get some sleep. I will see you in the morning." I grab my key, quickly entering my apartment. I lean against the door, my mind racing.

What the hell am I going to do? I will not give Theo up. I can't. But I also cannot carry on like this. I sigh.

Things just got even more complicated.

Chapter Twenty-Four

THEO

Greg shoots me a look that tells me he wants to kill me. I can't even blame him. This morning when Thalia got here, she told me he was waiting for her when she got back. He knows everything. You can tell he cares about her deeply, in a fatherly way. Which is why I am sure he hates me, wants to wrap his hands around my throat and watch the life drain out of me. He knows full well of my situation, how I am not a single guy. He also knows Thalia is way out of my league.

Still, it won't stop me.

Things are different between Thalia and me now. It's no longer just a fling. *She* is no longer the forbidden fruit that I can't have. Can't touch. She has become my everything.

She is mine.

And as I watch her on her horse, the improvement in her, I can't help but puff my chest out with pride. I am proud of my piccola. Not only because of her determination but because she chooses not to play it safe. This girl, who is too beautiful and tempting for her own good, can have anyone she wants. And yet, she chose me. A man twelve years older. A man who is taken. My chest tightens; my heart bursts. I am totally, irrevocably in love with her. I wasn't lying when I said it wasn't just sex. It's not. Somewhere in the last couple of months, she has become my everything. And I know what I must do. I will give it all up. Give everything up for her if it means I get forever with her.

"How was that?" Thalia asks, breaking me out of my thoughts. She is on her new horse. It's only the second time she has ridden him since he arrived. I am pleased with their progress already. They look great together.

"Good, cool him down and then get on the next one. It's going to be a group lesson with you, Carter, Marissa, and Kiara. We have one of our last competitions coming up before the Winter tour. This is the last time to show me that you are ready to step it up next year." She nods, determination flashing in her eyes.

It gets my dick hard.

It's one of the things I love most about her. Her passion for this sport. The way she does not give up.

"Oh, and Piccola, tell your shadow to take it down a notch with the death looks." She frowns, glancing over at Greg, shakes her head, then walks away.

———

After lessons, I decide to school my own horses. May as well make the most of them before Melody has them taken away. I briefly wonder if I can get an investor before I tell Mel it's over only to sigh when I know I won't. I have contacted a few people now and am still waiting to hear back. I am going to speak with Mel when she gets back before Christmas. She's been away for a while this time and I cannot decide if it's a good or bad thing. Good because I get to spend time with Thalia without having to sneak around. Bad because I get the feeling there is more to her trip back home than she was saying.

Finishing with the last one, I hand him off to Juan, one of my new grooms, and head to my office. I call Tess in, wanting to go through schedules for the holidays and the busy few months we have coming up in the New Year. I lean back in my chair, eyes on her.

"What's up, Theo?" she gets straight to it.

"I wanted to discuss the upcoming Winter tour. You have been with me long enough that you know how it all works, but I want you to bring all the newbies up to speed. It is imperative everything goes smoothly, especially with Thalia. It is her first tour and although she has competed at Royal Palm, you know how different it is compared to a normal competition."

Tess nods her agreement. A tour is completely different. There will be some of the best riders in the world competing there and for top prize money. But it's expensive to compete. This year, I won nearly half a million myself from competing for six weeks and only just broke even. Also, with high prize money comes bigger, more technical courses and better competition. I just know it will open Thalia's eyes; it will give her a feel of what's to come with Nations Cup teams and the Global tour. It's cutthroat. Nothing like she is used to.

Tessa and I finish up our meeting, with Tess promising to sort out the holiday schedule. I like all my staff to have time off and if they want to go home to their families, they can. But I do need some to stay here, and I always make sure to invite them for holiday dinner with me if they are staying. I push out of my chair and make my way to the golf cart. I want to shower and change before I go over to Thalia's. My cell ringing has me pausing and fishing it out of my pocket. I grimace when I see the name on the screen.

"Mel, how are you?" My voice sounds fake even to my own ears.

"Theodore, darling, I am good. I just wanted to check in. You didn't answer my calls last night." I flinch remembering the ten missed calls I found when my piccola left last night. I didn't return them, just went straight to bed. I clear my throat.

"Sorry, I had an early night." She laughs down the line, but it sounds off. Fake.

"What, at 8:00 P.M? I don't believe you." I sigh and jump on the buggy. Holding my cell between my shoulder and ear, I start it and make my way back to the house.

"I had a long day. I was beat. Is the purpose of your call to ask about my whereabouts or is there another reason?" The line goes silent for so long, I almost think the call has ended but then she speaks, her voice low and threatening.

"How dare you treat me like this, Theo. Remember my father made you and he can take it all away. I should not have to keep telling you this. I thought you were smarter," she tsks.

"Stop with the threats, Mel. You will not like the consequences if you keep pushing me." She chuckles, but it's not a nice sound.

"Oh, Theo, you seem to underestimate the lengths I will go. Anyhow, enough of that. I just wanted to let you know, I will be back around the eighteenth of December. I want to celebrate my father's birthday. A birthday you should also be attending."

"I can't so close to Christmas, with staff being off. You know this. The same happens every year."

"Yes, well, hopefully next year things will be different," she says ominously. Something cold slithers up my spine at her words. Like she knows something that I do not. Pulling up to the house, I say my goodbyes. I quickly make my way to the shower, wanting more than anything to be around Thalia's warmth after that call with Mel.

———

The door to her apartment is yanked open. She grabs my shirt and pulls me inside. I chuckle at the urgency of her movements and raise a brow.

"I didn't want Greg to see you," she huffs. I smirk, dropping my grocery bag before wrapping my arms around her.

"You are too adorable, Piccola," I murmur before taking her lips with mine. I kiss her with all that I am.

She is all I want.

All I need.

And I am past caring about the consequences of our relationship. So, I am older, who cares? We work. She makes me happier than I have ever been, and I will not give that up because people will judge me. Us. It's not like I am old enough to be her father. It's only twelve years.

Nothing really, when you know it is the person you are meant to be with.

And she is the person I am meant to be with.

I feel it deep down in my soul.

Pulling back, I stare deep in her amazing eyes.

"Come on, I brought groceries to make you dinner." I reach down, grabbing the bag as Thalia eyes me with an emotion in her eyes that I don't want to address right now. I feel it too but until things are clear for us to start something properly, I won't say it.

I make quick work of chopping the veggies, noodles, and chicken for a simple stir fry. I try to stay healthy; I need to, being an athlete. Especially a show jumper. It would be unfair for me to carry extra pounds and expect a horse to jump one-meter-sixty fences. So, I stay in good shape for myself and for my animals. Popping the veggies and noodles in a wok, I grill the chicken while Thalia sets the table and grabs a couple bottles of water. While it cooks slowly, I make my way over to where she is standing by the floor to ceiling windows watching the outside world go by. I wrap my arms around her waist, burying my head in her neck and taking a deep breath. Her scent instantly calms me. Her whole being is like a balm. I have never felt like this before. That's why I know what I must do. I can't risk losing Thalia. My mind is made up. The sooner Mel gets back here, the sooner I can end things and start fresh with the woman in front of me.

"What are you thinking?" I murmur. She sighs.

"Just how nice this feels, having you here. I want us—" I stop her, she trails off, looking back at me with her big eyes.

"Don't say it. Let me get some things in order and then you can tell me everything you feel. Everything you want." She stares at me for a long beat.

"Okay," she whispers, spinning in my arms and pushing up on her tiptoes so she can brush her lips against mine. "But then I am saying everything that is in my heart." My chest rumbles and I smile.

"As will I. There is so much I want to say, but not yet. When the time is right." She nods and nuzzles her head in my chest. I want to stay like this forever. Her and me in this bubble, in the safety of her condo. I pull out of her hold.

"Let me check dinner, it should be ready. Take a seat and I will bring it over."

Plating up, I serve dinner. Our conversation flows easily, we discuss everything from horses to where we see ourselves next year. What we want to achieve. It has never been like this with Mel. Not that I should compare it. What I have with Thalia is completely different and not something to be compared.

It's special.

Otherworldly.

After dinner and cleaning up, we do something so normal, so domesticated, I almost laugh at the absurdity of it. We cuddle up on the couch and watch Netflix. She falls asleep in my arms. It feels so natural, like she has always belonged here. I hold her tighter and study every single one of her features. A dusting of freckles across her nose. Full heart shaped lips. Sharp cheekbones. Long dark lashes. Flawless skin.

She is perfect.

And all mine.

My cock hardens in my pants, digging into her flat stomach. I pepper kisses over her face. She stirs, her eyes popping open.

"What are you doing?" she yawns.

"Just kissing what's mine. I can't get enough of you," I groan, grinding my dick against her to show her just what she does to me. She chuckles, eyes darkening with lust. She reaches down, shoving her hand in my sweats and boxer briefs. Wrapping her small hand around me, she starts to pump. I groan, capturing her lips with mine. She releases me, maneuvering herself until she straddles me. I grip her hips and grind her boy-short clad pussy against my hard cock.

"What do you want, baby?" she purrs so seductively my brain short circuits. I want so much right now. To be inside her. To eat her glorious pussy. To see her plump lips wrapped around me. Quickly going through my options, I decide to feast on her first. I flip us until I am on top of her. She giggles, the sound hitting me right in my chest. I remove her shorts, finding her cunt glistening and ready for me. My mouth salivates. I dip down, swiping my tongue through her wet folds. Jesus, she tastes like heaven. She tastes like mine.

"I am going to eat your pussy, then you are going to choke on my cock. Then I am going to fuck you so hard, you will feel me every time you move tomorrow." Her eyes flash with excitement making my dick pulse. I quickly shove off my sweats and boxer briefs and squeeze myself to release some of the pressure before moving back down to heaven. My lips wrap around her clit as my fingers play with her tight hole. I push two inside and she squirms beneath me. I growl.

"Stay still, Piccola. I don't want to tie you up," I taunt. She stills instantly. We have never done anything like that before, but I would like us to. And by the feeling of her getting wetter, she would like that too. I smirk, latching onto her little bundle of nerves again. I pump my fingers in and out, moving my free hand back and to her ass. She tenses.

"Relax. You like it when I put a finger in your ass," I murmur against her hot wet flesh. Yanking my fingers out of her pussy, I trail her wetness to her back hole, lubing it up some, so it doesn't hurt as much. I plunge them back in her pussy and gently push my thumb into her now lubed ass. She whimpers, making my cock leak. I want to be in her so badly, I physically hurt.

"Is that okay?" I look up at her to find her eyes already on me. She nods and I take that as my que to continue. I push into her ass further as my fingers pick up speed in her wet cunt and my mouth lavishes her clit with attention. Her legs begin to shake and seconds later, she screams out my name as her pussy walls and ass muscles clench around me like a vise. I pull all fingers out, bringing the ones that were in her pussy to my mouth and sucking them off like a lollipop. Her chest heaves, eyes wide as she watches me. I groan at the taste, my cock turning to granite. Her eyes drop down, lighting up when she sees how hard I am. She pushes up, getting on the floor and on her knees.

Fuck me.

She looks so hot, it should be illegal. I turn, placing my feet on either side of her and palm my dick.

"Come on, Piccola, swallow my cock," I grind out. She smirks, knocking my hand away and taking me in her own. My length jerks as her tongue darts out and swirls the tip where pre-cum leaks from me. I lean back against the couch, closing my eyes almost like I am in pain only for them to pop open when her mouth wraps around me and she takes me until she is deep throating me. I groan, my hips thrusting forward on their own volition. She gags, tears streaming down her face. I reach down, thumbing them. "Sorry, Piccola, I got a bit excited having your perfect lips wrapped around me."

She grins around my dick, then slowly works me. It takes everything in me to let her take control and not fuck her mouth. When my balls tighten, ready for release, I pull myself out, pick her up, and throw her over the arm of the sofa. She braces herself, looking over her shoulder at me as I thrust into her. If I am coming anywhere, it's in her cunt. I want to shower her insides with my seed and for a second, I pray that her birth control fails her. Pray that I can put my baby inside her. I shake my head at the thought.

Fuck. I really am gone when it comes to this girl. Kids are something I have not wanted, something I have never even really thought about. But I want them with her. I want everything with her. Getting close, I need her to come first.

"Play with your pussy," I growl. She reaches down and plays with her clit. I slam into her harder, making her orgasm come out of nowhere. She cries out my name, slumping forward as I roar out my own climax. I drop forward, peppering kisses on her sweat sheened back. She jerks as I pull out of her, no doubt still sensitive from my cock pounding into her.

I straighten. She looks back at me in her hazy, satiated state but doesn't move. I smile, liking her like this. Knowing it is me who did it to her. I grab her, lifting her into my arms.

"Come on, let's get cleaned up," I murmur, dropping a kiss to her forehead. She snuggles into me as I carry her to her shower, only releasing her when we step inside. I wash us both off, towel dry her, and put her into bed. Climbing in beside her, I tug her body close. It only takes minutes for her breathing to even out, me following not long after, content and happy, with my girl in my arms.

———

"When you jump the oxer, sit up straight, then it's around eight strides down to the combination. I don't want you to pull. I don't want you to kick. I want you to hit the fence in eight. Not seven. Not six," I tell Thalia as we walk the course for her first competition on JC. It is also one of our last before the winter tour. When she doesn't speak, I glance down at her to find her nibbling that bottom lip of hers. I inwardly groan. She really does not understand what she does to me. "Thalia?" Her eyes snap to mine. I see a flash of nerves in them. I pull her to a stop, avoiding the other competitors who are course walking.

"Look, I know you are nervous, but everything will be fine. You have got this. JC has got this."

She sighs.

"I know, I just want it to be perfect." My gaze softens as I watch her. I smile.

"You will be. *You are*," I whisper. She smiles, opening her mouth to speak when a deep voice interrupts us.

"Ah, Mr. Rhodes," Dean Carruthers drawls. I pin my gaze on him to find a smug smirk on his face. He glances at Thalia. I want to rip his eyes from their sockets when they darken with lust. His hand darts out and I take a step toward her. Something Dean doesn't miss if his smile is anything to go by.

"And you are the lovely Thalia Maxwell. I have been waiting for a chance to meet you. Theo here seems to keep you on a tight leash though. Hidden." She glances at me briefly, before taking his hand and shaking it.

"I am. And you are?" His smug grin drops only to be replaced by a fake one. Dean's ego is big enough to believe everyone in the equestrian world would know him. I cannot tell if Thalia is just messing with him or not, but I want to kiss her so hard right now.

"Dean Carruthers. If you ever want some proper training, please don't hesitate to contact me. I can promise you, I am better than this guy," he chuckles, playing it off as a joke but it isn't. He would do anything to have the clients I do. Especially one like Thalia. She snorts, yanking her hand out of his.

"Thank you, Mr. Carruthers. But I can assure you I am very happy with my current situation." He eyes her for a long beat but before he can say more, I turn to her.

"Come on, let's finish walking the course."

———

"Sit up, leg on," I mumble to myself as I watch Thalia come down to the last fence on JC. So far, she is clear. There were mistakes made but she came back from every single one of them which is the most important thing. We all make mistakes; it's how we react to them that is testament to who we are as an equestrian. What people forget is that show jumping is one of the toughest sports out there. You must try and set everything up perfectly every time—which is impossible—but we still try. Especially when you are competing at top level, and you have a five-to-six-hundred-pound live animal between your legs. Anything can happen. Which makes the trust between horse and rider important. If you don't have trust, you have nothing. The crowd cheering brings me out of my thoughts, and I see that Thalia has a clear round. I smile. I knew she could do it. She pulls to a trot, then a walk, and comes my way with a beaming smile on her face. Once out the arena, she hops off, handing him off to Maria. I open my mouth to speak when she cuts me off.

"I know there were some mistakes. I was off a couple of distances and buried him at the big oxer which he should have refused but didn't. It was our first competition. I can only improve, right?" I grin as the words rush out of her.

"Yes, there were mistakes. But you did well. Don't be so hard on yourself. It is still a new partnership." Her mouth drops open and eyes widen. No doubt that I have not chewed her out. I should, but I don't want to do that. She knows where she went wrong.

"Come on, let's get you on Roman."

Chapter Twenty-Five

THALIA

Thanksgiving has come and gone. I went back to the Hamptons with my family for a few days. I did not want to go. Although I miss my family, I wanted to spend it with Theo. I had visions in my mind about us being all domesticated, cooking Thanksgiving dinner together. But my parents insisted, and I knew they would grow suspicious if I had stayed in Wellington.

We have finished all our competitions for this year and now it's just a case of getting my horses ready for the Winter tour at Royal Palm, which starts in January. This will be my biggest competition to date with me entering the CSI3* star tour on Roman and JC and the CSI2** star on Zeus and Lolly. To say I am nervous is an understatement. Competing at this level will hopefully get me noticed and I can make the Nations Cup teams in Europe next year which is what I have been working toward.

"How does she feel?" I glance at Theo as we ride down to what I now call our trail.

"Yeah, she feels okay. The vet said it was just bruising of the foot, right?" Theo nods. While I was away for the holidays, he called me to say Lolly had gone lame while being out in the pasture. I panicked thinking it was something serious, like a tendon injury but turns out, she just stood on something hard like a rock and bruised herself.

"Right. He said just some light work for a week or two and then she should be good to go. It's nothing to worry about, Piccola. she will be fine for Royal Palm." I smile, unable to help it. I love how he knows what I am feeling. Without thinking, I pull Lolly to a stand. Sensing what I want, he does the same. We both lean in, meeting halfway, and he smashes his gorgeous lips to mine. It's at this moment that I know what I want more than anything and that's Theo Rhodes. I want him. This life. It just feels right, no matter the origins of our relationship, or even if he has a girlfriend. Theo and I are meant to be. I feel it in my soul.

I break the kiss, smiling shyly at him. He grins and says, "Come on, let's get back to the barn."

———

Later that day, I am getting ready to meet Kiara, Marissa, Carter, and some of the staff at a saloon type bar situated on Royal Palm. It's their end of season party. They have live singers, motorized broncos and cheap drinks. Everything you need for a good time. I wasn't going to go, wanting to spend the night in Theo's arms, but the girls wouldn't take no for an answer—much to Theo's annoyance.

I decide on some jeans, a simple black tank, my little black studded biker jacket and to finish the look off, my black suede Alexander McQueen sneakers. I pull my long dark hair into a high ponytail, pop on a lick of mascara, and a coating of red lipstick on my lips. I don't usually wear make-up. Never have done unless I have been on a modelling shoot or filming. But tonight, I feel like wearing a bit of color on my lips especially when my outfit is mainly black. My cell rings startling me out of my perusal in the mirror. I pad toward my nightstand, smiling when I see my mama's name flashing on the screen.

"Hey, Mama."

"Hello, Bambina, are you okay?"

"Yes, I was just getting ready to go out with some of the team from the farm."

"You are taking Greg with you, yes?" I roll my eyes even though she can't see me.

"Yes, Mama, Greg goes with me everywhere," I lie. I am not about to tell her I snuck out several times to go sleep with my trainer.

"Ah good, your papa will be happy." She clears her throat. "Two reasons for my call other than I miss you and wanted to hear your voice." I chuckle.

"I miss you too, Mama, but I did just see you for Thanksgiving."

"Yes well, I miss all my family, sweetheart. It's getting a lot to be away several months of the year. That's not why I called though. I wanted to tell you before it hits the media. I am in the running for another Darling award. The voting begins in January, the awards are in February as you know but my agent assures me it's in the bag." I gasp. The Darling awards are the biggest awards in TV and Film and what every actor aspires to win. The name came about because it represents the darlings of the industry. My mother won her first Darling award when she was just twenty-one. It was her first major movie role and a major achievement which skyrocketed her career.

"Mama, that is amazing." I smile. I am so proud of her.

"Thank you, sweetie. Now, the second thing. Luella called." I pause. Luella is my agent, and I haven't heard from her since I turned down a big modelling contract to focus on my show jumping career. "She has had interest from a big equestrian apparel brand. They want you to be the face of them, Bambina. To represent them. I thought because it would be involved with your horses, you would be interested?" My mom is right, I am interested. I do miss modelling; it is something I enjoyed but my horses will always be my first love. But being able to do the two together is the best of both worlds. Right?

"I am, can you get Luella to send me the details? I don't know why she didn't to begin with." My mother chuckles.

"Oh honey, she said you have been avoiding her." I snort. That would be correct. I was.

"Anyway, sweetheart, I must go. I will get her to send you the information. Have fun tonight and be careful. I love you."

"Love you too, Mama."

———

The bar is buzzing with excitement and people having a good time. I sit at a table with my group near the small stage, Greg not five steps behind me. I sip my water, while the rest drink beers. I was offered one, but I want a clear head.

"So, Thalia, how are things going with your new horse? He is a beauty," Kiara asks.

"Yeah, he is. It's going well. I just want to get going properly now. I can't wait to start the tour."

"I hear you. The Winter tour is completely different to what we have been doing. It's so competitive. But fun all the same. Some of the best riders in the world will be there. You will see what I mean. It's not too far away now."

"No, it's not. I almost wish we didn't have the Christmas break. I just want to get to it now," I say, making her chuckle.

"It will be here before you know it."

"What will be here before you know it?" a deep voice cuts in as an arm lands over my shoulders. My gaze snaps to Carter who has now joined us.

"I was just telling Thalia about the Winter tour and how different it is from what we have been doing." Carter nods.

"Yeah, it is. Completely different ball game. But don't worry, I have been watching you and you are ready. You also have some seriously talented horses." I smile at his compliment. I feel ready in one sense but then I also feel like I have imposter syndrome. Like I shouldn't be there. What makes me think I am good enough to compete at that level? What have I done to prove myself? I shake the thoughts from my head. I can't think like that.

Yes, I may have a father that will throw money at the sport for me but the ribbons I have won so far are from my own hard work and dedication. I can admit it helps that I have some good horses, but they don't do all the work themselves. The majority, yes. But if I wasn't good enough to ride them, they wouldn't do what I ask of them. With that in mind, I push the negative thoughts away and enjoy my time with the team.

Not an hour later, my skin prickles with awareness as I feel eyes boring into me. I know who it is without looking. Glancing over my shoulder, I see him standing by the door, leaning against a wall. His arms are crossed against his muscular chest. I swallow at the hunger and intensity in his gaze before turning back to the stage.

"I am just going to the restroom," I tell Greg. He pushes up to follow me, but I shake my head. He rolls his eyes but sits back down. I hop off my stool and make my way to the bathroom. Locking myself in, I lean against the door and take a deep breath. When did things get so complicated? I snort, knowing exactly when.

When I decided it would be a good idea to cross a line I never should have with my trainer. Sighing, I push off the wall, take a quick pee and wash my hands before exiting. I smile when I hear the words to The Sunday's *Wild Horses* sounding out around the bar. I only make it a few steps before someone covers my mouth and drags me through a staff exit door. I yelp, flailing my arms to try and get away. The warm Floridian air hits me as we make it outside and I am pushed up against the wall before being spun around. I relax when I see who stares back at me with a smirk.

"What are you doing, Theo? Anyone could have seen us. I thought you weren't coming tonight," I hiss.

"I needed to touch you. I was getting so hard just watching you in there," he groans before crushing his mouth to mine. I melt into his brutal kiss as he claims me, hooking my arms around his neck and grinding down on his rock-hard cock that now presses against my stomach. He pulls away, the look in his eyes making my stomach flip.

"Do you realize how ironic this song is right now?" he rasps. My brows furrow before I strain my ears to still find the lyrics to *Wild Horses* being belted out. "Wild horses couldn't drag me away from you, Thalia. Not now. Not ever," he whispers with so much emotion in his voice. I nearly say the words I have been dying to say.

I love you is on the tip of my tongue and as if he senses it, he shakes his head, dropping a kiss to my lips.

"Make an excuse to leave and meet me at your apartment. I need to talk to you." I nod. Pushing up on my tiptoes, I kiss him. In my heart, I know whatever he wants to say is going to change everything. Do I finally get the man I desperately want? Will he be mine? I break this kiss and smile up at him. He stares at me for a long beat before tapping my ass.

"Go. I will see you shortly." He pulls away and makes his way to what I assume is his SUV. I quickly make my way inside to find Greg in the hallway. He eyes me suspiciously.

"What are you doing? You have been gone a while." I shrug.

"My sister called. It was loud in here, so I stepped outside." He watches me before sighing and turning to make his way back to my friends. "Wait," he stops, glances over his shoulder. "I am not feeling too good. Can you take me home?" He nods.

"Say goodbye to your friends and we will leave. It was getting too loud in here anyway," he grumbles. I chuckle, pushing past him to say my goodbyes.

I pace my apartment while I wait for Theo to turn up. It's been nearly two hours. He should be here by now and quite frankly, him not being here is giving me anxiety.

A knock on my door has me freezing before rushing toward it and pulling it open. All the air leaves my lungs at the sight of him. He is so beautiful. Looks like a god.

"You going to invite me in?" he smirks, no doubt at the look on my face. I roll my eyes before pulling him inside.

"Where were you?" I hiss accusingly. He sighs as he drops down on the couch, taking me with him and pulling me into his lap. He looks tired, worn out.

"Melody is back. I had no idea. She said she wasn't coming here until just before Christmas. That's why it took me so long to get here, she didn't want me to go. I told her I had prior arrangements. She griped but eventually let me go." Worry twists in my gut. I wait on tenterhooks for his next words. His eyes bore into mine. I know whatever he says next is going to change everything, his next words confirm it.

"I am going to end things with her," he blurts. My eyes widen, mouth drops open in shock. Never in my wildest dreams when we started this did I think Theo would leave *her*. He is so tied up with her—in the business sense—I never thought it was a possibility, especially since he will lose all his top horses. I know he doesn't love her, but I thought his career was more important to him than me. Guess I thought wrong.

"What?" I whisper, wanting him to confirm the words he just said to make sure I am not hearing things. He wraps his arms around my waist and smiles. It's his real genuine smile that he seems to reserve only for me.

"I am leaving Mel," he repeats. "I want to be with you, give things a go. Obviously, we will need to work out the logistics with telling your parents. But you are what I want, Piccola. Just you. Only you." He drops a kiss to my forehead. I stare at him.

This man. Who I was never supposed to touch. Never supposed to love. Yet I do. With everything in me, I love him.

"But what about your horses? Your career?" He smiles, tucking a loose strand of hair behind my ear.

"You are more important than any of that. It may have taken me a while to realize that, but you are. I have found another investor. I won't be able to keep them all, but he will invest enough that I can keep some of them. I have thought about it, I want to start over. With you. With a new team of horses. Sometimes change is good, Thalia. I know with everything in me, you are the change I want. Need." I swallow. My eyes search his for any sign that he is unsure, that he is lying. All I see is his honesty and truth staring back at me. I am so overwhelmed with love, with emotion, I blurt the words before I can stop myself.

"I love you, Theo. I want to be with you." He grins before crashing his lips down on mine. We are both breathless when he pulls away. His cock is hard beneath me, I want to show him how much he means to me. I push out of his lap, quickly unzip his pants, and free his massive cock. He smirks at me as I remove my sleep shorts and tank. His gaze rakes over every inch of me and I know I will never find another man who looks at me the way he does.

"Come and ride my dick, Piccola," he rasps. I don't need him to ask twice. I jump on his lap and lower myself, taking every inch of him. He groans as he finds me wet. It's what he does to me. Just from looking at him, I am soaked. I ride him until we both find our release, coming apart together. Me soaking his cock and him painting my insides with his hot seed. I collapse on his chest as I try to catch my breath. He peppers kisses in my hair, whispering soft words to me. I don't know how long we stay like that but all too soon, he is shifting me onto the couch next to him.

"I have to go, baby, but I will be back. I promise. Let me sort things out tonight and then we can start our forever." My heart jumps at his words. Forever with this man doesn't sound like long enough but it's a start. He tucks his dick away and pushes off the couch but not before kissing me. As he makes his way to the door, I think about the three little words I said. Although he has not returned the words, I know he feels the same. I feel it in the way he kisses me. The way he makes love to me. I don't need the words right now; I know they will come. He has a lot to sort out before they do. He grabs the knob but I speak before he can open the door.

"Theo?" He glances at me over his shoulder.

"Yeah?"

"Thank you." His eyebrows furrow in confusion so I elaborate. "Thank you for making me the happiest woman alive. I love you." He smiles, pulling the door open.

"No. Thank you. For choosing me. For making me the happiest I have ever been." And with that, he steps through the door. I smile.

The next time I see him, he will officially be mine.

Chapter Twenty-Six

THEO

I pull up to the house, my thoughts racing with how I am going to approach this. Melody is inside, she has no idea what is about to come. Part of me hopes she is asleep, but then I will only be putting it off for another day and I want to be able to claim my girl. Show the world Thalia Maxwell is mine.

I cannot believe Mel just showed up tonight and didn't tell me. I haven't spoken to her in a few days but as far as I was aware, she wasn't flying in until around the eighteenth of December.

It's just like her to do something like this and I am sure her motives aren't exactly pure. I don't care though. Tonight, I end things with the woman I have spent six years with. A woman I never loved but felt forced to be with for the sake of my career.

Tomorrow though, I get to start my forever with the girl I love.

Hopping out of my SUV, I make my way up the steps and to the front door. Before I can shove in my key, it is yanked open, a smiling Melody on the other side.

"Jesus, Mel," I bark. She chuckles but it sounds off.

"Theodore," she breathes in her strong British accent. I step inside and past her. She closes the door and I spin to face her.

"Mel, we need to talk." She stills, her eyes narrowing on me before she schools her features and plasters a fake smile on her wrinkle free face.

"Okay, let's go to your office," she murmurs, pushing past me and heading in the direction of said office. I trail behind her, my chest tightening with every step I make. I know she will not take this well. She is expecting an engagement. Marriage. But that isn't going to happen when I am in love with someone else. And I am in love with Thalia. Hearing her say those three little words made my heart burst in my chest. I wanted to say them back, but I couldn't. Not when I am still with Mel. Not when there is still so much for us to overcome. When I say those words, it will be the first time I have ever said them to another person who isn't my parents and I want to be free from my current relationship. I want Thalia's family to know. I want to be able to shout the words, so the whole world knows how much I love her.

Stepping inside my office, I round my desk as Melody takes a seat on the couch. She looks like the picture of calm, but I know she is worried. I see it in her eyes.

"What is this about?" she asks as I take a seat in my leather chair. I clear my throat, my eyes locking on hers.

"I want out of this Mel. I can't do it anymore. I don't love you and if you really think about it, you don't love me either. You love the lifestyle that comes with being with me but not me," I tell her straight, because what is the point of beating around the bush? Anger flashes in her eyes as she stares at me. "Obviously the contracts I have with your father regarding horses will need to be sorted out and I am sure we can do it in a professional manner. I have no ill feelings toward you or your family. I just think the relationship has run its course."

Her face is a mask of calm. When she doesn't speak, I continue. "You know I am right, Mel; we have been having problems for a long while now. I think it's best..." I trail off when her face transforms into something dark. Someone I don't recognize. Her lips tip up into a sinister smirk making my stomach turn.

"Well, well, well, Theodore. I was wondering when you would do this," she starts. My brows furrow in confusion. "You think I don't know about you and your little whore?" she spits the words. My eyes widen and jaw tics. She cannot know about Thalia. No way. Her next words prove me wrong. "Thalia Maxwell, Theo. Really? She is barely legal. You think her parents won't ruin you if they find out?" My heart beats in my chest frantically at the mention of my piccola. I must do everything and anything to diffuse this. So, I lie.

"What are you talking about? Thalia is training with me, that is all. You are delusional if you think there is anything else between us." She chuckles darkly. Her eyes flashing triumphantly. And I know. I just know she has a trump card. She pushes to a stand, pulling her cell phone out of her pocket and flicking through it. She glances at me quickly before speaking.

"Now this is what is going to happen, Theodore. You are going to marry me. I don't care if we fly to Vegas tonight or have a big wedding in six months. But you WILL marry me." I scoff, eyeing her in disbelief. The woman is crazy.

"Never going to happen. I don't care what you think you know, but me and you are over." She grins almost manically, stepping around my desk towards me.

"I don't think, I *know*. I *do* know. I have the proof." She thrusts her cell in front of my face and a video plays on the screen. I hear the moans before I see us.

Me and Thalia.

In one of the stalls as I fuck her against the wall.

I swallow, remembering this night. Thalia was convinced she heard someone. I told her she was being paranoid. Now I know she was right. Melody was fucking filming us. The clip comes to an end and so does my life as I know it. Melody shoves it back in her pocket, smiling down at me. But it's not a nice smile, it's a smile that tells me she has won. But then I remember something.

"You signed an NDA. You can't release anything." She cackles.

"I didn't sign anything, Theo." I shake my head. I had everyone...fuck. Mel was away. And then with everything going on, I forgot to get her to sign it when she got back.

"FUCK," I roar.

She laughs, the sound like nails on a chalkboard. I want to wrap my hands around her. Throttle her. "I didn't. It must have slipped your mind. Now Theo, you will marry me. If not, I will release this video of your precious Thalia to every news outlet and gossip magazine out there. It will ruin you and her. Her mother is building up to awards season and I am sure she doesn't need a scandal like this. Her barely legal daughter fucking around with an older man who has a long-term girlfriend? I cannot imagine the bad press this will bring to the otherwise perfect Maxwell family," she tsks, making my heart drop to my stomach.

I stare up at the women who I have spent six years with. I thought I knew her, but I don't. I never thought she would stoop this low to get what she wants. What choice do I have now? I cannot let her put a video like that out there. She is right. It will ruin Thalia, portray her as someone she is not. A homewrecker. A whore. The bad press it will bring to her family is something I cannot allow when I can prevent it. I stare at the vindictive bitch in front of me.

"Leave my office. I need to make a call." For a second, I don't think she is going to listen, but she smiles and leaves. I pick up my cell, scrolling to a name I haven't used in a while. We haven't had the best relationship since I decided not to follow in his footsteps but if anyone can help me now, it's him. I need him. I hit dial and wait for the call to connect which it does a few seconds later.

"Theo?' I hear the confusion in his voice.

"Dad, I need your help," I croak.

"Okay," he says warily.

"How bad would it be for the Maxwell family's reputation if a sex video of me fucking their eighteen-year-old daughter was released?" I get straight to the point. He hisses, followed by a sharp intake of breath. My heart jackhammers in my chest and I swear it is going to beat all the way out.

"As in one of the richest families in the world? As in Elena Maxwell?"

"Yes,"

"Jesus, Theo. Fuck," he curses then is silent for a long beat. No doubt processing this news. "Do you want me to be honest or tell you what I think you want to hear?"

"Honest." The emotion in my voice is raw. I am raw.

"You have a girlfriend, Theo. If that video gets out, she will be made out to be a homewrecker. Her image, reputation, ruined. Her mother is seen as America's sweetheart. I am sure you have seen she is up for some big award. It will jeopardize all that and can potentially ruin her chances of winning. People don't take kindly to cheating. The family will be vilified. Embarrassed. What did you get yourself into?" He's angry now. I scrub a palm down my face as I feel tears build in my eyes and a lump form in my throat.

"I fell in love with the wrong girl. Mel found out. She has a video. Has threatened me. If I don't marry her, she will release it. What do I do?" He is quiet for so long; I think the call has ended.

"You give Mel what she wants, if you want to protect the girl. If you love her like you say you do, then you have no other option." And with that, he ends the call, making my heart crack painfully in my chest.

I know what I must do.

I only have one choice.

I just wish now I had told Thalia I loved her when I had the chance. Wish she knew how much she means to me, that she is the love of my life. But I can't. I must do the right thing and protect her. Even if it will break us and me in the process. My chest tightens with thoughts of what this will do to my piccola. It will break her heart. I see no other way though. I can't allow Mel to ruin the Maxwells or me, for that matter.

Mind made up and as if she knows she has won, she saunters back into the room. I look at the bitch in front of me. Her eyes sparkle triumphantly. I have never hit a woman before, never thought I would. But damn, I want to smack her right in her smug face. I let out a breath and push to a stand.

"Pack a bag. We are going to Vegas."

To be continued...

AUTHORS NOTE

Thank you for reading Thalia and Theo's story, I hope you enjoyed it as much as I enjoyed writing it. I can't wait for you to see what happens next.

I would like to say thank you to my family, partner and friends for supporting me on this journey and believing in me when it gets too much.

I also want to say a HUGE thank you to Keri, my PA aka wonder woman. Thank you for pushing me and making this experience in the book world even better. Your belief in me knows no bounds and I will forever be grateful.

For all things Kelly Kelsey, you can follow me on social media.

Facebook Readers Group – Kelly Kelsey Readers Group
Instagram – Kellykelseyauthor
Goodreads – KellyKelsey
Tiktok - Kellykelseyauthor

BOOKS

Standalones
Sweet Temptation

Jump Series
Elimination
Checkmate – April 2022
TBD – May 2022
Aria's book - Winter 2022

Beautiful Beaumont
The Secrets we Keep – February 2022
The Pain we Hide – Autumn 2022

Anthologies
Used and Bound Anthology – March 2022
Seeds of Love - April 2022

Printed in Great Britain
by Amazon

17420079R00142